DESTINATION DANGER

Quist sets off for Quivira City to clear up the murder of one Whitney Clayton, a man who had no mourners at his funeral. No lack of suspects, though, as both Clayton's widow and her brother — children of the powerful cattle baron Grizzly Baldridge — readily confess. Add the reappearance of a hoard of lost gold, plus the presence of killer Cobra Macaw, and Quist realises he's in for a pile of trouble . . .

WILLIAM COLT MACDONALD

DESTINATION DANGER

Complete and Unabridged

LINFORD
Leicester

First published in the United States by
Lippincott & Co.
First published in Great Britain by
Hodder & Stoughton

First Linford Edition
published 2021
by arrangement with
Golden West Literary Agency

*A catalogue record for this book is available
from the British Library.*

ISBN 978–1–78541–965–2

Published by
Ulverscroft Limited
Anstey, Leicestershire

Printed and bound in Great Britain by
TJ Books Ltd., Padstow, Cornwall

This book is printed on acid-free paper

1

Switched Guns

During a lifetime a man may hear many varied sounds that, at a distance, resemble momentarily those made by gunfire. For instance, the sharp cracking of a whip may approximate, on the ear, an explosion from a Winchester repeating rifle; or two heavy objects coming forcefully together can carry the sound made by a detonating forty-five six shooter; a certain variety of rock, splitting violently and abruptly, under intense heat, has been known to assume the auricular aspect of burned powder projecting a missile from a gun barrel. But when an actual shot has been heard, the experienced man rarely retains in his mind any confusion as to its identity, by the time the final echoes have died away.

Thus it was with Chris Baldridge. There wasn't the slightest doubt in his thoughts that what he had heard was a shot. No cracking of a whiplash there, nor yet two ponderous objects colliding in violence; no sharply splitting rocks. What he had heard had been a shot, all right — probably, at a quick guess, from a six-shooter. He'd been guiding his horse leisurely through a small stand of blackjack oak when the sound had reached him, but had swiftly pulled his chestnut pony to a halt. Now he sat silently in the saddle, straining his hearing for any further shots that might follow.

Baldridge frowned. 'That sort of sounded like it might have come from the house. That direction, anyway.'

Still, he sat waiting. Ahead of him rose a short rise, obstructing his view of the small house he knew lay beyond. Still farther on the Montañosa Mountains lifted broken outlines against the turquoise morning sky, flecked but slightly with small drifting clouds, driven on by the same breeze that rustled the leaves of the blackjacks around Baldridge. The Montañosas really shouldn't have been called mountains: they were actually a chain of jumbled hills of broken rock, bare surfaces exposed to the open, studding thickly growing grass and stretching to a higher range farther to the southwest.

The lines in Baldridge's face relaxed. 'I could have been mistaken,' he told himself, even doubting the thought as it took form in his mind. 'Anyway, I guess it doesn't amount to anything. Howsomever, we'll see what's what.'

Kicking the pony in the ribs he moved on up the slope ahead, a slim-hipped, broad-shouldered figure in faded Levi's and weathered sombrero, with good features that were yet too young to present any particular lines brought on by responsibility.

Topping the rise, he paused but an instant to gaze a couple of hundred feet down the slope where stood a small house — it was but little more than a shack — constructed of unpainted but nearly new lumber, with a sort of small roofed porch built across the front. The porch was in shadow at the moment, but there didn't appear to be anyone there. Except for an occasional post oak or small blackjack, with now and then a clump of prickly-pear cactus, the way to the house was clear. So far as Baldridge could determine, there wasn't a human being anywhere near the house. A corral to the rear and one side, held a single horse, still saddled. Nearby grew a tall pecan tree.

'Must be someone around,' Baldridge mused, as he urged his pony down the grassy slope toward the building. A moment later he had dismounted near the porch, and lifted his voice, 'Hello — inside!'

There was no answer. The front door stood slightly ajar. Baldridge's forehead creased slightly. He wasn't sure of the reason, but something about the quiet made him uneasy. His brow cleared momentarily. 'Must be, he's gone down to the creek — ' glancing beyond the house where thick brush and tall cottonwood trees, forty yards distant, attested a damper soil for growing.

Bluebottle flies droned in and out of the open front door. Baldridge glanced about uncertainly, noticing old newspapers and empty tin cans cluttering the earth in the vicinity of the house. His nose wrinkled in distaste. 'No wonder she couldn't take it,' he speculated. 'Still, of course, living alone, I shouldn't expect him — ' He broke off, then, 'Could be the buzzard's drunk in there.' Baldridge's face darkened. 'That'd be just my luck, when I came here to talk sense to him — make him see he's got to behave, or clear out. Well, I reckon I might as well take a look-see.'

Still obsessed with a premonition that all wasn't quite right, Baldridge stepped reluctantly to the porch and, shoving back the partly opened door, stepped inside. An exclamation burst from his lips and he halted abruptly just within the entrance.

'Cripes A'mighty!' he blurted. 'Somebody's played all hell here.'

The room looked as though it had been struck by a cyclone. Two chairs lay overturned. A couple of Navajo rugs were rumpled at one side. A variety of objects — newspapers, magazines, a smashed lamp, an odd stirrup — had been flung to the floor from an upset table which lay with one side resting on the floor, directly opposite Baldridge. It was a rather large, oblong-shaped table which previously had stood in the center of the room. Beyond the table a doorway led to the rear of the house.

Baldridge's dark eyebrows gathered in a scowl. 'If that dirty son has been trying to beat up — ' The words broke in sudden, bitter oaths. 'Blast his crooked hide! I sure aim to tell him a thing or two. He's likely sleeping off a jag in the bedroom.'

Stepping wide around an overturned chair and past the broken lamp which had leaked kerosene on the floor, Baldridge started for the rear of the house. He was moving angrily around the overturned table when the sight at his feet brought him to an abrupt halt. A swift intake of breath whistled through Baldridge's lips, and he drew back a pace, jaw dropping, eyes widening in horror.

His voice shook a little, a moment later, when he muttered, 'No, I reckon I won't tell you a thing or two — Clayton — not ever.'

A dead man lay crumpled at Baldridge's feet — anyway, he looked dead — a man named Whitney Clayton, whose still form had been hitherto hidden from Baldridge's view by the overturned table. The body lay partly on its side, one knee drawn up. The left arm was doubled beneath the chest, the right was stretched out on the floor, fingers wide, with beyond them a Colt's six-shooter, as though the weapon might have been dropped as Clayton went down.

For a brief moment, Baldridge entertained a notion that Whitney Clayton had committed suicide, but almost instantly dismissed the thought. In the first place, Clayton wasn't the type to kill himself; in the second, how to explain the overturned furniture and general wreckage throughout the room? No, some sort of a struggle had taken place here, Baldridge mused, a struggle that had ended in Clayton's being shot to death. In addition, Clayton, apparently, hadn't been wearing a gun.

He moved nearer, stooping down to examine the body. Blood dripped from a dark hole in the neck, just below the left ear, and formed a pool of blood on the floor, which was already commencing to congeal about the head of sandy-colored hair. Clayton's eyes were half-open, glazed. His jaw sagged.

Baldridge rose slowly to his feet. The gathering flies scattered at the movement, buzzing angrily. Baldridge sniffed the air, catching the scent of spilled blood through a faint smell of burned gunpowder. 'No,' he told himself, 'that's not suicide. Never yet heard of a man shooting himself in the throat.' He stood a moment looking down at the corpse. 'Somebody come here and just caught up with the bustard, I reckon. Maybe I shouldn't be the one to say it, but Clayton sure got what he deserved.'

Another thought struck him: perhaps

the killer was hidden at the rear of the house. Baldridge stiffened, listening, then relaxed. There was nothing to be heard except the droning flies. It might be just as well to have a look, though.

Drawing his six-shooter, Baldridge stepped cautiously around the corpse and through the doorway in the rear wall, into the kitchen. Beyond a couple of straight-backed chairs, a depleted shelf of groceries, a table and a stove, there was little to be seen by the light of the kitchen window. The kitchen door, leading from the back of the house, was closed.

A doorway at Baldridge's left led into a bedroom. Nothing to be found there, either, aside from the usual bedroom furniture. Here a window was tightly closed. Baldridge drew a deep breath and reholstered his six-shooter. Seizing a blanket from the rumpled bed, he once more stepped into the kitchen.

'Whoever it was,' he muttered, 'sure made time getting away after I heard that shot.'

Crossing to the kitchen door he found it unlocked. The knob turned easily under his hand and he flung it open. Outside, there was nothing to be seen that could tell him anything. The earth showed a few old hoof and footprints; there were many rusted tin cans scattered about. A tall clump of prickly pear grew near one corner of the house. A few weeds and scattered cacti, clumps of buffalo grass and young mesquite, were all that barred the eye to the thick brush and cottonwoods, forty yards distant, growing along the creek.

'A man could be hidden in that brush,' Baldridge speculated. 'Or the killer could be miles away from here by now. Still I didn't hear any horse leaving. Anyway, any hoof beats would have been drowned out by the sound of my own pony when I was arriving.'

He studied the brush and trees growing along the creek, and finally shrugged his shoulders. 'I guess it's not my business to go hunting the hombre who shot Clayton, in case he's hidden down there.

I might be forced to stop a slug of lead if I get too nosy.' Eyeing the brush a moment longer without detecting any movement beyond that made by the breeze rustling through leaves and branches, Baldridge withdrew once more to the kitchen, shutting the door behind him.

An instant later he was back in the front room where Whitney Clayton lay still in death. Swearing angrily at the droning flies, he waved them away, then spread the blanket over the motionless form. 'Next thing to do,' he told himself, 'is to make a beeline for the sheriff's office and tell what's happened.'

He had started for the front door when a cartridge belt and holster hanging on the wall, near the door, caught his eye. The holster was empty. Baldridge stopped dead, then half-fearfully, gazed back over one shoulder toward the gun on the floor, resting just beyond the outstretched dead fingers. Reluctantly, he turned back and stooping, picked up the gun to examine it.

Quite suddenly, all the color left his face

and he drew a quick shuddering breath, as he straightened up. Swirling emotions clouded his thoughts. An anguished look twisted his features. 'Good God,' he groaned — 'no — no — '

After a moment some of the color returned to his cheeks, and he commenced to marshal his thinking into clearer channels. 'This will sure raise hell,' he muttered bitterly. 'Dammit! What a fool thing to do. But maybe it couldn't be helped.'

Various thoughts ran through Baldridge's seething mind. The condition of the room showed there'd been a struggle. And there were all the other happenings this past year. Sometimes, murder, a killing, could be justified by a plea of self-defense. But you couldn't count on it. No telling what a trial jury might do nowadays. Trial juries were beginning to grow skeptical, having heard so many self-defense pleas the past few years.

Doubtless, Whit Clayton deserved what he had got. At the same time, a judge or jury — perhaps both — might take a biased view. Baldridge frowned, glanced again at the six-shooter he held in his hand. Finally, his face cleared, as a solution occurred to him. For a few moments he concentrated on the idea, then with a careless shrugging of wide shoulders, came to a decision.

'I reckon,' he said, half aloud, 'that's the best thing to do about this business. Anyway, it's the only way I see, at present.'

Drawing his own six-shooter from his holster, he leveled it through the open front door and pulled trigger. The heavy detonation of the shot shook the rafters of the building, as a spurt of dust was ploughed up on the earth, twenty feet beyond the porch fronting the house. Powder smoke swirled through the room and vanished in thin air.

Baldridge cast another look at Whit Clayton's corpse, then tossed down the gun he'd just fired in approximately the same position from which he'd lifted the other gun. Then, jamming the death weapon into his holster, he strode from the house and climbed into his saddle. Wheeling his pony, he thrust in the spurs, then almost as quickly, as another thought struck him, he jerked the horse to a stop.

'Damn!' he mused. 'I'd better get rid of this other gun before I talk to the sheriff.'

Thoughts of burying the gun came to mind, but he rejected that idea. He twisted in the saddle, eyes scanning the surrounding landscape and came to rest on the brush and trees bordering the creek. As if satisfied, Baldridge nodded. 'I don't figure anybody's going to have any reason to go looking there.'

He turned the pony and directed it toward the creek, then when he neared the thick growth, he lifted the death weapon in his hand and hurled it into the tangle of mesquite, tall grass and catclaw, where it landed with scarcely any sound. That accomplished, he once more wheeled his pony and, face grim, loped off at a swift ground-covering pace toward the southeast.

Baldridge had hardly disappeared over the low rise of ground fronting the house, when a girl emerged from the brush lining Montañosa Creek, leading behind her a bay pony. Once in the clearing, surrounding the house, she paused a moment, looking about, a slim figure in divided riding skirt and flat-crowned sombrero. Her shirt was a mannish dark-red flannel and there was a red bandanna tied about her throat.

The saddled horse in the corral whinnied, but she gave it only scant attention before resuming her advance toward the house. Here she halted near the kitchen door, dropped the pony's reins on the earth and, opening the door, stepped inside. The door closed at her heels.

Later, the girl was unable to state with any certainty how long she had spent within the house. It was probably not more than six or seven minutes when she again emerged through the kitchen doorway, looking white and shaken, and carrying in one hand the gun Baldridge had dropped near the corpse a short time before. The girl swayed as she reached the pony's side and clutched at the saddle for support.

For a few moments she just stood there, shoulders shaking, head bowed against the saddle.

Finally, with an effort she lifted her head and climbed to the horse's back, still carrying the six-shooter in her hand. With bowed head, she started the pony slowly into motion, and rounding the front of the house, headed off in the direction taken by Baldridge, without once turning to glance back. Ten minutes later she had topped the hill and was urging the bay pony along the trail that ran through the small stand of blackjack trees.

2

'Murder Changes Things!'

Long before the trial of the freight thieves had been concluded, Quist was ready to leave the Dallas courtroom. It hadn't been much of a trial; Quist's testimony and guilty pleas on the part of the miscreants had clinched matters. The judge had scarcely pronounced sentences when the crowd started to file out of the stuffy courtroom, jamming the center aisle in its haste to escape to the fresher air of the street, after the humidity of the courthouse.

A couple of newspaper reporters had detained Quist a few minutes with questions but he had brushed them off as soon as possible and, not even waiting for the railroad's lawyer to join him, had caught up with the tail end of the audience pushing through the wide doorway to the sidewalk. There was the usual buzz of conversation all around. Quist sauntered easily along with the throng, a wide-shouldered man with thick tawny hair, smooth-shaven in a day when most men wore beards and mustaches. His features were rather bony, the nose high-arched, the skin deeply tanned from long exposure to southwest suns. He wore a coat, somewhat faded across the shoulders, over his woolen shirt; tan corduroys were cuffed at the ankles of his high-heeled boots; a flat-crowned sombrero slanted across his forehead.

The crowd from the courtroom had bunched before the building by the time Quist reached the steps beyond the exit doorway. He paused there a moment, sniffing the fresher air, seeing across the street the two, three and four story buildings that attested Dallas' booming growth, and the sidewalks thronged with pedestrians. Someone pushed from behind and Quist started to move on.

At that moment, he heard his name called: 'Greg — this way.'

Quist's topaz-colored eyes flitted swiftly over the massed heads and shoulders on the sidewalk, until his gaze picked out a tall spare figure in citizen's clothing and derby hat, standing at the edge of the roadway. Lifting one hand in quick greeting, Quist rapidly shouldered his way down the steps and pushed through the crowd. The man who had called to him advanced, palm outstretched.

'It's good to see you, Greg.' They shook hands.

'Same here. I didn't see you in the courtroom, Jay.'

'I left right after you'd given your testimony.' Jay Fletcher, Division Superintendent of the Texas Northern & Arizona Southern Railroad, smiled. 'I thought I'd give myself the pleasure of coming to watch the great Gregory Quist in a courtroom role. You see — '

'Bosh!' An expression of annoyance flitted across Quist's tanned features. 'That doesn't go down, Jay. There's something else behind your being here, or I'm a liar. Just exactly what are you up to? El Paso and Dallas are miles apart.

You're out of your territory — '

'Where the T.N. & A.S. is concerned, I'm never out of my territory.'

'By cripes,' Quist chuckled, 'truer word was never spoken. Come on, let's get away from here. I'm thirsty.' Working their way through the throng, they fell in step on the plank sidewalk. Quist went on, 'Where you staying?'

'Same hotel as yours — the Le Grand.'

'Thought these days you'd hit one of the more stylish hotels.'

'Jeepers,' Fletcher laughed. 'I remember the day when the Le Grand was called magnificent. First hotel I ever stayed at in Dallas. I recollect when it was being built — man named Smith put it up. And on a shoestring too. It used to be said that there was a chattel mortgage on everything in the Le Grand, except the smoke from drummers' cigars — and no one was too sure about that either — '

'Jay,' Quist broke in, 'what really brought you here? You know right well I've been planning to get away — I still am and nothing's going to stop me.'

A mule-drawn streetcar went clanging and rocking past. When the noise had subsided, Fletcher said, 'You certainly wrapped up that trial in a hurry. You're mighty dependable, Greg.'

Quist frowned and said inelegantly, 'Buffalo chips! There wasn't much work for an investigator on that job. Bunch of wet-nosed kids, practically, with no more sense than to try to get rich robbing freight cars. The oldest was only twenty-one — '

'The fact remains they were armed when you rounded them up, apprehended them in their hideout. You nipped something in the bud that might have led to train-wrecking in time, and they'll go to the penitentiary — '

'Yes.' Quist scowled. 'And that's exactly what I don't like about the business. I've yet to see the man who was improved by a term in the pen.'

'Those fellows broke the law. They're dangerous malefactors. What would you do with them?'

'I'm damned if I know,' Quist conceded bluntly. 'There's just something wrong with the system, that's all. Frankly, I couldn't find it in my heart to blame those hombres too much for stealing. I've talked to all of them. When they were kids they never had enough to eat, or sufficient clothing in winter. That's why I tried to get them the lightest sentence possible.'

'Hah!' Fletcher jeered. 'You're getting soft, Greg. That doesn't sound like the great manhunter, our best operative, the T.N. & A.S.'s very top special investigator — '

'Investigator hell,' Quist growled. 'Changing the name doesn't make me any different than any other private detective. To be frank, I'm a railroad dick.' He dropped aside to allow a woman to pass, then caught up with Fletcher again, a savage note in his voice, 'I'm getting pretty damn sick of the business, Jay. Hounding my fellow man, chasing killers. And for what? So the T.N. & A.S. can pay better dividends to the stockholders and extend its lines.'

Fletcher didn't reply for a moment as they strode along side by side. Carriages and buggies rolled along the street. Fletcher said soberly at last, 'There's a heap of people think better of you than that, Greg. That article that was printed in *Karper's Weekly* called you the smartest investigator — '

'That *Karper's* writer had a rush of imagination to the brain,' Quist snapped disgustedly. 'Just because I happened to be lucky clearing up a couple of murder cases — oh, cripes, let's forget it.'

'That *Karper's* writer,' Fletcher said slyly, 'seemed to think you were quite some man. What was it he said? Oh, yes, something about your having a way with women.' He ignored the irritated snort from Quist and went on, 'You're too cynical, Greg — '

'How in God's name can a man be anything but cynical in this world?' Quist snapped. 'And particularly in a job like mine.'

'What you should have, Greg, is a

good wife. It would mellow you —'

'Now I know you've gone crazy,' Quist exploded with considerable exasperation. 'A man with a job like mine has no business with a wife. You know that as well as I do, Jay.'

Fletcher didn't reply. A moment later they turned into the granite-flanked entrance of the Le Grand Hotel. Quist said something about getting a drink, but Fletcher urged him on. Quist shrugged his shoulders, stopped at the desk for his key and the two men made their way to the second floor of the hostelry.

Quist's room contained the usual hotel furniture, somewhat worn in this case, but clean. What he noticed first, as he and Fletcher stepped inside the room and closed the door, was a tray on the table, holding half a dozen chilled bottles of beer, glasses and an opener.

'A rather beautiful sight,' Quist said softly, 'to a man as thirsty as I am.' Tossing his sombrero on the bed he ran long fingers through his shock of tawny hair and quickly strode to the table. 'Just cold enough. You know, Jay, most people chill their beer too much. My favorite beer too. 'The beer that made Milwaukee jealous.' Employing the screwdriver-like opener he quickly pried out the cuplike stoppers from a couple of bottles and poured the creamy amber liquid into glasses, handing one to Fletcher, then sat down on the bed, glass in hand, to quaff a long draught.

Fletcher sank into a chair. His rather tired-looking eyes gleamed thoughtfully behind glasses. There were deep lines in his face and his thin hair was rapidly whitening. As a Division Superintendent of the Texas Northern & Arizona Southern Railroad, he had watched the company grow, extending its lines wherever possible. Shrewd investments in company stock had made him a well-to-do man, and though he had long ago been offered higher positions with the company, his present situation suited him. His word was law with the eastern heads of the T.N. & A.S. — and western heads as well. Realizing that to Jay Fletcher, the development of the road was his whole life, the board of directors was deeply influenced by any pronouncement that Fletcher might make, and to date this trust had been more than justified.

Such thoughts were passing through Quist's mind as he finished his first bottle of beer and opened a second. Two thirds of the second bottle had been consumed, while Fletcher was dawdling over a half glass, before Quist spoke:

'All right, Jay. I'm much obliged for the beer. So you come here from your office, not to attend a trial, but to arrange to have been waiting for me when the trial is over — and your office is hundreds of miles from here. So, again, all right. I'll concede that I'm in a better humor. What do you want from me?'

Fletcher studied the glass in his hand, then his gaze ranged toward the afternoon sky, seen through a front window. He didn't reply at once. Finally, he reached over and placed his partly-filled glass on the table. 'Greg, you and I have been friends for a lot of years now,' he commenced.

'Admitted,' Quist nodded, 'long enough for you to know that I'm leaving on the first vacation I've had in years. I'm leaving tonight. I've friends in San Francisco expecting me. It won't be long before the weather will be getting nippy nights, in Texas. Out in California I'm going to hunt and fish and just loaf in the sun — '

'Greg,' Fletcher broke in, 'I'm in a jam — rather the T.N. & A.S. is in a bad way, unless matters can be adjusted.'

'What's wrong,' Quist jeered, 'did some engineer kill a ranchman's cow — and you can't make him settle for less than the price of the critter?'

'Let's be serious, Greg.'

Quist sighed. 'All right, I'll be serious, on condition that you take the same attitude and remember I'm pulling out of Dallas for the Coast. Tonight.'

Fletcher drew a sigh to match Quist's, then asked, 'What do you know about Quivira City?'

Quist considered while he rolled and lighted a brown paper cigarette, setting his beer on the floor during the operation. Blue smoke mingled with gray, curled through the hotel room. He said finally, 'Not a great deal. Out road runs through the town. I haven't stopped off there in years. Back in the days before the railroad came through, Quivira was a pretty rough burg for a spell. Lot of rustling thereabouts, but I guess that's been pretty well cleaned up. Back in Civil War days there was cotton raised around there too. Now it's cattle, of course. Let me see . . . I think a man named Baldridge is the big beef raiser around there —'

'Do you know Baldridge?' Fletcher asked quickly.

Quist shook his head. He said dryly, 'I know how to read, though. Sometimes I find time from company duties to read newspapers.'

'And *Karper's Weekly*?' Fletcher smiled.

Quist flushed and ignored the question. 'To sum up,' he concluded, 'Quivira City is a right thriving town these days. No crime that I've heard of, and it gives the T.N. & A.S. quite a bit of business.

Now, what's on your mind?'

'Greg, we're having trouble getting a right-of-way through some property near Quivira City.'

'That's a job for the company's legal sharps.' Quist finished off a bottle of beer.

'Ordinarily, yes, but not this time. Let me show you.'

Fletcher drew a folded map from his pocket and rose to approach the bed where Quist was seated. Quist said, 'Fetch me a bottle of beer on your way, Jay. Please.'

A bottle was opened and handed to Quist. Fletcher seated himself on the bed and spread his map. 'Now here,' — indicating with a pencil on the map — 'is Quivira City. The railroad runs east and west through the town. Baldridge's holdings — the Bee-Hive Ranch — lays northwest of the town, clear over here until they reach the Montañosa Mountains. It's a big ranch. Now here,' — Fletcher's pencil traced an opening in the Montañosa Mountains — 'is what is known as Estrecho Pass. We've got to have a right-of-way through there.'

'Why?' Quist queried bluntly.

'To expand our lines, of course.' Fletcher sounded a trifle sharp. 'From the main line through Quivira City, we want to run the road up toward the northwest. We got word a while back that the Rock Buttes Southern & Silverado road is planning to build down to the south, and if so they'll be after the pass — Estrecho Pass — too. We've simply got to beat them to it. While the Montañosa range isn't high, there's a lot of broken country there — up-and-down stuff. Blasting for level grades costs money, money that can be saved if we can secure the right to go through Estrecho Pass. Do you see?'

Quist didn't appear much interested. 'To me it looks like a matter of paying the owner the price asked, price depending on how badly you need that right-of-way through the pass.' He glanced at the map. 'The proposed road would have to cross Baldridge holdings, wouldn't it?'

'Part of the route, yes. But we wouldn't

have to start laying rails north, from our established line, until nearly to the Montañosas. Then we'd parallel the mountains on Baldridge property until we turned left through Estrecho Pass — '

'And Baldridge refuses to sell the necessary right-of-way?'

'Baldridge will sell. We have no trouble there. But sometime back he sold his son-in-law, named Whitney Clayton, a half section of land that lies smack-dab in front of Estrecho Pass, controlling the entrance. And Clayton is proving mighty damn stubborn.'

'Clayton refuses to sell?'

'He'll sell, but only at an exorbitant price — twenty thousand dollars. We've offered two thousand — a mighty fair figure, considering.'

Quist chuckled. 'The old holdup game, eh? Well, Jay, it's up to the company to pay if it wants the right-of-way bad enough — '

'Greg! You can't mean that.' Fletcher looked aghast. 'What would our stockholders say? They'd think we'd gone criminally insane.'

'My heart bleeds for the poor stockholders,' Quist said caustically.

'Now, now, Greg, don't take that attitude. You know there isn't a fairer dealing road with both stockholders and public — '

'Never mind making speeches, Jay. What do you expect me to do about all this? If your legal department is any good, it will be able to handle the business —'

'I just thought, Greg, that you, being a westerner, might be able to talk some sense into this Whitney Clayton man. You see, our men from the law department are easterners and they don't understand the western mind. Those people in Quivira City just clam up when an easterner comes around. Now, Greg, you can see it's a simple matter for you to take care of. You've the ability to make people listen to reason and — '

'Cut it short, Jay. You're holding something back. What's the whole story? You're not just asking me to go to

Quivira City and beg somebody to peddle a right-of-way. If you expect me to believe that, you're more stupid than I think. Come on, cough up, what's back of all this?' He rolled another cigarette and took a sip of beer, meanwhile an eyeing look in his topaz-hued eyes.

Jay Fletcher drew a deep breath. 'Frankly, Greg, I'm not sure,' he admitted in tired tones. 'I stopped off in Quivira City on my way here. I thought maybe I could talk to Baldridge and see if he couldn't do something with his son-in-law, Whitney Clayton. Baldridge sent word he had no time to talk to me. It seems Clayton had pulled a gun on old Baldridge. That's the talk I picked up around town. And no one seemed to know where Clayton was at the moment. I —'

'Clayton shoot Baldridge?' Quist asked quickly.

Fletcher shook his head. 'The trouble was quieted, before any shooting was done. What the quarrel was about, I don't know. Clayton's wife figured in the trouble, somehow. No one in town seemed to know exactly what was happening. On top of that, our legal man was shot at one day, on the way to see Clayton. He admits the bullet flew wide, so maybe it was just some sort of warning, but he refused to drive out and see Clayton again. Says he'll resign from his job first. So the board put it up to me to see what I could do. I at once thought of you and — '

'You can forget me,' Quist said tersely. 'I said I was leaving for the coast tonight and I mean it. Buying rights-of-way isn't in my contract — '

'But, Greg — ' Fletcher started a protest.

'But me no buts, Jay. You know you've no right to ask me — '

'It's within my power to *order* you,' Fletcher flared. 'Now you know blame well — '

'Order and be damned,' Quist snapped. 'You know as well as I that my contract reads I'm to have a free hand in any job I take, and I can refuse a job if

I don't like it. For that matter, the company can have my contract any time it likes. I've had enough of — '

'Now, now, Greg,' Fletcher said placatingly. 'No use of you flying off the handle like this. We've been friends too long to scrap over trifles. I just thought maybe you'd be willing to help me out in a small matter.'

'Small matter,' — sarcastically. 'Clayton pulling a gun on his own father-in-law, and somebody shooting at the company law sharp.'

'Well, you know what I mean,' Fletcher said lamely. 'Sure, I'll admit there's a certain element of danger if I ask you to go to Quivira City, but I've never known danger to hold you back, Greg.'

'You know damn well that's not what I meant either,' Quist growled. 'What gripes me is, here I've made all preparations to get away for a spell. We've got damn nigh thirty operatives on the company payroll — but you have to come to me with your blasted request.'

'There's no one has your ability — '

Fletcher commenced.

Quist swore, low-toned. 'Cut out the palaver, Jay. I'm not going to Quivira City — danger or no danger. Send somebody else.'

Fletcher's shoulders slumped. 'There's no good man available, right now. Of course, I could pull Frank Bowdoin off that job he's working on. It's not important — merely a matter of checking through some recovered stolen goods. Next to you he's got the best mind for detective work and that sort of thing —'

Quist cut swiftly in, 'Bowdoin's got a wife and a couple of children, hasn't he?' Fletcher nodded, adding that the kids were pretty good size, though. Quist went on, 'And wasn't Bowdoin due to retire with a pension this year.' Fletcher admitted this was so, but that quitting so soon in life wouldn't bring a large pension. Quist said, 'But large enough to help him get started on that chicken farm he's planned on for some years now.' He added that there weren't many operatives who lived long enough to retire.

'That's all true enough, Greg,' Fletcher agreed, 'but when I need a man for investigation, I need him. That's all there is to it.'

'You bustard.' Quist swore long and bitterly. When he had run out of breath, Fletcher smiled and said:

'So you'll go then, Greg?'

Before Quist could reply there was a knock at the room door. Quist rose and answered it. He came back with a telegram for Fletcher, tossed it in the Division Superintendent's general direction and proceeded to open another bottle of beer. He was midway through his glass, when he caught a sudden exclamation from Fletcher.

'What's up?' Quist asked, noting the look of concern on Fletcher's face. 'Something wrong, Jay?'

Fletcher looked back at the telegram then raised his head. 'This telegram is from Quivira City. From our lawyer there. He says,' — Fletcher's voice quivered a little — 'that Whitney Clayton died yesterday — '

'So?' Quist didn't appear greatly concerned. Standing beside the small table, he raised a glass to his lips and drank deeply. 'That'll probably simplify matters for you. His widow will inherit the property. As Baldridge's daughter she'll be amenable to reason, so long as her old man is willing to sell. So matters are cleared up, Jay, and I'm heading for the Coast tonight.'

'Simplify matters hell!' Fletcher jerked out irritably. 'All I can see is more trouble. Clayton didn't die a natural death. He was murdered. Shot by young Chris Baldridge — the daughter's younger brother. There's bound to be a lot of delay in a situation of that kind . . . ' His voice fell off as his gaze went back to the telegram held in his hand, and he didn't even hear Quist's reply.

Eventually it was borne in on Fletcher's consciousness that Quist was hurriedly jamming articles into an open satchel resting atop the dresser. Drawers were jerked out, contents removed, slammed shut again. Quist worked fast, whistling softly to himself.

Glumly, Fletcher eyed the proceedings. He said rather peevishly, 'So you're leaving me in a mess, just when I need you. I'm blasted if I can see the reason for all this rush though. That Coast Limited doesn't leave until eight-nineteen — '

Quist turned momentarily back from his packing. 'My train,' he corrected, 'leaves in exactly twenty-one minutes.'

Fletcher frowned, considering. 'But — but where do you think you're going?' He gained his feet, staring at Quist.

'You're asking my destination?' Quist smiled mockingly. 'Quivira City, Jay. No, don't waste time talking. Murder changes things!' He jammed on his flat-crowned sombrero, jerked up the closed satchel. 'I'm on my way, Jay. *Adios!*'

Crossing the room in quick strides, he pulled open the door, slammed it behind him. Almost instantly the door was reopened and Quist's head reappeared. 'Jay, take care of my hotel bill, will you? It'll save time for me. And wire that law-sharp in Quivira City to clear out. I don't want him cluttering up my path, when I get to work. You'll hear from me, eventually. S'long!'

The door banged to once more. Fletcher could hear Quist's steps retreating rapidly down the hallway, then the clatter of booted feet on the stairs. Speechless, Fletcher sank slowly back to his seat on the bed, mouth half open at the sudden turn of events. 'Good Lord,' he said finally, 'Greg surely moves fast, once he's made up his mind.'

3

Twisted Facts

Once the railroad had come through, Quivira City had boomed rapidly. Mostly the town had built north, from Railroad Street which paralleled the T.N. & A.S.'s shining steel rails. Next came Blackjack Street — a name long since forgotten since the inhabitants of the town insisted on calling it' Main Street. A block farther to the north ran Lamar Street, mostly a thoroughfare of residences. Crossing Main, and running north and south, were several cross streets: Laredo, Austin, Alamo, Bowie and two or three others. Both north and south of Quivira City was a scattering of houses, set down helter-skelter where no regular streets existed. Southwest of the railroad the population was largely Mexican. Here, also, had been placed the town cemetery. North of the rails, at the far western end of town were the whitewashed cattle pens and loading chutes, generally idle except in the fall after beef roundup had taken place across the range.

Business buildings occupied most of Main Street, naturally. There were two hotels; a brick bank — where the majority of buildings were of rock-and-adobe or frame with high false fronts — half a dozen saloons and as many restaurants; two feed and hay stores; a couple of liveries; three general stores; a weekly newspaper titled the *Quivira Blade;* clothing establishments and various other buildings of commercial enterprise. The combination jail and sheriff's office stood at the southeast corner of Main and Laredo streets, its rear wall facing the tracks on Railroad Street. Directly across from the sheriff's office, on Main, was the County Building and Court House, a two-story structure of sun-blistered paint and wind-blasted pine. None of the streets were paved and they were dusty in summer and muddy when the winter rains came. But, as all too many real-estate agents proclaimed,

Quivira City possessed the finest climate in America. Dozens of other growing towns throughout Texas disputed that claim. It was mid afternoon when Gregory Quist stepped off the caboose of a westbound T.N. & A.S. freight train, to the raised-dirt platform of the depot, a red-painted frame building from which issued the continual *clickety-click-clickety-click-click* of a telegraph instrument. Up ahead a locomotive panted furiously and threw up clouds of black smoke, hissing steam and cinders. As the stop had been made only for the purpose of depositing Quist, the train quickly got under way again, and in an instant the platform was cleared of the shadowing smoke. And in that instant Quist felt the burning sun strike him like a furnace blast. 'Whew! Plenty hot today,' he grunted, and nodding briefly to the usual loafers collected around the station he stepped down from the platform and strode up Austin Street until he'd reached Main, satchel gripped in his left hand. On the corner he paused a moment to glance in both directions along the street. On either side ran an almost unbroken line of hitchracks; waiting ponies and vehicles were spotted here and there. Pedestrians moved along the sidewalks; more people were to be seen sitting or standing in shadows, out of reach of the torrid sun. A vagrant breeze swept down from the Montañosas, to the west, stirring brief 'dust devils' along the roadway, but there was nothing cooling about the breeze.

'This burg has sure grown some,' Quist grunted. 'Must be folks thrive in ovens nowdays. I could use a beer right now.' He glanced longingly at a saloon across the way, then shifted his gaze diagonally to the opposite corner where a wooden building constructed on a high cement-block foundation, bore a sign proclaiming it to be the QUIVIRA HOUSE — ROOMS BY DAY OR WEEK. Quist crossed over, quickening step to avoid an approaching surrey, and mounted a flight of eight stairs to the roofed porch of the hotel, the porch fronting on Main Street and turning to face Austin Street as well. Quist noticed, just before he stepped into the lobby, there was an entrance to the hotel bar on the Austin side.

He approached the desk and registered. The clerk looked up with sudden interest. 'Oh, yes, Mr. Quist, we've been expecting you. A Mr. Fletcher telegramed to Mr. Dowd — '

'Dowd?' Quist didn't recognize the name, for a moment.

'C. F. Dowd — the T.N. & A.S. lawyer — '

'Sure enough, I'd forgotten. Is Dowd still here?'

The hotel clerk shook his head. 'He took the eight-thirteen from town this morning. But we've arranged everything to his orders. It's a good room, Mr. Quist — one at the rear where it will be quiet. And the beer's taken care of. Mr. Dowd saw to that personally — '

Quist looked blank. 'Beer?'

'Beer,' the clerk insisted. 'The telegram to Mr. Dowd read explicitly. Mr. Fletcher told Dowd that he'd 'better damn well have some beer on hand' when you arrived.' The clerk looked apologetic.

Quist threw back his head and laughed, secured the key to his room and mounted the stairway from the lobby to the second floor. Not far from the stairway he located his room, Number 23, which on entering he found to be a fairly large airy chamber situated at the northeast corner of the building, with open windows in either wall affording a cross current of air. The furniture was about as usual: double bed, dresser, a couple of chairs, a commode and washstand, clothes rack. The walls had been papered with a floral pattern of purple-red roses and poisonous blue forget-me-nots. One wall held a framed engraving of 'The Stag at Bay'; over the commode was a small mirror. Towels hung from a rack. Probably the first thing that caught Quist's eye was a wooden case of bottled beer placed on a small table near a window.

Dropping his satchel to the bed, Quist crossed the room to the case of beer.

Something like a groan parted his lips and he swore. 'Wouldn't you know that damn legal sharp would ball things up! On a day like this he leaves me warm beer. And not even an opener. Of all the stupid idiots — '

A knock at his door interrupted the tirade. Quist went to the door and opened it. A man entered the room carrying a galvanized bucket in which reposed a chunk of ice and four bottles of cool beer. He was a tall bonily constructed man with rugged features and the bluest eyes Quist had ever seen. His features were freckled and he had brick-red hair — so much of it as could be seen beneath a slouch-brim weathered sombrero. His spare legs in black trousers, tucked into boots, were slightly bowed. He wore a denim shirt, open at the throat, and a stringy vest on which was pinned a deputy sheriff's badge. Quist judged him to be close to thirty.

'Where do you want this put?' — indicating the bucket of beer bottles and ice. He had an easy drawly way of speaking.

'Can you think of any better place than down a throat?' Quist asked.

'Now that sounds right laudable,' the redhead grinned. He placed the bucket on the table, next to the case of beer, and extracted two bottles, replacing them with ones from the case. From a pants pocket he produced an opener, used it, and passed a bottle to Quist. The two men stood in the center of the room, uptilted bottles at their lips. The bottles were lowered almost simultaneously, followed by exclamations of satisfaction.

'That's a godsend,' Quist commented, 'on a day like this.'

'Mighty hot, all right,' the other agreed. 'Folks been having trouble with their shadows all morning.'

'Shadows?' Quist inquired politely, raising the bottle again.

'Yeah,' the redhead explained gravely. 'They won't lay flat. Keep curling up like a slice of bacon in a hot pan. Makes folks uncomfortable to have to drag a shriveled shadow at their heels.'

'I imagine,' Quist said dryly. 'Likely

gets tangled between a man's legs now and then — might throw him.'

They drank on that one too. The redhead added, as though he'd just thought of it, 'Name's Sargent, Mr. Quist — Todd Sargent. Deputy here.' The two men shook hands. Quist liked the firm grip Sargent gave him.

He said, 'Apparently you knew I was coming, but you haven't explained the beer yet.'

'Hell's bells! Practically the whole town knew you were coming. And with your rep — ' Todd Sargent broke off. 'Y'know, Mr. Quist, that railroad lawyer — '

'Anybody brings me beer like that calls me by my first name, Todd.'

'If you say so,' Sargent drawled. 'But to get on — I don't figure that C. F. Dowd hombre was too bright. 'Stead of taking care of things himself, far's possible, he talks too much to the hotel clerk downstairs. As I'm on better than speaking terms with the clerk, I hear things about you. And a lot of other people do too. So this whole town is primed to see some unusual detecting on your part — '

'Bosh!' Quist frowned.

'As to the beer,' Sargent continued. 'When I learned that Dowd had just left a case of warm beer here, I set about to amend his plan some.'

'Let's amend it some more.' Quist nodded toward the bucket.

The two men finally took seats, each holding a cold bottle. By this time, Quist had doffed his coat and loosened his tie. Quist said, 'So now we come to why you're so interested in my welfare.'

Sargent didn't reply for a moment, as he slouched down in his chair. Finally, 'I'd like a chance to work with you — watch your methods. Pike Wolcott won't always be sheriff of Blackjack County. Some day I'd like to have his job and do right by it — '

'Oh, a politician,' Quist said dryly.

'Let's say,' Sargent put in, 'an *honest* politician. There's a difference these days.'

'I stand corrected,' Quist nodded. 'So I'm to take it this — Pike Wolcott? — the present sheriff — isn't honest?'

'Cripes, no!' Sargent sat straighter in his chair. 'I don't want to give that impression at all. Pike's straight as a die.'

'Did he send you to talk to me?'

The deputy shook his head. 'That I did on my own. Fact is, Mr. Quist — Greg — this Clayton killing is sort of messed up — '

'Murder's a messy business.'

'I didn't mean that way. It's just — just —' Sargent seemed at a loss for the proper words. 'Let's put it this way. I'm not sure the Baldridges welcome your coming here. There seems to be a feeling they can settle matters without outside interference. Old Grizzly Baldridge is sort of a law unto himself in these parts. Folks generally do as he says. So I just sort of figured that — that — well, hell, you'll want to talk to somebody, and I might be able to give you straighter facts than — than —'

'Than Pike Wolcott?' Quist asked shrewdly.

'Now, understand, I'm not saying a

word against Pike —'

'Maybe you've already said it, without intending to,' Quist said quietly. 'I've rather gathered that you don't like the way things are going. So I conclude that Grizzly Baldridge, as you called him, plays the tune that Wolcott dances to. Am I right?'

'I didn't say that. It's just that I want you to get facts right, as I know 'em — and Lord knows they're in a muddle. Your company wants a right-of-way. I'd like to see this murder business cleared up soon's possible. There's been blame little crime in Quivira City. I like this town and —'

'Let's get straightened around a mite, Todd. You can give me a quick run-down on what's happened here. As I get it, there's been trouble with the Baldridge son-in-law who owned the right-of-way to Estrecho Pass. Why he didn't get along with the Baldridges, I don't know. We'll get to that later. Whitney Clayton tried to gouge a big price out of our representative. Later, somebody threw a shot at Dowd and scared him spineless. Who did it?'

'That I don't know. I went out there near Clayton's house, where Dowd claimed he was shot at, but couldn't pick up any sign. I really looked too' — earnestly.

'I'll take your word for it. Now as to the Baldridges — who are they?'

'Grizzly Baldridge, the father, is one tough old root and owns more cattle and acres than you can shake a stick at. Then there's young Chris, his son, 'bout twenty years old. And a good hombre. And,' — Sargent drew a long breath — 'Chris's sister, Laurinda. Laurinda Clayton, now — Whit's widow. She left Whit Clayton a few months back. They were only married about a year ago. I can't say I blame her. Whit Clayton was a skunk.'

'In what way?'

Sargent hesitated. 'I'd rather not say. You'll hear — '

'You came here to give me facts,' Quist said tersely. 'Pretty good friend of

Laurinda's, are you?'

'I didn't say that,' Sargent snapped.

'I can guess at it. Maybe you were better than good friends. Maybe you might even have married her, except that Whitney Clayton beat you to it. And now you figure I think anything you say against Clayton will be biased, so you want me to learn about him someplace else. Right?'

'Blast you, Greg Quist,' the deputy said ruefully. His face was redder than usual. 'All right, it could be you've come close to the truth, though I never really had a chance with Laurinda. Too many other men felt like I did — '

'We'll get to them later. What, exactly, was wrong with Whit Clayton?'

'He turned out just plain no good. When he got his hands on any money he gambled it away. He couldn't handle liquor — not the way he drank it. He was a liar by the clock — '

'That's enough for the present,' Quist said dryly, 'to tell me he didn't run on standard time. I've heard he once pulled a gun on old Baldridge. Did Clayton consider himself a gunfighter?'

'Only when he was drunk. Cripes! That business was some time back. Dowd must have picked it up someplace and you got it through him — '

'I'm waiting to get it through you. What was the fuss about?'

'I haven't the least idea. I reckon it didn't amount to much. It started down near the depot one day when I happened to be standing on the platform. I could hear Whit and Grizzly squabbling, but couldn't distinguish the words. Finally Clayton reached for his gun. It had scarcely cleared leather when Grizzly was on him like a wildcat, and yanked the gun out of Whit's hand. Then he slapped him across the face with the barrel and knocked him down. I'd come up to interfere, but there was nothing for me to do. Clayton had been drunk, but he was sobering up fast. As Grizzly left, he tossed me the gun, and told Whit if he ever saw him with a gun again, he'd gunwhip him to death. And I never saw Whit Clayton wear a six-shooter from that day on, either. I've still got his gun down to the office —'

'So Clayton wasn't armed when Chris Baldridge killed him?'

'Not so far as we know — ' Sargent broke off suddenly, his blue eyes widening. 'Sa-a-ay, sounds like you don't know — oh, cripes, I might have known Dowd wouldn't have had time to send you word. I guess I was just taking it for granted — '

'What in the devil are you driving at?'

'Look here, Greg,' the deputy said earnestly, 'I've been trying to make it clear that facts are mighty twisted. Sure, Chris Baldridge come into town yesterday and gave himself up to the sheriff. Said he'd just killed Whit Clayton. Wouldn't give any explanation, or anything. Seemed right upset about the whole business. But now, we don't know what to think — '

'Why? What's happened?'

'It's Laurinda. She showed up late yesterday and told the sheriff *she'd* killed Clayton.'

4

Warning?

Quist whistled softly as he absorbed the information. A cooler breeze came through the open windows. 'I didn't think when I came here,' he said finally, 'there'd be much for me to do. Now I'm not certain about that.'

'You agree something sounds fishy about the setup ?' Sargent asked eagerly. 'That's a fool question, I suppose.'

'Any time you catch two trout on one hook, it's mighty interesting. I've never known it to happen. So either Chris, or Clayton's wife — widow — isn't dropping a straight line. They're covering up something.'

'What you got in mind ?'

'Mostly,' Quist evaded, 'that I'm a lot more comfortable than I was when I arrived. It's cooled off a heap.'

The deputy looked disappointed. 'Yeah, the heat was unusual for this time of year. Why only last week, one night, I thought we were due for a frost. But, what do you figure — ?'

'I figure I'm going to get cleaned up a mite. I had a long hot ride. I need washing and a shave. You keep talking, and keep that beer chilling.' He opened his satchel and got out shaving things, then went across the room and poured water from a pitcher into a washbowl. Next he peeled off his shirt and started working up a lather on his face. 'So,' he said finally, 'am I to understand you got the brother and sister both in cells ?'

'Hell's bells on a tomcat no!' Sargent exclaimed. 'You don't put a Baldridge in a cell in Quivira City — and Laurinda's still a Baldridge, even if her name was changed by marriage.' He sounded rather aghast at the thought of a Baldridge being kept behind bars.

Quist spoke over his shoulder while he continued shaving. 'How'd Chris Baldridge act when he came in to give himself up?'

'Like I said — upset. Nervous. Just

announced that he'd shot Clayton. Refused to give details. Said he'd tell the story at his trial —'

'Probably wanted time to think up a story,' Quist commented. 'Didn't the sheriff even put him in a cell then?'

'No. Pike told Chris to stick around the office and he'd see about getting a hearing right off with the Justice of the Peace. Word was sent to Grizzly Baldridge to come in. Hell, hearing was had and bail set even before old Baldridge arrived in town.'

Quist said caustically, 'The Baldridges seem to have things tough in this town, don't they?'

'I've been trying to make you see how it was. I noticed when Chris first come in to surrender himself that he wasn't wearing his forty-five. I asked him what became of it, and he told Pike and me he'd dropped it near Clayton's body in his excitement.'

'Is Chris generally what you'd term the excitable type?'

'Not on your tintype, Greg. He's pretty

levelheaded as a rule, but I must admit he seemed right upset. Anyway, bail was set, and Grizzly arrived and got things fixed up. The undertaker was told to go out and get the body. Pike told me I'd better go out and take a look — '

Momentarily, the razor paused in its ringing sounds. 'Do you mean to say Wolcott himself didn't make an investigation?'

'That's the way it was. Shucks! That doesn't mean anything. Pike's no longer young. He's put on a lot of fat the past years.'

'Mostly above the ears, I imagine.' The shaving continued. 'Let's not hold it against Pike, Greg. He's been a mighty good sheriff in his time. He figures I'm capable of handling things. I rode out to Clayton's house, which lies not far from the Montañosas. Things were about as Chris had said, the corpse covered with a blanket and so on. What Chris hadn't told us was that there'd been a struggle of some sort. Furniture had been knocked galley-west. I noticed Laurinda's belt and empty holster hanging on the wall, but thought nothing of it at the time. My mind was occupied with the body. The bullet had entered Clayton's neck. I reckon it severed a jugular. Blood had soaked into the board flooring — '

'Was the gun there on the floor as Chris had said?'

Sargent hesitated a moment. 'Weell, there was a gun there. But it wasn't Chris's forty-five. It was a thirty-eight caliber. Later — last night — Laurinda admitted it was her gun. I'd recognized her initials, LB, stamped into the butt. I'd seen it before, of course. That sort of puzzled me at the time, but I didn't know but that Chris had had her gun for some reason or other. Anyway, I waited at Clayton's place until the undertaker's wagon arrived, then I headed back to town. On the way I met Chris and we stopped to talk a minute or so. I asked him if he was sure he had dropped his forty-five six-shooter beside the body — and I emphasized 'forty-five.' He insisted he had, and asked if I hadn't found it.

I told him I hadn't. Chris allowed that was damn funny. It seemed to worry him. Finally he came up with some feeble idea that I must have overlooked it. I laughed at him and said anyway the coroner's jury would probably insist on the bullet being probed out — words to that effect. Right away, Chris got mad. Said he couldn't see any reason for an inquest or any probing out of bullets. He'd confessed to the shooting; that should be enough, and so on in that strain. He was pretty riled and excited when I left him and continued on toward town.'

'You didn't mention finding the thirty-eight near the body?' Quist toweled himself and dug a clean flannel shirt from his satchel, after pausing for a swallow of beer.

'No, I didn't tell him, nor Pike Wolcott either, right away. I got hold of Doc Twitchell, soon's I got back and told him to probe for the bullet as soon as the undertaker got the body to town. It proved to be a thirty-eight from Laurinda's gun — from a thirty-eight caliber weapon, at least. And then, last night, Laurinda came to town and made a confession to Pike and me that she had shot Clayton. She wouldn't give any details either. She'd brought Grizzly in with her, and I could see he'd been trying to dissuade her from talking. He tried to shut her up all the time she was at the office. Grizzly was boiling mad over the whole business. Anyway, another hearing was held and more bail set. Then Laurinda went back to the Bee-Hive with her father.'

'Was an inquest held?' Quist asked.

'It was concluded shortly before you hit town. Grizzly and Pike told Doc Twitchell — he's coroner here you know — that things should be held off a spell, but Twitchell ain't the sort of man you can boss around.'

'Verdict?' Quist asked.

The deputy laughed bitterly. 'This will show you how this town can be buffaloed. The coroner's jury brought in a verdict that Clayton had met his death as the result of a gunshot, and while both Chris

Baldridge and Laurinda Clayton might be held under suspicion, there may have been exonerating circumstances, and any verdict given must be considered as open to reversal if and when the sheriff's office turned up fresh evidence.'

'And it is up to *you* to dig up said evidence?'

'If you knew Pike Wolcott you wouldn't expect it of *him*.'

'That's all you've got in the way of evidence, so far, then?'

'That's all — except the fall sessions of circuit court are due in about a month. I'm dumping it in your lap, Greg.'

Quist stared questioningly at the red-headed deputy. 'What in the devil are you expecting of me?'

'I want you to get Laurinda out of this business.'

'And see that Chris gets the blame — ?'

'I just can't believe Laurinda would do a thing like that. Someway, she's trying to cover up for Chris.'

Quist laughed shortly. 'My God, but some men are susceptible. A pretty face can turn a man's head — ' He broke off, then, 'I'm assuming she's pretty. You say there were several men — '

Sargent's face had reddened. 'Now, look here, Quist — '

'You look here,' Quist interrupted brutally, 'what do you expect? I've been taking you at your word. Now I'm going to do some talking. I'm asking exactly what you plan to gain if I can work things to get Laurinda Clayton off scot-free? What's in it for you? Or do you want me to tell you ?'

The deputy was on his feet now, facing Quist, angry lights burning in his eyes. 'If you mean what I think you mean — '

'I'm not giving a damn what you think,' Quist sneered. 'I'm telling you how things shape up to me. How do I know you haven't rigged this whole business to get rid of Whit Clayton? You come to me — without your sheriff's knowledge — and talk of political ambitions. You admit you're interested in Laurinda Clayton. Grizzly Baldridge is a rich man. Some day, Laurinda Clayton will own part of that money. Why shouldn't you marry her, if you can push yourself high enough in the world to meet her standards? In short, how in hell do I know you didn't kill Whit Clayton yourself, or arrange to have it done?' He laughed nastily.

Todd Sargent was white as a sheet. Tiny bulges of angry muscle worked at the corners of his mouth. He half raised one clenched fist, then swung about and headed for the door, not trusting himself to speak.

The door was half open when Quist caught Sargent's arm and whirled him around. Even through his anger, Sargent was impressed with Quist's strength. Quist shut the door. There was a rueful smile on his face, as he drew Sargent back into the room.

'I'm sorry, Todd,' he said sincerely. 'I can be such an awful bustard at times.'

Sargent glared at him uncertainly. His voice shook a little when he said, 'If you'd had a gun on you . . . ' He allowed the sentence to go unfinished. The color was returning to his face now. 'I still don't understand what in hell — '

'I had to do it, Todd. There wasn't any other way. Not that I know of — '

'But you were hinting that I — I — '

'Hell! I did more than hint, and I'd not have blamed you if you'd knocked all my teeth down my throat.' He said again, 'But I had to do it that way. Y'see, Todd, when I go on a job like this, I commence by suspecting everybody connected with the case. Then I ferret out those I can trust from those I don't trust. I've got to trust somebody. I was hoping it was you, but I couldn't be sure until you'd passed the test — '

'Test? You mean you were just putting on an act?'

'It was just an act,' Quist admitted. 'I wanted to see your act — if you had one — when I made certain accusations. You didn't have an act. You got mad as hell. You rung true as the devil. I could tell.'

'Aw, cripes A'mighty,' the red-headed deputy grinned self-consciously. 'Let's forget it.' He added, 'There should be a couple of more bottles cold by this time. But, jeez,' — an afterthought — 'you sure made me boilin' for a few minutes.'

'We'll get back to where we were,' Quist said, after a few sips of beer. 'Now, you refuse to believe Laurinda killed her husband. That means you think Chris did it.'

'It had to be one of the two — '

'That's a possibility,' Quist conceded.

'And yet,' the red-headed deputy scowled, 'I can't overlook the fact I picked a thirty-eight six-shooter from the floor near Clayton's body, and a thirty-eight slug was probed from his carcass.'

Quist pondered the question. 'How often have you ever seen Laurinda Clayton wearing a belt and gun?'

'We've known each other since we were kids,' Sargent said, 'and I could count the times I've seen her with a gun, on the fingers of my two hands — and have some fingers left over, too. Oh, she knows how to shoot all right. Grizzly Baldridge saw to that. She was a kid when he gave her that gun — not more'n twelve or thirteen. Just as he gave Chris his forty-five. Had their initials stamped on both weapons.'

'Laurinda and Chris get along together?'

'They've always been mighty close. Laurinda sort of acted like a mother to Chris when he was a kid, after their mother died. And I know Chris didn't like it one bit when she married Clayton.'

'What's the possibility of old Baldridge having killed Clayton?' Quist asked.

'It could be that way.' Sargent shrugged his shoulders. 'He hated Whit enough, Lord knows.'

'Yes, but I gather both Chris and Laurinda did too — '

'But I'm sure Laurinda wouldn't — '

'Don't ever be sure of anything, or anybody, Todd. It doesn't pay.' He added, 'Not until they've actually assayed up to your satisfaction.'

'That sounds pretty cynical, Greg.'

'If I'm cynical,' Quist replied gruffly,

'it's my job that's made me that way. Well, I don't know as there's anything more I can learn from you, right now. Oh, yes, was Whitney Clayton a long resident here?'

Sargent shook his head. 'It's less than two years since he came here.'

'Where from?'

'I haven't the least idea. I think he mentioned Colorado once, though I'm not sure. Actually, he didn't seem like a bad hombre at first. No,' — at a question from Quist — 'he wasn't a cowman. But he did know horses, right well. Claimed he came here for his health — some lung trouble or other — and he did look rather peaked when he first arrived — you know, washed out, pale-looking. Howsomever, he seemed to recover fast.'

'I've always understood Colorado was good for the lungs.'

'Maybe it wasn't in his case.'

'If,' Quist said, 'old Baldridge didn't have any use for Clayton, how come he ever let him have that half-section over near Estrecho Pass?' Quist expanded on the question. 'What I'm wondering, did Clayton bring some sort of pressure on Baldridge to make him turn over that chunk of land?'

'That I don't know. He bought the land, or so he said, after he and Laurinda became engaged. Claimed he intended to raise polo ponies for some market he knew of back east. At the time he told it, it sounded like a good setup. We thought he was in earnest when he threw up that little house on the land — though none of us ever figured it was any place to bring a bride — not a bride like Laurinda that had always been used to the best. But she took some furniture out there and, so far as I know, tried to make a go of it. It wasn't too long before she left him and returned home.'

'Did he ever do anything about the polo ponies?'

'Not one damn thing. Fact is, he didn't seem to show any ambition at all, except when it came to a matter of get- ting drunk, playing poker or stud, or fooling around with women.'

'The more I hear about this Clayton hombre,' Quist laughed shortly, 'the more I wonder why I should bother trying to decide who killed him. The killer sounds like a real benefactor of humanity.'

Sargent grunted assent. Quist rolled and lighted a cigarette. Tossing the burned matchstick through an open window, he noticed the sun was nearly gone. With the cooling of the day, there was more activity in Quivira City. Horses and vehicles, moving on the streets, mingled their clatter with the sounds of voices and footsteps along the sidewalks. From somewhere back on Lamar Street, which was mostly populated with rooming — and boarding-houses, came the monotonous *thwack-thwack-thwack* of a carpet or rug being beaten.

Quist continued, 'Right now I'm just certain of one fact, and that is that my stomach is beginning to think my throat's been cut.' He blew a gray spiral of cigarette smoke into the room. 'What's the best place for chow in this town, Todd?'

'At this hour,' the deputy replied, 'I don't think you can do better than the hotel dining room, downstairs. I'm ready for a bite, too. How'd you like to have supper on me?'

'I'd like. Thanks. I'll be ready in just a minute.'

Quist donned his sombrero, smoke from the cigarette in his mouth curling up past the slanted brim, then going to his satchel he drew out a leather under-arm gun harness, which he fastened about his body. Next, he picked from the satchel a short-barreled Colt's six-shooter of .44 caliber and shoved it into the holster.

From his chair, the deputy eyed him curiously. 'That's quite a contraption, Greg.'

'Best rig I've been able to work out to date,' Quist answered, approaching to allow Sargent to examine the harness. 'With this type holster I can just draw my gun straight out, through the open side. With a belt holster, I'd have to draw up, then out. It's a fraction of a second faster this way — and sometimes that fraction spells the difference between firing or being fired on.'

He demonstrated several draws, and the deputy's eyes widened at the smooth, effortless speed with which Quist got the .44 weapon into action. Sargent nodded, saying, 'But what I don't understand is what holds that gun in place? Doesn't it ever just fall out of that side opening in your holster?'

Quist shook his head. 'There's a flat steel spring sewed inside the leather, which holds the gun in place until it's needed. This is a sight more comfortable than toting a gun on your hip.' He dipped into a box of .44 cartridges and slipped them into a pocket.

'Don't you even wear a ca'tridge belt?' Sargent asked.

'One belt supporting my pants is enough around my waist,' Quist replied. 'No, Todd, if a man can't do his job with what's in his gun, plus an extra handful of ca'tridges, he hasn't any business carrying a gun. And with this caliber six-shooter, should I ever have need for a rifle, I can use the same caliber .44. Saves me toting two kinds of loads.' Tying a blue bandanna around his throat, he slipped into his coat. 'I'll be with you just as soon as I draw these shades and light the lamp.'

'Lamp?' Sargent frowned. 'Already? It's still light out.'

Quist nodded. 'I generally leave a lamp burning low when I'm on a job and go out for a spell, in the evening. If the lamp is out when I return, I take it easy entering my room, until I've learned just why it's not burning. If the lamp is still lighted on my return, I can size up my room faster, in case anyone is waiting to take a shot at me.'

'Jeepers! You don't take many chances do you, Greg?'

'Not any that can be avoided. I can't afford to in the life I lead.'

He crossed to the open window to draw the shade, facing out on Austin Street, stooping down for a moment to glance outside. Instantly, and with considerable alacrity, he jumped to one side. Something had whined past his head and struck the opposite wall with a solid thud. Quist swore in surprise.

Sargent had leaped to his feet. 'What the devil was that?'

'I'm a liar.' Quist laughed softly. 'No! Stay back. Keep away from those windows.'

'But what—'

'I'm a particularly stupid liar,' Quist continued. 'I do take chances—Todd, somebody outside took a shot at me.'

'T'hell you say! I didn't hear any report.'

From over on Lamar Street, still came the sounds of somebody beating dust from a carpet. 'I didn't either,' Quist replied, 'but that was one mighty cool breeze that whipped past my head.'

Todd Sargent hadn't waited to hear more. Leaping halfway across the room to the door, he flung it open and went clattering down the stairway to the lobby and street below.

'I'll say one thing for that deputy,' Quist mused, 'he doesn't lose any time going into action — though I doubt it will do him any good.'

Even as the thought was crossing his mind, Quist, staying well back from the windows, was glancing sharply outside. There was no unusual movement to be noted anywhere. Directly across Austin Street, the roof of a general store met Quist's eye. Beyond that, two and three story buildings caught the late rays of the dying sun. Quist shifted his gaze toward Lamar Street, where across the roofs of houses and other low buildings he saw an almost unbroken line of tall cottonwood trees. Branches showed barely, here and there, where some leaves had already fallen, but of a sign of anything human, there was none to be seen.

'Probably ducked from view as soon as he fired,' Quist speculated. 'The question is, was the bustard actually trying to kill me, or was that just a warning not to meddle around here? For a warning, it came mighty close.' He added grimly, 'All right, somebody wants to play rough. I'll have to try and satisfy him.'

5

Trouble

By the time Todd Sargent returned, a half hour later, the shades at the windows had been drawn and the small kerosene lamp lighted. By the light of the lamp, Quist had located the spot where the bullet had penetrated the wall, almost directly opposite the window through which the shot had come, and had succeeded in digging it out of the wall with his pocketknife.

The deputy entered the room and said disgustedly, 'No luck, of course. There wasn't a soul on the street that looked suspicious.'

'You didn't think there would be, did you?' Quist asked. Sargent shook his head. 'Whoever did it, lit out fast after shooting. I just figured somebody might have seen him, or heard a shot — or something. Nobody did that I talked to.'

'Anyway,' Quist pointed out, 'that shot

didn't come from the street below.'

'It didn't?' The deputy looked surprised. 'But, where — ?'

'Whoever fired that shot,' Quist explained, 'was stationed on just about the same level I was — '

'A rooftop!' Sargent exclaimed. He moved quickly across the room, drew back the shade and peered out, then, 'Damn! It's too dark to see much. Let me see,' — frowning as he came back into the room — 'just across from here, on the corner of Main and Austin, there's Deming's General Store; next to that stands Merker's Drug Store — that roof would be below Deming's; then comes the Green Bottle Saloon — single story, too; adjoining the Green Bottle, is the *Quivira Blade* building — that's a two-story — '

'Forget it, Todd,' Quist advised. 'There's all those house rooftops over on that next street, paralleling Main — '

'Lamar Street,' Sargent supplied.

'All right, Lamar. The shot might have come from any of those roofs, or even higher — '

'Look here, Greg,' Sargent asked, 'what makes you so certain that shot wasn't fired from the street below?'

Quist indicated the point on the wall from which he'd extracted the bullet, about four feet, or a little more, from the floor. 'I judged by the direction the slug took when it ploughed into that wall,' he explained. 'It took a mite of time to dig 'er out, but there it lies, on that table.'

Sargent crossed the room and took up the slightly battered chunk of lead. He examined it a moment, then turned to Quist. 'I figure it for a forty-five slug.'

'We agree on that,' Quist nodded. 'Whoever fired it, knew guns — he had to figure his elevation, trajectory and so on. And still he almost accomplished what he set out to do, and a forty-five six-shooter might not be too accurate at such range — '

'How do you know what the range was?'

'I know it was far enough away so neither of us noticed the report. With that heavy *pow* that a forty-five makes, it had to be some distance off or we'd have heard it. About that time somebody was beating the stuffing out of a carpet or something over there on Lamar Street.'

Sargent's eyes narrowed. 'Folks don't beat carpets this late in the day generally. So maybe this whole business was arranged.'

'That's possible,' Quist said dryly.

'What I mean, I thought there was a chance the gun might have been fired by accident, perhaps.'

'I doubt that too.'

'But why, Greg? You've not stepped on any toes yet.'

'I likely stepped on several toes just by coming here, Todd. Folks don't like private investigators coming into their business. You say, the whole town knew I was coming, due to that jackass, Dowd, talking too much. It wouldn't be difficult to learn what room I was to have. The whole setup could have been arranged by the time I arrived. All that was necessary was to have some gun-slinger wait opposite my room. Eventually I'd be almost certain to appear in the window.'

Sargent nodded reluctantly. 'It sure looks like somebody didn't even want to give you a chance to get started. It could have been just a warning, of course.'

'I thought of that too. But whoever shot at Dowd a spell back, fired plenty wide. That slug,' — nodding toward the bullet the deputy had replaced on the table — 'came just too damn close for comfort. Let's forget it. I'm ready to eat anything that doesn't start biting on me first.'

Quist turned the lamp down and the two men left the hotel room, descended the carpeted stairs to the lobby and started to turn right, toward the dining room beyond. Sargent caught Quist's sleeve. 'Just a minute. There's Chris Baldridge standing near the window. Want to meet him?'

'You bet your life.'

Sargent hailed Baldridge who crossed the lobby, dark eyes intent on Quist. He was a good-featured young fellow, with hair that was almost black, a solid jaw and straight nose. He shook hands somewhat reluctantly with Quist.

'Fact is,' he continued, 'I knew you were here, Quist — is there anyone in this town who doesn't? — and I wanted to talk to you. Maybe we can make a deal.'

'It's possible,' Quist replied quietly, though he'd had no intimation of what sort of deal Baldridge had in mind. 'Had your supper?'

'Not yet, but I don't want to take time to — '

'I've put off eating long enough for one day,', Quist smiled. 'And I'm damn sure I don't intend to talk any business until I've let my stomach know it's not forgotten. Better come along with us.'

'If you insist,' Baldridge said coldly, though it was clear he didn't relish the prospect of eating supper with Quist.

The three men entered the dining room, which had begun to fill up, and found a table against the far wall. There were probably two dozen tables in the room, with straight-backed chairs for customers. Kerosene lamps suspended in brackets around the walls furnished light. A larger lamp with wide reflecting shade hung from the center of the ceiling. A waitress arrived, spoke to Sargent as though he were an old friend, nodded shortly to Baldridge and said 'Good evening' to Quist. After she'd taken the orders, Quist said, 'And, miss, please bring a lot of coffee, right now.' The girl nodded and hurried off.

Quist said, chuckling, to Chris Baldridge, 'Todd poured so much beer into me this afternoon, I practically gurgle at every step. Figured coffee might make some sort of antidote.' It wasn't humorous to Baldridge. He acknowledged Quist's words with no answering smile; merely nodding. 'As I understand it, Quist, you're here to get a couple of rights-of-way for your railroad. Is that correct?'

'That's incorrect,' Quist said promptly. 'Our legal department takes care of that sort of thing. I'm here to learn what is holding up the proposition — '

'Amounts to the same thing,' Baldridge said brusquely.

'Now here's what we're willing —'

'Do you mind holding up business habla until I've got some food in me?' Quist said pleasantly.

'I just thought we could get things settled.'

'There's too much to be settled,' Quist stated, 'before I've eaten. And I've a hunch it will take quite some time longer, too.'

Chris Baldridge's face reddened. A sharp retort rose to his lips but he held it down. 'Just as you say,' he said coldly, and relaxed back in his chair.

Coffee arrived and a few minutes later the waitress again appeared bearing steaming platters of roast beef, mashed potatoes, canned corn and tomatoes. Bread and butter was distributed around the table. For some time there were no sounds to be heard except that made by cutlery and dishes.

Baldridge tried again, after a time, 'It's

this way, Mr. Quist. Todd has no doubt given you the details of the — the killing of my sister's husband. Now, actually that is no concern of yours. What you're after is to get this railroad business settled. Isn't that right?'

'Go on,' Quist said, and forked a chunk of roast beef into his mouth.

'Here's our proposition. We Baldridges like to clean up our own troubles without outside interference. This — this present affair, can be handled by us. There's no call for any of your famous detecting. We know what's happened. If we don't care to talk about it, that's our business. Now here's what we'll do. My father will give your company the right-of-way it wants, with it not costing the T.N. & A.S. a cent. Is that fair?'

'More than fair,' Quist acknowledged, 'but it's the right-of-way through Estrecho Pass that caused the hitch.'

'I figured you'd understand that was included in the deal,' Baldridge said impatiently.

'But, Chris, how could it — ?' Todd

Sargent broke off.

'Todd's right,' Quist put in, 'in what he intended to say. How could you give us that right? It's my understanding Clayton owned that property.'

'Only partly. My father, Griswold Baldridge — Grizzly as he's known around here — holds a mortgage on the Clayton half-section. On top of that, my sister, Laurinda, will inherit from Clayton. As his widow — '

Quist interrupted tersely, 'You make it sound very simple, Baldridge, but it's not as simple as all that.'

'What do you mean?' Baldridge bridled.

'Exactly what I say. I'll explain in a minute.'

Dried-apricot pie and more coffee were arriving. Quist commenced on his pie and commented that it was extra good. Finally he pushed the plate away and drew out his sack of Durham and brown cigarette papers, offering them around the table. Baldridge refused shortly. Sargent had produced his own tobacco. When smoke was rising from the cigarettes, Quist continued,

'Baldridge, you're out on bail for murder. Right?'

'Right,' Baldridge snapped. 'But what — ?'

'Just a minute.' Quist raised a protesting hand. 'For a murder you didn't commit.'

'That's not true,' Baldridge insisted.

Quist didn't reply at once, only stared steadily at Baldridge. When Baldridge's eyes finally dropped, Quist went on, 'Todd's given me the story. Sure, you appeared at the coroner's inquest and stated that you'd shot Clayton to death, but you didn't give any details. You didn't even know that it was a .38 slug that had killed him — or you pretended you didn't, I don't know which — until your sister confessed to the killing, and the doctor probed out a .38 bullet from Clayton's body. Previously, you'd tried to put across the idea you killed Clayton with your forty-five. By the way, I noticed you weren't wearing a gun. Haven't you found your forty-five? According to you, you dropped it by the body. What did happen to it?'

'I'm damned if I see that it matters to you,' Baldridge burst out angrily. 'What became of that gun is none of your business.'

Quist smiled thinly. 'Much obliged, Baldridge.'

Baldridge stared at him. 'For what?' he asked uncertainly.

'For telling me you don't know what happened to that .45. If you knew, you'd have said so. Eventually we'll learn what happened to that gun. That should prove a lesson to you, Baldridge, not to lose your temper and blurt out things you don't care to reveal.'

Baldridge bit his lip, then forced a wry smile. 'All right, Quist, maybe you're right. Maybe you're not. I don't care, either way. I'm only interested in making a deal with you, like I — '

'One thing I'd like to know,' Quist interrupted, 'is just how your father happened to sell Clayton that particular half-section near Estrecho Pass. And when?'

Baldridge considered. This time he'd not be trapped into blurting out information that should be kept secret. Finally, he replied, 'I didn't care for the idea, but after all, it was Dad's property. I suppose Laurinda was responsible in a way. The deal was made when she became engaged to Clayton. They talked of building a house. It was Clayton who wanted to be near Estrecho Pass. Claimed it would be good horse-grazing country. Dad was dubious, but Laurinda persuaded him to sell the half-section to Clayton. She could always wind Dad around her little finger. The house Clayton had built was a pretty shoddy proposition.'

'How much did Clayton pay your father for the land?'

Baldridge shrugged. 'I don't know. Never gave it any thought. Not much I know. Clayton claimed to be momentarily short at the time, though said he had money coming. Dad accepted an initial payment of two hundred dollars for the land. A mortgage was drawn up for the balance. Clayton promised to pay the full price in quick time, but he never did. He kept putting Dad off, with one excuse or another. We'd all believed him at first, especially when he had that shack built up there. That was to be the nucleus of a larger house, but Clayton never went farther with it, after he and Laurinda were married.'

'At any rate,' Quist nodded, 'it was Clayton's idea to buy that particular chunk of land. I wonder why?'

Baldridge shrugged. 'Perhaps he had an inkling that your company would be interested in it, and he'd make a profit.'

'That I doubt,' Quist said. 'The T.N. & A.S. doesn't make public its ideas that far in advance, even if they've been formulated.'

'Anyway,' Baldridge continued impatiently, 'I don't see what difference it makes now. Laurinda only lived with Clayton a few months, then left him to come home. Dad sort of felt they might get matters straightened out, after a time, so he didn't do anything about the mortgage payments not being kept up. But Laurinda was through. At least, it must all be clear to you now that we can give your company what it wants, so I can't see any reason for you hanging around Quivira City. We Baldridges like to settle our own troubles. So what do you say?'

'I say no, of course,' Quist replied shortly. 'Now, wait' — raising one protesting hand to silence Baldridge's angry outburst — 'try to see my side of it, Baldridge. I'm sent here to do a job. The T.N. & A.S. has a stake in this town too. We can't afford to lose business —'

'How would you lose business?'

'The company lays tracks through here with the idea that Quivira City will continue its growth. But people will start moving away, and other people will refuse to come here and invest money, if the town gets a name of hushing up killings for the sake of one powerful family that apparently runs things hereabouts. Once this town hits the downgrade, what do you think would become of railroad business?'

Baldridge said hotly, 'Aw — w, you're crazy as hell, Quist. How do you figure a killing could be hushed up?'

Quist laughed scornfully. 'Look at the weasling inquest that has been held, already. Sure, it produced two — what'll I'll call 'em, suspects? So two suspects, to use a polite word, will go to trial, both claiming to be the killer of Whitney Clayton. And both will likely refuse to give any detailed testimony. So what have you got? I'll tell you — a jury that will disagree. Clayton's rep — and I'll concede that it's a nasty one — will get a thorough airing. The jury will decide he only got his just deserts. It's probable the jury may free both you and your sister. Or you may get a few months, with a suspended sentence, something of the sort, or a justifiable homicide verdict. At any rate, with the Baldridges running things, I just can't see anything serious happening to you.'

'By God, I don't like your attitude, Quist.' Baldridge was on his feet, now, face flaming angrily.

Quist glanced up at him. 'Do you expect me to like yours, Baldridge?' he snapped. 'If you had the sense the Almighty gave you, you'd know better than try to run me out of town — '

'We're not trying to run you out — '

'Do you deny that you, or somebody you hired, fired on me through my window a spell back?' Quist asked quietly.

Baldridge stared at Quist. The hot color faded from his face. Slowly, he sat down again. 'Just exactly what did you say?'

Quist repeated the words.

'Good Lord, no!' Baldridge exclaimed. 'Quist, you're all wrong if you think I'd do a thing like that. When did this happen? I haven't heard about it — '

'I'm telling you it happened, that's enough,' Quist said tersely. 'So think it over, Baldridge. Maybe now you'll realize why I'm not leaving Quivira City. I don't like to be pushed around.'

Baldridge seemed at a loss for words. 'I've got a hunch,' he said finally, 'that you and I got off on the wrong foot, Quist. I'll — I'll talk to you again — later.'

Rising hastily, he tossed some money on the table to pay for his supper, then strode quickly from the dining room.

Todd Sargent looked after him, then, 'Whew! You sure threw a jolt into young Chris, Greg. Look, have you actually got any proof he was connected in some way with that shot?' Quist drained his coffee cup and laughed softly. 'Not the slightest. It was just as you said, I wanted to throw a jolt into him — make him realize that I'm not ready to leave here — not yet.'

The deputy nodded. 'If you're through supper, maybe you'd care to amble around town a mite, get acquainted. You'll want to meet Sheriff Wolcott, likely.'

'Good idea. I'm ready when you are. And thanks for the feed.'

The waitress came and Sargent handed her some money. Receiving change, the deputy examined each coin carefully, before dropping a tip on the table and putting the rest in his pocket.

The two men rose. Quist said, as they were going out, 'Something wrong with your change, Todd?'

'No — no, it was all right.' He made no explanation of his examination of the coins.

Passing through the lobby, they stepped out to the hotel porch where Quist paused a moment to roll and light a cigarette. It was completely dark by this time. Lights shone spottily along Main Street; pedestrians passed on the sidewalks.

Now and then a rider or vehicle raised dust along the roadway.

Sargent said suddenly, 'Well, that's surprising.'

'What is?' Quist asked.

Sargent gestured to a point a few doors along the street, where light from a window threw into bold illumination the figures of two men, one of them Chris Baldridge. The two were absorbed in an intent discussion of something or other. Quist studied the pair a moment. Baldridge's companion was a rather slight, undersized figure, in cowhand togs, and with a holstered gun swung at his right hip. Quist turned back to the deputy. 'Who's the other hombre, and what's so surprising?'

'In the first place,' Sargent replied, 'it's surprising that Chris Baldridge would even have anything to do with that bustard. I've never even known those two to speak before. Chris always sort of ignored him.'

'Just who is he?'

'Cobra Macaw — he calls himself. Bronc peeler for Gene Martinsen who runs the G-Bar-M spread, which same is a rather rough outfit — '

'In what way?'

'Martinsen hires a gang that likes to raise hell when it comes to town. They just about had Pike Wolcott buffaloed. I had a couple of talks with Martinsen. He didn't like it, but since then he's more or less held his crew down. Generally on paydays I have a couple of 'em to arrest on peace-disturbing charges. No — no, I wouldn't say I know of anything downright crooked about the G-Bar-M, but those hands will sure run roughshod over anybody who lets 'em.'

'Which brings us to this Cobra Macaw hombre. What about him?'

'He could be mean, Greg — he is, in fact. Fancies himself as a gunfighter, and fast, I guess. Got a couple of notches carved in his gunbutt. I've heard he played quite a part in a couple of cattle wars. He's quarrelsome. I've had to warn him more than once, not to start anything in this town, but he gets away with all he can. Greg, I just don't like it. There's something in the air that spells trouble.'

6

Cobra Macaw

Even while they were watching the two men, Chris Baldridge moved rather angrily away and strode off down Main Street. Cobra Macaw looked after him a moment, then walked leisurely after the man.

Quist asked Sargent, 'What exactly spells trouble to you, Todd?'

The deputy frowned. 'Not one damn thing I can put a finger on. But it's just damn queer to see Chris Baldridge talking to Macaw that way. What was being cooked up — if anything?'

Quist smiled. 'Forget it. You're seeking trouble before it happens. Is this Macaw hombre sort of a vicious-looking rat, with queer eyes and kind of muddy-colored hair?'

'Yeah. Do you know him?'

'I can't say for sure. He looked sort of familiar, but he was too far off to distinguish features. I never knew him under that name, for certain. Maybe we'll run across him again before the night's over. C'mon, let's get moving. My legs need stretching. You fed me too well, Todd.'

The two men descended the steps from the hotel porch to the sidewalk. The deputy spoke to various men they passed on the street. Quist said, 'I believe you mentioned, Todd, that Laurinda Clayton didn't appear at the coroner's inquest.'

'Doc Twitchell didn't subpoena her. As a matter of fact, after she came to town and confessed to killing her husband, she was just about on the point of a breakdown —'

'Do *you* believe that?'

'Yes, I do,' Sargent stated seriously. 'I've known Laurinda quite a number of years now. She — she's pretty damn sincere. She wouldn't fake an illness she didn't feel.'

'All right,' Quist smiled. 'I'll take your word for it. So what did the coroner do about her testimony?'

'Pike Wolcott testified to what she had

said. I corroborated Pike's testimony. That satisfied the coroner's jury.'

'Seems to me it's right easy to satisfy juries in this town,' Quist grunted.

'Where a Baldridge is concerned, it is. I thought I'd made that clear to you.'

Quist changed the subject. 'Anything special you can tell me about that shot that was thrown at our legal sharp? Dowd?'

'Damn little,' Sargent replied. 'What I know I got from Dowd. He'd hired a horse at the livery and rode out to see if he couldn't make a deal with Clayton. Didn't find Clayton at home, so he pushed on a mite farther, in the hope of seeing him someplace in the vicinity. Suddenly, from the top of a hill, somebody fired on Dowd. The bullet didn't come near, but it scared him into making tracks back to Quivira City. I rode out to see Clayton, myself, when I heard about it, but Clayton wasn't near the house. Fact is, I didn't see him again, until I looked at his dead body.'

'Did you know, Todd, that previous

to that business, when Dowd first saw Clayton, here in town, that Clayton had offered to sell a right-of-way for twenty-thousand dollars?'

'Jeepers! Nothing hoggish about Clayton — oh, no! No, I hadn't heard the amount mentioned.'

'You wouldn't have any idea, then, as to why Clayton had asked that particular figure?'

'Not the slightest,' the deputy replied promptly.

For the next hour and a half, Quist and the deputy strolled around the town, dropping into saloons here and there, where Quist was occasionally introduced to someone Sargent thought he might care to meet: business men of Quivira City, a couple of ranch owners, a cowhand here and there. There seemed to be no doubt in anyone's mind that Quist was in town to work on the Clayton killing, though just why he was needed, no one was quite sure, considering that two people had already made confessions. None of the men Quist met were particularly friendly, though there was no downright hostility evidenced either.

Drinks were bought and accepted; each time, although Quist took beer, he drank little. He did notice that when it was Todd Sargent's turn to pay for drinks, the deputy always scrutinized his change with unusual care. This aroused Quist's curiosity, though he didn't ask questions. As he and Sargent were leaving the Bluebonnet Saloon, they encountered Chris Baldridge. Quist nodded and started on through the swinging doors. Baldridge turned and spoke to him. Quist halted on the sidewalk outside.

'What's on your mind, Baldridge?'

'I just want to speak to you a minute, Quist. I won't detain you but a little. Do you know a man by the name of Cobra Macaw?'

Quist said quietly, 'I've heard of him. Why?'

Baldridge said, 'He wanted to make a deal with me a while back.' Quist asked for particulars. Baldridge continued, 'Macaw said he knew your presence in town wasn't welcome to us Baldridges. For five hundred dollars he offered to see that you left Quivira City.'

'And so?' Quist said softly. 'Isn't it worth five hundred to you?'

Baldridge stiffened. 'It's worth a hell of a lot more,' he said bitterly. 'But the Baldridges haven't yet descended to the point where they'll make deals with scum like Cobra Macaw. We handle our own troubles.'

'So you've said before,' Quist replied dryly. 'Why are you telling me this, Baldridge?'

'If anything happens, I wanted you to know we're not back of it.'

'What could happen?'

'I don't know — and I care less. I'm just telling you it won't be any of our doings if it does happen.'

Without another word, Chris Baldridge spun around and entered the Bluebonnet Saloon. Quist stared at Todd Sargent. 'Well,' he said softly, 'looks like that hombre aims to keep the family skirts clear — or should I say skirt?'

'You can depend on it, Laurinda would never have anything to do with Macaw either, Greg. I don't know, but I somehow feel that Chris was shooting straight with us. That sounds like Macaw.'

'In what way?'

'I've heard of a few deals of the sort he's made in this neck of the range. Say two fellows have a grudge against each other. For a certain price — though nothing like five hundred bucks — Cobra Macaw offers to get rid of one of 'em. No, wait — I don't mean it comes to gun fighting. Macaw just throws a few threats around, and suddenly somebody leaves town.' Quist swore disgustedly. 'Do you know this for a fact?'

'Hell, no, or I'd do something about it. I've just picked up rumors to that effect. I've questioned Macaw, but he'd never admit anything. Just sneers at me. Now, with Baldridge's word to go on, I'm going to look for Macaw and — '

'Don't, Todd. Leave Macaw to me. If, somehow or other, he happens to be mixed into this Clayton killing, I want he's at liberty. It's right hard to pick up clues on a man when he's in a prison cell, as a rule. Anyway, about all you could do would be to have him bound over to keep the peace. If he's set to make trouble, that wouldn't stop him. So leave him to me.'

Sargent said reluctantly, 'All right, if you say so.'

The two men continued their walk and stopped next at the sheriff's office, a rock-and-'dobe building with a wooden awning above its narrow porch. From one of the uprights, suporting the awning, was suspended a sign which read, SHERIFF'S OFFICE — BLACKJACK COUNTY. A light from within shone through a window, and next to the window was an open doorway. Todd Sargent led the way into the office. As he entered, Sheriff Pike Wolcott swung around from the roll-top desk at which he'd been seated.

'Where in hell you been, Todd?' he queried peevishly. 'I wanted you should help me on the monthly expense account.'

'I been around town,' Sargent replied. 'Pike, this is Greg Quist. I've been making him acquainted with our town. Greg, Sheriff Wolcott.'

Quist extended his hand and got a limp handshake from the sheriff. Wolcott was a fat-bodied man with a double chin and wide, sun-bleached mustaches. His eyes were a watery blue and he was around fifty years of age. He said in rather unfriendly tones, 'Heard you was in town, Quist — reckon everybody in Quivira City did too. Don't know what you expect to do here, though. I'm capable of handling any law enforcement necessary.'

'I imagine you are,' Quist said quietly, 'with Todd's help. I'm here on company business. You probably know that too.'

'Feller name of Dowd — T.N. & A.S. attorney — allowed you was coming to mess into this Clayton business.'

'Don't you think that's necessary?' Quist asked.

Pike Wolcott scowled and ran one hand across his nearly bald head. 'Can't say I do,' he grunted. 'We got two confessions to that killing. I reckon 'fore many days pass, I'll ferret out which one of them two Baldridge youngsters is speakin' truth. Then a trial will be held. That's all there is to it. So there's no need for you to hang around, Quist.'

'Sorry to disappoint you, sheriff, but I'm staying,' Quist said curtly.

'Suit yourself,' Wolcott shrugged. He turned back to his desk and fiddled with the wick of the kerosene lamp. 'But I tell you you're just wasting your time, Quist.'

'I think I'm the best judge on that score,' Quist replied.

A few minutes later, he and Todd Sargent were again on the street. Todd said, 'You don't want to take Pike too seriously — '

'Hell! I don't take him at all,' Quist laughed. 'This isn't the first time I've hit a town where the law was hostile to me.'

'What do you usually do?' Sargent asked curiously.

'Things generally work out,' Quist replied.

'People learn I'm not so bad as I'm painted.'

'You've got the rep of being a rough customer to tangle with, Greg. I read a piece in a magazine about you — it was *Karper's Weekly* — '

Quist groaned and lifted one protesting hand. 'Don't even talk about it, Todd. Everywhere I go I run into that damn article. If I ever get my hands around the throat of that blasted writer — ' He broke off, swearing softly. Sargent let the subject drop.

The two men strolled down Main Street, until they'd reached Laredo, then crossed over and started back. The deputy said, 'The Green Bottle Saloon is just ahead. Do you want to drop in?'

Quist shook his head. 'I've had enough saloons for one night, Todd. No, I figure I'll drift back to the hotel and get some sleep. I've had a long day, and I don't think there's anything more I can learn tonight. This town's practically gone to bed.'

As they neared the Green Bottle, a man

pushed through the swinging doors and headed toward his pony at the hitchrack. Quist suddenly raised his voice, 'Hey, Truchas,' he called.

'That's Cobra Macaw,' Sargent said.

Quist didn't reply, but quickened pace a little. The man had paused, momentarily, and then swung back to the hitchrack again. The light from the saloon shone on his form, picking out clearly every movement. Quist called again, 'Truchas — just a minute.'

'Where do you get that Truchas stuff?' Sargent frowned.

'That's Macaw.'

'Alias Macaw,' Quist corrected. 'I got a good look in the light from the Green Bottle. You notice he stopped and waited for us.'

Quist and Sargent approached the hitchrack. Macaw — or Truchas — waited with his back against the tierail, his expressionless eyes on Quist and his companion. He said, ''You gents call me? There must be some mistake —'

'I called you,' Quist replied. 'And

there's no mistake. You used to be known as the Truchas Kid, seven or eight years back.'

'You're wrong, hombre,' Macaw said in a flat, toneless voice. He was undersized, with muddy-colored hair. A holstered forty-five six-shooter hung at his right thigh. His clothing was that generally worn by cowhands — faded denims, slouch-brim sombrero, cotton shirt, spurred boots. He spoke again, 'My name's Macaw. I reckon you got me wrong — '

'I doubt I could get *you* any way but wrong,' Quist smiled thinly. 'Think back, Truchas. El Paso. Tolliver's place. You used to hang out there. When you left, reports drifted back from Tucumcari. They weren't flattering reports. As I heard it, you moved out fast, only a jump ahead of a United States Marshal. Remember?'

There was no expression at all in Macaw's features. His queer eyes slid sidewise from Quist to Sargent and back again to Quist. There was something flat, opaque, about those eyes — like eyes of a dead fish — giving no hint whatever as to the thoughts that functioned behind them. An evil vicious something about Macaw reminded Quist of nothing so much as a sidewinder about to strike. His head gave an almost imperceptible jerk, after a moment, and he said, 'All right, so you've got a good memory. Who in hell are you to be questioning me, hombre?'

'Don't try to come that game on me, either,' Quist snapped. 'You know damn well who I am and what I'm here for, Truchas.'

'Y'know, you're beginnin' to sound interestin', Quist,' the man sneered. 'Maybe I've underrated you some. All right, as to the name. These days I prefer Macaw — Cobra Macaw. So what? You ain't got anything on me. It's my own monicker. What you aimin' to do about it?'

'I haven't said I've got anything on you — yet. Of course,' Quist pursued softly, 'I might mention a little matter of five hundred bucks to get rid of me. Wasn't that your price?'

Again that flat stare from cold eyes. 'I ain't no idea what you're talkin' about, Quist.' His gaze dropped to a point below Quist's coat and seeing no gun holster there, moved over to Todd Sargent's weapon. The glinting stare came back to Quist, 'What's more, if there wa'n't two of you — and one a deputy at that — you wouldn't be bracin' me like this, railroad dick.'

Quist spoke quietly to Sargent, 'Drift along, will you, Todd. I'll catch up in a few minutes.'

'But, Greg —'

'Please do as I say, Todd.'

'I don't like it, Greg — — '

'I like it fine,' — shortly. 'Now, drift.'

Reluctantly, the deputy turned and sauntered away. Quist's gaze came back to meet Macaw's. They stared steadily at each other until Sargent was half a block away. Faint surprise showed in Macaw's almost toneless voice as he sneered, 'You must be big medicine around here,

Quist — orderin' the law around that way.'

'I'm too big for you, Macaw, and don't forget it. And don't try making any more deals to get rid of me, either.'

'I already told you I don't know what you mean.'

'And I've warned you not to lie to me.'

'All right, so what about it ?' Macaw sneered defiantly. 'A man's got a right to go after business.'

'Not when said business includes me, without my consent.'

Macaw spat an oath. 'I'll tell that Baldridge hombre a few things — '

'You'll not do that either,' Quist said coldly.

Macaw spoke bitterly, calling Quist a name. Swiftly, Quist struck him a back-handed slap across the face. The color fled from Macaw's features, he swayed back a step, one hand flashing toward his holster. Quist's left hand darted out, seizing Macaw's right wrist. A brief struggle took place, but there was no doubt as to its outcome. Within seconds, Quist had wrested the gun from Macaw's grasp.

Macaw staggered back, panting. 'Lemme have that gun — '

'Get on your horse and ride,' Quist ordered.

'Give me that gun, you — '

Again Quist struck him a resounding slap across the lips. 'I'll give you this gun in a way you won't like, Macaw. Now climb into that saddle and make dust. *Pronto!*'

Macaw hesitated but an instant longer, then coolly shrugging his shoulders, he rounded the end of the hitchrack, mounted his pony and went loping off down the street. Quist looked after him until he'd disappeared in the darkness, then swung back to rejoin Todd Sargent. There were very few people on the street by this time.

Just beyond the corner of Main and Austin streets he caught up with the deputy. 'Look here, Todd, please don't get an idea I was trying to order you around, but I didn't want to take time to be polite.'

'Forget it, Greg. I was just sort of worried — what happened, anyway?'

'I had to take his gun away. Here, you keep it. Let him have it tomorrow if he wants it bad enough to ask for it.'

'Good Lord! He drew on you — '

'I can't say I blamed him any. I taunted him into it — slapped his face when his tongue got nasty.' Quist related details. He concluded, 'Yeah, I know what you're thinking. You're thinking I had an advantage in weight and height and reach. All right, so I'm a bully. But don't forget, Todd, that a Colt gun is a great equalizer. I had to act as I did, or shoot him. And you can't ever get any evidence out of a dead man.'

7

Baffled

It wasn't quite yet eight o'clock, the following morning, when Quist, after having breakfast in the hotel dining room, once more ascended to his room, with the intention of writing a brief letter to Jay Fletcher, to outline for Fletcher the situation as it existed in Quivira City. Hearing sounds within his room, he cautiously opened the door and peered inside, then relaxed. A young Mexican girl had just finished making his bed and was sweeping up. Quist tossed the girl a half a dollar and hurried her on her way. Then getting writing paper and a lead pencil from his satchel, he got busy.

He had just sealed the envelope and was addressing it when a knock sounded on his door. Quist called, 'Come in.' He was still occupied with the letter when he heard the door open and close and a voice said, 'Mr. Quist?'

Quist's head jerked up, he got to his feet, removing his sombrero. 'Well,' he said softly, and again, 'Well. This is a pleasure.'

A girl was standing, facing him, her back against the door, as though uncertain of her reception. She had thick black hair gathered at a heavy knob at her nape, beneath the flat-crowned sombrero. She was a tall girl, and very slim, in her divided riding skirt and mannish flannel shirt. It was her eyes that Quist noticed most. Dark and with unbelievably long lashes. The nose was straight, the mouth a trifle wide perhaps. A lot of strength in the chin too. These thoughts coursed swiftly through Quist's mind. A damnably pretty woman, he told himself, and immediately supplemented that. It wasn't mere beauty; something else that had to do with character, as well.

The girl's left hand lingered nervously at the blue bandanna at her throat. 'May — may I come in?' she asked, something pleading in the tone.

Quist smiled. 'I thought you were already

in.' He hurried to place a chair for her.

The girl thanked him and sat down. 'Of course.' Her smile was rather wan. 'I'm afraid I'm not thinking quite straight lately. Mr. Quist, I'm Laurinda Clayton.'

Quist merely lifted his eyebrows a trifle and waited for her to continue, feeling himself strongly attracted to her.

'I suppose,' she stated somewhat defiantly, 'you expected me to be wearing widow's weeds.' A bit of color came into her face, and she looked not quite so pale and drawn.

'I expect so few things nowdays, Mrs. Clayton, that I hadn't given the matter a thought.'

'Mr. Quist, I want to talk to you. I've thought matters over and come to a decision. I need your help.'

'I'll be pleased to do anything possible. Do you prefer to talk in the lobby?'

Laurinda Clayton shook her head. 'No — under the circumstances. I think we can talk better here.'

Quist bowed. 'And how can I help you?'

'I want my brother, Chris, cleared of the murder charge that's placed against him.'

'I had an idea that you — well, that you — ' Quist hesitated.

The girl swiftly took up the thought. 'I'm not sure that my admission — my stating I — shot Whit Clayton — is quite enough. I want Chris cleared beyond the shadow of any doubt.'

'Have you any idea of what that means?'

'I think I have. It's a matter of finding evidence to prove he had nothing to do with the murder. I'm willing to pay you well.'

Quist raised a protesting hand. 'I'm not thinking of money. Anyway, I'm under contract to the T.N. & A.S. Railroad. I'm not free to take other jobs. But that is not what I meant. Have you considered the fact that in clearing your brother I may find evidence pointing to you?'

'I've considered it,' the girl said briefly. 'It doesn't matter I've done a lot of thinking about it. I've moped in bed like a silly schoolgirl. I've refused to talk to people. I finally came to a decision to see you. This morning, before I had a chance to change my mind, I rose early and rode in. And — and — ' again that wan smile — 'here I am.'

'Why are you so anxious to clear your brother?'

'I don't want his life ruined. Because I've made a mess of mine, is no sign — ' She broke off. 'There's no need going into that. The point is, Chris is taking the blame to protect me, I'm sure. Or if he isn't, he was — ' Again she halted. 'Look here, Mr. Quist, what happens to me doesn't greatly matter. But I do want Chris to be happy. He is just about engaged to be married — '

'So? I hadn't heard that. Who's the young lady?'

'Priscilla Kiernan. She runs a small shop here in town.'

Quist asked quietly, 'Did Whit Clayton know Miss Kiernan?'

Laurinda Baldridge drew a quick

breath. For a moment she didn't reply, then she said low-voiced, 'I believe he did.'

'You're not sure?'

Again the hesitation, then, 'Yes, I'm — I'm sure he did.'

'How well?'

'Mr. Quist,' — a certain dignified resentment in the tones, 'is it necessary to go into all this? Priscilla Kiernan has nothing to do — '

'All right,' Quist smiled, 'I'll not press the question. Is there anything else you want to tell me?'

'We — ell, I thought you'd ask questions. I could tell you about — about the shooting — and all that.'

'Are you considered a pretty good shot, Mrs. Clayton?'

'Dad taught me when I was a child. Around here, the answer to your question would immediately be 'yes.' Dad is known to be pretty good at that sort of thing.'

Quist considered a moment. 'Do you mind going over what happened that day you — that day that Clayton was shot?'

When Laurinda spoke it sounded like a well-rehearsed act. 'There's little to tell,' she said promptly. 'Whit and I had had a falling out — we couldn't agree on things. To save my marriage I thought I'd try once more. I'd been living at home. I saddled up and rode over to our house. Whit was there. He had been drinking. He wasn't at all — well, agreeable. He became abusive, both physically — ' she hesitated.

'And there was some sort of struggle,' Quist prompted.

'How did you know that?'

'I've talked to Todd Sargent. He was out there, you know. And from him I learned what happened at the inquest.'

'Of course,' Laurinda Clayton nodded. 'I hadn't thought of that.'

'It might have been a good idea for you to attend that inquest.'

'But, I couldn't, Mr. Quist. It — it — the whole business was so — so horrible. It was bad enough to have to tell Sheriff Wolcott — and Todd — '

'Skip it,' Quist said shortly. 'Let's go back a little. You must have been expecting trouble with Clayton that day, otherwise you'd not have worn your gun to his place. Am I right?'

'That's correct,' the girl said after some momentary hesitation. 'Whit was unpredictable and I thought it safer — '

Again Quist interrupted. 'Quite so. So while you were struggling with your husband, your father entered the house and — '

'That's not true,' the girl exclaimed. 'Wherever in the world did you get that idea?'

Quist smiled rather sheepishly. 'It just popped into my head. It could have happened, you see.'

'But it didn't,' Mrs. Clayton said earnestly. 'Dad was nowhere near the house — so far as I know — when it — it — '

'Let's stay on the subject,' Quist flashed his next question, 'and tell me exactly what position you were in when you fired your gun?'

The girl stared at him a minute. 'Well,' she said, low-voiced, her eyes downcast, 'Whit had seized me in his arms. I was struggling to get free. Finally, I jerked my right arm loose and drew my gun. Then — well, then — I pulled the trigger — '

'Without cocking the weapon?'

'Naturally I had to cock it first. It's a single — action.' Quist smiled thinly. 'Just where did you aim the gun?'

Again Laurinda Clayton hesitated. 'I'm not exactly certain. Toward some spot in the body. Dad always said if you want to stop a man fast, shoot for his middle.'

'That's good advice,' Quist nodded. 'What did you do next?'

'Whit fell to the floor. He died almost instantly.' The girl's voice sounded rather toneless. 'I got a blanket and covered him, then mounted my pony and rode home — to the Bee-Hive.'

'What did your father say to all this?'

'I didn't tell him at first. I was frightened. I went to bed. It was only later when I learned that Chris had confessed to the shooting, that I decided to act. Then I told Dad what I had done. He didn't believe me. I was determined to go to town and tell Sheriff Wolcott. Chris had arrived at the ranch, then left again. We didn't know where. Dad tried to dissuade me, but finally consented to ride into town with me. He was very angry about the whole business.'

'You've talked all this over with your brother by this time — '

'No. There's been no chance. Such times as I have been at the ranch, he's been in Quivira City. I've been staying in my room. I've seen scarcely anyone.'

'And you're willing to go to town to save Chris Baldridge?'

'I want to! He mustn't suffer for something I've done — '

'You feel certain no jury in Quivira City would convict a Baldridge?'

Laurinda Clayton's chin came up. Color flooded her cheeks. 'I hardly think that's called for, Mr. Quist.'

'I'm not so sure,' Quist snapped.

'Do you doubt my word in anything I've told you?'

'Let's say I'm just plain baffled,' Quist replied. The girl asked his reasons, but Quist brushed aside the question and went on, 'You're sure, after you placed the blanket over Clayton's body, you did nothing else except leave the house, get your horse and ride home?'

'That's all,' the girl insisted.

'You didn't even take time to remove your cartridge belt and holster and hang them on the wall — just threw your gun on the floor, near the body and ran out of the house?'

'Why — why — ' the girl floundered in words. Then, nervously, 'I'd forgotten that. Come to think of it — '

'It doesn't go down, Mrs. Clayton. You'd forgotten that holster all right — forgotten it altogether. Before you start trying to hook anyone, you'd better get your line straightened out first.'

Crimson spots burned in Laurinda Clayton's cheeks. 'You talk as though you don't believe what I'm telling you.'

'In heaven's name how can you expect me to?' Quist demanded. 'That's why I say I'm baffled. It's known that you've only worn a gun a few times in your life. You tell me you went to the house that day to try and make peace with your husband — yet you buckled on your gun. You state you're a good shot with a six-shooter — '

'Mr. Quist!' She was on her feet now. 'I don't like your attitude.'

'It's the only one I have to offer at present,' Quist smiled coldly. 'Look here, Mrs. Clayton, if you aimed at a man's body where would you expect to hit him when you fired?'

'In the body of course,' the girl said instantly. 'But I don't understand what you — ' She broke off and reseated herself. 'You don't understand where Whit Clayton was hit, either,' Quist said swiftly. 'The bullet entered his neck.'

Mrs. Clayton paused to marshal her thoughts. 'To tell the truth,' she said nervously, 'I didn't really notice — I — I — well, I was excited of course, it is possible that I aimed high.'

'Not with your training, if what I hear is true. You don't even seem to remember what you've told me. Think back. You told me Clayton had seized you in his arms and you just managed to get one arm free. As I understand it, that would bring you quite close to him. With one arm free and your gun drawn, it seems to me you would have fired instantly — and struck him in the body. But, no, as you tell it, you would have to take time to bend your elbow and point the gun toward his neck.'

Laurinda Clayton lifted her handkerchief and dabbed at her lower lip. She wasn't meeting Quist's gaze now. Finally she said, 'I remember now. Whit grabbed at my arm. I suppose he jerked the gun barrel up towards his neck at the time I pulled the trigger — '

'It's no good, Mrs. Clayton.' Quist shook his head, smiling. 'You've made a nice try. Now why don't you just decide to tell me the truth for a change? You've done your best to save your brother, but a little straight talk would have done you more good — '

The girl rose from her chair. 'Mr. Quist, I think you've said quite enough,' she flared. 'I was prepared for a certain amount of cynicism, perhaps. In a magazine article I read that you were hard, ruthless — '

Quist said, 'Oh, Lord, not again.' He rolled his eyes toward the ceiling and ran long fingers through his thick tawny hair.

' — but *Karper's Weekly* did say that women liked you. I remember the exact words. The writer said that you 'had a way with women.' But I fail to — '

'I wish you'd remember other things as well,' Quist said ruefully, 'things not in that article. I never will live it down.' He added ominously, 'If I ever lay hands on that writer — '

'You can hit him for me too,' Laurinda Clayton snapped. 'I'm sorry I've taken your time, Mr. Quist. I expected something different. I — I — ' She paused and her voice broke a little. Half way between tears and rage, or a combination of both, she whirled about, flung open the room door and departed. An instant later the door crashed shut with a jolt that shook the wall.

Quist stood gazing at the door a moment, then drew a long breath. 'Whew! A mite of temper, too.' A smile twitched at his lips. 'But she's a sweetheart for looks. Lord, I wish she'd tell me what she really knows about Clayton's killing.'

Five minutes later he was on the street, carrying his letter addressed to Jay Fletcher. The post office, he learned, was in Deming's General Store. He bought a stamp, posted the letter and again stepped into the street. There was a good deal of morning activity along Main, the day being much cooler than the previous one. The sun was bright and clear. A few banked clouds moved with dignity across the turquoise sky.

Glancing diagonally across the street, Quist saw Todd Sargent just emerging from the Cattlemen's Commercial Bank.

Quist crossed over. Sargent had come to a halt on the corner and was examining a handful of coins in one palm. Quist hailed him, chuckling. 'I never knew a deputy sheriff to make a salary large enough to have bank business. What'd they do, short change you!'

Sargent's head jerked up, and he shoved the coins in his pocket. 'Oh, hello, Greg. No, I was just inside getting a bill changed. All the bank business I do you could stick in your eye. What's new?'

'What's new with you?' Quist countered.

'I was wondering if it wasn't about time for you to be around. Figured you might sleep late, after your long drag, yesterday, though. I was down to the Lone Star Livery a spell back. Figured you might be needing a horse, and wanted to make sure Stinson didn't palm off any of his old hire crowbaits on you. Picked out a buckskin pony for you. Told Stinson not to let anybody else have it.'

'I appreciate that, Todd. Save me time looking over livery stock. Anything else doing?'

'Saw Laurinda Clayton a little while before I went into the bank. Guess she's feeling better. She sure looked mad as the devil about something though.'

'What was wrong?'

'She didn't take time to say. Just asked me if I'd seen her brother, Chris. Told her I'd seen Chris lining out on the Bee-Hive trail just a short spell before. She jabbed spurs to her horse and headed after him. Wish I could figure what she's mad at.'

'Me,' Quist gave the information. 'She's a nice-looking girl, Todd.'

'You aren't wrong there. But — but why should she be mad at you? Where did you ever meet her?'

'This morning. She called on me.'

'T'hell you say!'

They rolled cigarettes while Quist related details relative to his discussion with Laurinda Clayton. Todd Sargent's mouth was hanging open when Quist had concluded. 'Judas priest!' the deputy exclaimed. He looked rather pleased.

'Greg! You make it sound like Laurinda didn't kill Clayton.'

'Not I.' Quist shook his head. 'The story Laurinda told makes it sound that way.'

'And you don't believe her story?'

'Not much. Now wait, can't you see yourself that it was something she made up?'

'That very fact should exonerate her — as you tell it.'

Quist laughed good-naturedly. 'All right. But, Todd, keep an open mind until all the evidence is in. Also, don't tell anybody what I've told you — not even Pike Wolcott. Let's watch and see how things shape up.'

'Just as you say, Greg — '

'Mornin', Todd,' spoke an elderly voice at the deputy's rear.

Sargent turned. 'Hi-yuh, Lennie, you ol' gaycat,' he grinned. 'Lennie, I'd like to make you acquainted with Mr. Greg Quist. Greg, this is Lennie Plummer. Likely the *Quivira Blade* couldn't run every week without Lennie.'

Quist found himself shaking hands with a somewhat stooped individual with weak blue eyes and a wrinkled countenance. Lennie Plummer's hair was snow-white — what was left of it. His short straggly beard wasn't quite so white, being copiously stained with tobacco juice; the beard looked as though it had been chewed off by rats and only partially covered the collarless soiled shirt beneath. A greasy-looking vest and patched trousers completed his attire. After shaking hands he donned his battered felt hat which he'd removed for the occasion.

'Newspaper man, are you?' Quist smiled.

Lennie Plummer looked uncertain. 'Well, I aims ter lend a hand 'round the office a mite,' he admitted in his cracked voice. 'Reckon the *Blade* will be a-printin' a piece 'bout you comin' here, Mister Quist, to do some *de*tectin'. Pro'bly ye realizes some folks ain't taken to yer bein' here, but don't let it fret ye none. I've hearn tell of ye afore this, and if ther's truth to come out, I'm thinkin' ye're the man to fetch 'er.'

'Well, much obliged, Lennie,' Quist smiled.

'Suppose you'll be at the funeral this afternoon, Lennie,' Sargent put in.

'Pervidin' my health holds up, I'll be thar. Been feelin' sorter puny of late though. The old bones can't take sudden changes in weather.'

They talked a few minutes longer. Quist turned to watch Plummer as he departed, noting the shuffled, dragging step and bent back. He turned back to Sargent, chuckling, 'Must have a right lively force on the town newspaper.'

Sargent laughed. 'Poor old Lennie. He landed here about six months back, looking for some sister or other. Couldn't find her, but he's been here ever since. Probably would have turned into the town bum, if it wasn't for Nugent, publisher of the *Blade*. Nugent pays him a few bucks a week to come in early and sweep out the place. Lennie hangs around the newspaper a lot. Now and then he even brings in some item of interest that can be printed.'

'Nugent let him sleep there, too?'

Sargent shook his head. 'There's a broken-down shack out where the Mexes live. It's such a wreck that nobody would live in it but Lennie Plummer. He took it over and nobody's thrown him out. I'm not certain who owns it — if anybody does.'

'What funeral were you talking about?'

'Whit Clayton's. He's to be buried out in Boot Hill this afternoon. Grizzly Baldridge sent in word he'd stand the expenses of burial. Likely wishes he could have done it months ago.'

'I imagine.' Quist looked thoughtful. 'Todd, I think I'll ride out and look over that house where Clayton was shot. I might be able to pick up some bit of evidence or other.'

'Good. I'll go with you.'

Quist shook his head. 'I'd rather you stayed here to check on two or three things.' Sargent nodded agreement. Quist went on, 'I suppose you locked the house when you left it.'

'Yes. I'll get the key at the office before you leave.'

'I'd like to have you sort of mosey around town and see if you can learn who was beating that carpet last evening. And why it was being done at the particular hour somebody chose to shoot at me.'

'I'll take care of it, Greg. What else?'

'You might attend Clayton's funeral if you have time.'

'What am I expected to look for?'

Quist shrugged his shoulders. 'I haven't the least idea. It could be somebody will bear watching. Todd, who is Priscilla Kiernan? I told you Mrs. Clayton mentioned her.'

Todd stiffened a trifle, his eyes narrowing. After a moment he said seriously, 'She's one darn nice girl, Greg. Runs a novelty store here — y'know, pins, needles, thread — ribbon — stuff of that sort for the female trade. She's right popular in Quivira City, and I hope you don't get any ideas that she — '

'What was her connection with Clayton?'

'Who said there was any?'

'I guessed it from Laurinda Clayton's manner.'

The deputy said, 'Oh, hell, I suppose you might as well know. Clayton was pretty sweet on Priscilla, before and after he was married. But don't get any ideas — '

'The only idea I get is why in hell you didn't tell me this before, Todd,' Quist said irritably.

'Well, I didn't see any use dragging her into the business,' Sargent explained apologetically. 'She's a sweet, decent kid and she and Chris — '

'Dammit, Todd! If you're going to help me I don't want information held back. I want to learn everything possible about Clayton. It's the only way I can ferret out knowledge about him. All right, we'll forget the Kiernan girl for the present. I want to get headed out of town. Let's get that key.'

8

Powder Smoke

It was nearing eleven that morning when Quist rode out of Quivira City on a chunky buckskin gelding horse. Sargent had given him directions for reaching the house where Whitney Clayton had been killed; being certain of finding the place without trouble, Quist loped easily along, not pushing the buckskin to any extent until he could get acquainted with the horse. At the end of three-quarters of an hour Quist admitted he had a good mount. He commented mentally, 'Todd must have talked turkey to that livery man. He even furnished a near new saddle, and stuck on a throw-rope to boot. Dam'd if I know what Todd expected me to do with a lariat, today. Rope a few clues, maybe.'

The trail he was following was well rutted and hoof-chopped, with a climb so gradual it was scarcely noticed, by horse or man. Ahead lay a series of low rolling hills, grass-covered and conditioned by the season for excellent cow fodder. Here and there were to be seen mesquite, pecan and blackjack oak trees. Prickly pear grew in tall thick clumps, many of the past summer's blossoms already ripening fruit on the wide spiny pads of green.

After a time, Quist began to see small bunches of white-faced cattle, branded on the left ribs with the Bee-Hive iron — a design in the form of a rounded top bee-hive enclosing a large letter B. 'Those cows look to be in prime condition,' Quist mused. 'I wonder how that old Grizzly Baldridge would take it should he meet me riding along his trail.' He spoke to the buckskin, touched it lightly with spurs and it responded instantly with a quickened gait.

At the end of an hour-and-a-half's loping, Quist reached the trail to Clayton's place. It had never been much of a road in the first place, little used as it had been, and now it was overgrown with grass and low growth. Still it wasn't at all difficult to follow. Here, Quist swung his pony from a northerly to a northwesterly direction and pushed swiftly along. There were more cows to be seen now, on either side, and after a mile of riding, Quist saw to his left the long line of cottonwoods and other trees that marked the course of Montañosa Creek flowing down from the mountains of the same name. Reining the pony off the trail, Quist headed it for the stream. It was far from reaching river proportion when Quist reached the water, but the creek was clear and running with some speed. At this point it wasn't more than thirty feet across. Reining the pony down the grassy bank to the firm footing of the gravelly bottom of the stream, Quist drew to a halt and rolled a cigarette while the buckskin quenched its thirst. Five minutes later he turned back from the creek, and sent the animal loping along the trail. He glanced again at the sky which had become overcast. Clouds scudded down from the north; the breeze quickened.

'Sure hope I don't run into a norther before I get back,' Quist frowned. 'Likely too early for a norther yet, though. Still, with Texas weather you don't ever know for sure.'

He glanced ahead. The Montañosa were nearer now, and rugged tops silhouetted against a gray sky two miles farther on, the trail crossed the creek. Here it was barely twenty feet wide and only a trifle above the pony's fetlocks, though the trees were taller, the brush much thicker on either side. Guiding the horse up through the heavy growth, Quist emerged to find himself in a small stand of blackjack trees. He pushed on through and a few minutes later was urging the horse up a slight rise. Reaching the crest, he gazed down a long easy slope toward the Clayton house. He drew rein a moment to scrutinize the surrounding terrain, then moved on down the slope.

Dismounting before the house, he tethered the pony's reins to one of the uprights supporting the porch roof, drew out the key and inserted it in the front door lock. Then, opening the door, he stepped within and closed it softly behind him. At first glance there was nothing of fresh importance to see; Todd Sargent had explained in what condition the house had been found. The furniture was tumbled about as Todd had said. Rugs were crumpled to one side. An ominous dark stain colored the floorboards. Quist's gaze swept quickly over the room, noticing at once the cheap construction of the building. Jerry-built. That was the word for it. 'Clayton sure didn't spend much money on this place,' Quist mused. 'Probably hired wood-butchers instead of carpenters. But I suppose he had to throw up some sort of shack to show his good faith. The thing is, why in the devil did he want this particular half-section?'

His eyes again swept the room, dwelling on the wreckage about the place. 'Whoever put up the fight, it was one hell of a tussle. That's a right heavy table knocked over there. Now if that Laurinda girl had been sent crashing against it, I doubt she'd been able to do any shooting. Whoever hit it, ended up with a jolt — probably got knocked off their feet. Could have been Clayton, just before he was shot. But unless she's a devil of a lot stronger than I give her credit for being, I doubt she'd be able to knock Clayton around in such fashion. Yep, the girl has been telling fibs; no doubt about that.' He noticed a cartridge belt and empty holster hanging on one wall near the door, and crossed to examine it. It wasn't particularly new, though it was little worn. He judged it to be the one which had formerly held Laurinda Clayton's .38 six-shooter; the belt seemed about the right size for a woman of Laurinda Clayton's build. On another wall hung a small chimayo blanket by way of decoration. There were no pictures. All the interior was of bare, unpainted wood. 'Not much of a home to offer a bride,' Quist speculated, ' — not a girl of Mrs. Clayton's position, leastwise.'

He moved around the overturned table and entered the kitchen with its small window and bolted door. There were dirty pans and dishes about. The stove hadn't been cleaned for months. Glass chimneys of kerosene lamps were smudged with thick smoke-soot. The bare table was spotted with grease. 'Not much of a housekeeper this Clayton hombre,' Quist mused. 'Things must have went to pot after she left.'

The bedroom doorway was to his left. He entered and looked around, noting the wooden bedstead, with its soiled rumpled sheets and blankets. There were a couple of chairs, a commode with wash set and a dresser. A pair of Indian rugs were spread on the floor. These showed dirty footprints. Quist crossed to examine the dresser. The mirror was cracked. On the top of the dresser was an assortment objects: a hairbrush and comb matted with hair of a sandy-blond shade; the butt of a dead cigar rested at the edge of the dresser; there were a couple of neckties and a bandanna handkerchief; a pamphlet on horse-breeding and a bottle of hair tonic; a couple of matches;

other odds and ends usually found on a man's dresser, including shaving articles. A photograph of a man, mounted on board, rested against the mirror. Quist picked it up and saw a rather handsome, but weak, face, above a wing collar and cravat. The hair was slicked back. Written across the bottom of the photograph were the words, in a scrawling hand, 'To Laurinda, with love — Whit.'

Quist studied the picture. 'I can't say I'd count too much on a man who looked like that,' he commented. 'I reckon Laurinda told him what she thought of his love when she left it behind, on departing.'

The dresser had two small drawers at the top, three long ones, the width of the furniture, below. Quist yanked out the small drawer at the right. It was empty, except for a few glass beads broken from a string, a couple of bits of ribbon, and an empty bottle which had contained some sort of scent. A faint fragrance still hovered about the drawer, reminding him of Laurinda Clayton. He picked up a bit of torn cambric handkerchief. The scent was stronger. There were a couple of metal hairpins on the bottom of the drawer, and a woman's backcomb of celluloid. Quist shoved shut the drawer.

The other top drawer was full of male articles — handkerchiefs, socks and so on. The first wide drawer proved to be empty, as did the second, excepting for that faint elusive scent. What was it, lavender? Quist shrugged his shoulders and jammed shut the drawers. He jerked open the bottom container. Nothing much there to interest him, he guessed: shirts, underwear, some stiff collars, soiled and otherwise. Quist scowled and straightened up. 'Damn! You'd think a man would have some papers, or something, around. Probably all his papers are in his clothes at the undertaker's.'

A clothes rack near the bed held a nightshirt, a pair of torn trousers with suspenders attached and a felt hat. Quist went through the pockets, but they were empty. He returned to the dresser and tumbled the various articles out on the floor. There were several papers on the bottom of the drawer. Quist scowled when upon scrutiny they proved to be unpaid bills and dunning letters from firms in Quivira City. At one side lay a couple of short sections of blue ribbons, notched at one end, such as are awarded for prizes. One end of each was torn. Quist grunted. 'Huh! If he ever got any medals with these, he probably pawned 'em.'

He was about to replace the articles of clothing when a small pasteboard card caught his eye, stuck in the bottom of the drawer where it joined the side. He picked up the card and turned it over. There was printed a written signature on the pasteboard, which proved to be a membership dues card of the Artexico Horse Breeders' Society, dated some years back. Interest quickened in Quist when he read the name of the man to whom it had been made out: Mr. Clay Whitney.

'I'm damned if I know what this proves, though,' Quist grumbled, after a time, 'beyond the fact that Whitney Clayton was once known as Clay Whitney.' After a few minutes he replaced the various articles in the drawer, excepting the dues card which he stuck in one pocket.

Half a minute later he had returned to the kitchen. His eyes roved around the walls, then studied the rafters overhead, between which could be seen the shingle roofing. Here and there daylight showed between shingles. 'Yep, jerry-built, all right,' Quist commented. He unbolted and flung open the kitchen door and stepped from the rear of the house. By this time the sky was entirely overclouded and a few drops of rain splashed down.

Quist glanced around. A few old footprints showed on the earth here and there, but there was little of definition remaining. Rusted tin cans had been scattered far and wide among the clumps of buffalo grass; there were green spots of small mesquite. Off to Quist's left was a tall pecan tree, and to this side of the tree stood an empty corral constructed of poles. Considerable cactus spotted the terrain. A tall clump of prickly pear grew near the corner of the house at Quist's right, reaching above the eaves of the house, which were low. The roof was peaked, slanting from the top to the front, and from top to rear. Unplaned shingles, already curled from the summer's heat, showed raggedly at the edges. An old packing case stood near the clump of prickly pear, one broad pad of which had been broken off in the past, and lay drying on the gravelly earth.

Quist stepped to the packing case and hauled himself to the roof. Here he stood upright gazing around. Running diagonally about forty yards to the rear of the house was Montañosa Creek, flanked thickly with cottonwoods and high brush. Quist shifted his gaze off to the left, where a break in the tumbled Montañosa Mountains showed clearly against the leaden sky. 'Thought I might be able to spot Estrecho Pass if I got high enough,' Quist told himself. He glanced at the sky. 'I'm due to get wet, mebbe — However, so far as I'm this near, I might as well ride over and look at that Pass that's got Jay Fletcher so het up. Might be something to be picked up there.'

He got down from the roof, without the aid of the packing case this time, landing lightly on the earth. Re-entering the kitchen, he closed and rebolted the door, went through the house and emerged at the front. Here he locked the front door and mounted his pony, heading it first toward Montañosa Creek. Approaching the brush, he dismounted and penetrated the tall grass and bushes. Now from where he stood, he could see the house plainly. Ten minutes was spent pushing around through the brush, under the tall cottonwoods, in a search for sign of some sort. Finally he returned to his pony and headed it in a southwesterly section toward the Montañosas.

It wasn't long before the way through Estrecho Pass became clearer as his pony climbed ever higher between the rugged hills. Finally, he reached the pass, cutting between low rocky bluffs, and pulled the pony to a halt. There was the pass all right, almost straight through the mountains. The grade looked fairly level too, as Fletcher had said.

Quist prepared to turn back. There was a steady drizzle in the air now. 'Might as well slope back as soon's possible. I'll bet I'm due for a soaking as it is — ' He paused suddenly. Near the entrance to the pass, his roving gaze had spotted a shovel and pick. Somebody had been digging there. Quist urged the pony to motion and a few moments later was gazing down on the tools. Whoever had been working at this spot, hadn't gone deep. Suddenly, Quist became aware there were other holes dug in the vicinity. Several shallow excavations and heaps of broken rock and earth showed at various spots.

Quist considered the setup. All of the digging had been done in the immediate vicinity of an unusual-shaped rock only a few rods from the entrance to Estrecho Pass. The rock was tall, slim and eroded almost smooth by centuries of sand-blasting wind and wet weather. It jutted rigidly from the earth, forming a sort of spire to the massed jumble of blocky rocks below from which it seemed to lift.

'Damned if it doesn't look like a church steeple,' Quist observed, 'though I'd lay a ten to a plugged peso that whoever did all this digging, wasn't any church-goer.' He frowned. 'Now what was the idea? Did Clayton have secret information about minerals hereabouts? Is that why he wanted holdings around Estrecho Pass? Was he prospecting for silver? Copper? Gold? I doubt there's any gold ore in that sort of geologic formation. All those times nobody knew where he was, he was probably prospecting, 'stead of being off on a drunk. And it commences to look more and more as if the bustard just married Laurinda, so he could get hold of this property. Damn poor taste, I'd say. The gal outranks the land. Of course, I don't know that Clayton did this digging, but I'd be willing to bet on it. The son-of-a-bustard!'

The rain was coming down harder now. Reluctantly, Quist turned away and started back. ''I'll be blasted if I don't come out here again some day and look around some more.' He consulted his watch. 'After four now. I'd better get pushing.' Rather than return to Clayton's house, he decided to travel straight east across the hills, until he struck the trail to Quivira City. He touched spurs lightly to the buckskin and they picked up speed.

Silver lances of rain slanted down. Quist turned up his coat collar and huddled down in the saddle. After a time, horse and man topped a low rise and started down across a wide depression between hills, thickly grown with tall mesquite and huisache bush, forcing the pony to an irregular progress through the trees. It was about then that Quist fancied he heard shooting, but the thudding of horse's hoofs across wet sandy earth, blurred the sounds. He pulled to a halt, listening. Then he was certain. There came two more quick shots, followed by a third.' Winchester fire, he guessed.

A moment later, through the downpour of rain came a horse's shrill neigh, the cracking of whipping branches and a scrabbling of hoofs. Then silence again. Starting on, once more, eyes straight ahead, Quist almost missed the other man and horse. The man was down on the wet soil, off to one side, near a clump of mesquite, struggling futilely to arise. A few yards away from the stricken man, the horse was moving excitedly, but not making any attempt to run. It was the movements of the two that had caught Quist's attention.

Quist jerked his buckskin to a halt, and slid to earth. Even before he reached the man, the fellow had ceased his struggles and was stretched face down, prone on the earth, one clenched hand extended before him. As Quist turned him over, the man rattled out his dying gasp. Quist gently laid him back and felt for his pulse. There wasn't any. Already the eyes were set, staring.

Alert for the approach of some enemy,

still Quist took time to study the man. It was no one he'd ever seen before. The dead man was shabbily dressed, with patched boots and clothing. Thick, uncut gray hair reached to his coat collar, where it had been raggedly trimmed. The work appeared to have been done with a dull butcher knife. A dirty gray beard reached to the man's breast. Something glistened through the tangled hair of the head. Upon examination, Quist found small round gold earrings attached through the lobes of both ears. The old man had been struck twice with gun shots. A wound showed high in the left shoulder; a second bullet had penetrated just below the left shoulder blade.

Quist frowned. 'And once more I'll be damned,' he exclaimed. 'Now what — ?'

The thought wasn't destined to be finished. A leaden slug furrowing savagely through the earth, sprayed wet sand into his face and eyes. At almost the same instant his ears caught the far-off report of a rifle. Moving fast, Quist flung himself to partial concealment behind a mesquite tree. A second bullet came dangerously close, even as he ducked for safety.

Quist peered through green foliage and slanting rain in the direction from which the shots had come. There was no movement to be seen through the trees. Then, raising his gaze a trifle, above the broad expanse of mesquite tops, he saw the summit of a low brushy hill. He was never sure, but through the gray rain haze, he thought he momentarily caught sight of a small patch of drifting powder smoke, against the hilltop growth.

Instantly, the underarm .44 six-shooter was in Quist's fist, jumping violently with each detonation of the heavy explosions, as he sent a wide pattern of leaden slugs toward the hilltop brush, where he imagined the hidden rifleman was concealed.

9

Clues

Powder smoke from the six-shooter drifted across Quist's face through the wet air, as his narrowed eyes searched the hilltop for movement. So far as he could determine, there wasn't any. After a little, he relaxed a trifle and moved out from his point of concealment, alert for the first flash of rifle fire. Nothing happened.

Quist grunted impatiently, 'Damn that bustard! Why doesn't he show himself? And that's a fool question, too, I guess. My shooting must have thrown a scare into him. I doubt any of my slugs found a mark at this distance — '

He broke off, strode quickly to the buckskin and vaulted into the saddle. Rain beat into his face as he urged the horse toward the hilltop, guiding the animal with his knees while he reloaded the .44 Colt gun. Then with the gun clutched in his right hand, he spurred the buckskin up the irregular slope of the hill, expecting every second to hear the crack of the hidden rifleman's weapon. Still no shots came.

Nearing the top of the hill, he drew rein, and climbed down from the saddle to approach on foot, the six-shooter still gripped in one fist. There was nothing to be seen against the leaden sky, except the summit of tangled brush-scrub oak and cedar, chaparral and prickly pear. Quist's eyes searched the brush, but could detect no hostile movement of any sort.

'The son-of-a-bustard has had plenty chance to throw down on me,' he muttered. 'Must be he's lit out.' He moved around the side of the hill a trifle, gaze ranging along the horizon. Finally, through the teeming rain he caught sight of a rider, moving fast, some distance off across the top of a far hill toward the southeast. Quist lifted his gun, then lowered it again. 'No use at this range,' he scowled. Even as he watched, the rider disappeared beyond the top of the hill he'd been crossing. The distance was too great for either horse or rider to be recognizable; it was only by chance that Quist had been able to distinguish movement through the gray dark atmosphere.

'Blast this rain,' Quist grunted. 'It'll wash out any sign that hombre might leave. I'll just have to guess he was heading for Quivira City, and let it go at that. Or some point farther east.'

He returned to the edge of the brush where he'd left the buckskin. The animal waited, head down, its hide streaked with running water. 'Be with you in a few minutes, horse,' Quist muttered, and pushed into the brush. Thorny branches caught at his clothing as he moved here and there, through wet grass and shrubs, trying to find the place at which the rifleman had been concealed.

After a search of nearly fifteen minutes he was rewarded. At a point behind some low mesquite and cedar, matted grass showed where a form had crouched. A few yards away were horse droppings.

Quist moved around, looking for ejected cartridges, or other sign. Whoever had fired the shots had been smart enough to pick up the empty shells. Quist studied the matted grass which wasn't packed hard. 'Hmm!' he speculated, 'not a very heavy cuss, I'd say. With this rain and grass, bootprints don't show — '

He paused as something white caught his eye a couple of yards off. Moving over, he picked up a small square of cambric — a woman's handkerchief. Nearby, three metal hairpins lay scattered on the grass. These, Quist also retrieved. Quist held the handkerchief to his nostrils, and recognized the faint lavender fragrance. Drawing a deep breath, he shoved hairpins and handkerchief into one pocket and pushed back through the brush, reholstering his six-shooter as he moved.

Quist's features were a study in frowning concentration as he climbed into his saddle and returned down the slope to the point where he had left the dead man. Here he dismounted, noticing that the other horse hadn't moved far from the corpse. The animal was rib-thin, and appeared not to have had too much care in the past. The saddle was old and worn; at spots on the horn and cantle, wood showed through the scuffed leather. One stirrup strap had been mended with a length of haywire. Eyeing the gaunt form of the pony, Quist shook his head, 'What a miserable specimen of horse-flesh. Pony, you're just about due for the boneyard.' He turned back to the dead man and stooped at his side. Blood had dripped into the sodden sandy earth. Disturbing the form as little as possible, Quist went through the pockets in the clothing, replacing articles as soon as he had looked at them. The pockets revealed nothing unusual: some tobacco, a couple of soiled bandannas, a dulled and rusty pocketknife; one dollar and sixty cents in silver. That was all. No letters, or writing of any sort that would lend a clue as to the corpse's identity.

Quist remembered now how the man had looked when he had first seen him prone on the earth, right arm extended as though about to throw something. He glanced at the right hand. The fist was tightly clenched.

'I wonder if he was trying to get rid of something — throw it away,' Quist speculated. 'If he had anything in his fist, it should be still there.'

Rigor mortis having not yet taken hold, it was a simple matter to force back the lifeless fingers and learn what the man had been holding in his clenched fist at the moment death struck. Quist's eyes widened as he gazed at the object he had taken from the dead hand, and a sudden exclamation parted his lips.

Forgotten now was the downbeating rain as Quist studied the flat metallic object he held in his palm. It appeared to be made of gold and was octagonal in form. Quist guessed it was about an inch-and-a-half across. Probably somewhat larger. 'Heavy enough to be gold and looks to be,' he muttered interestedly. 'Must weigh up to two or three ounces.'

He gazed at the flat octagonal-shaped

form, one side of which showed a circle, stamped or molded, just within the edge. In the exact center was a much smaller circle with a dot in the middle, the space between the two circles being filled with a sort of curved cross-hatching design. 'Some sort of medal, I suppose,' Quist mused, his mind now returning to the bits of blue ribbon he had found in Whitney Clayton's dresser drawer.

He turned it over and a look of disappointment crossed his features. Whatever wording the reverse might have showed, had long since been obliterated, either by a grindstone or continued rubbing on some flat piece of granitic rock. Here and there a letter, or portion of a design showed faintly, but there was left too little of either to be intelligible to Quist.

In place of the original design, someone had scratched with the point of a sharp instrument — perhaps a small knife — certain lines and figures in the metal. A sort of wavy line ran across one side, with at one end of the line a letter W. Almost below the wavy line was a sort of quarter-circle, with extending from the quarter-circle what looked like a letter Y. Near the bottom of the Y were the figures one hundred fifty-two. There were other figures near the two arms of the Y, a thirty-one and a forty-six. Near the thirty-one arm was a short straight line with some zig-zag scratches across it.

'Looks like somebody tried to make his own medal,' Quist frowned. Drawing out his knife, he opened it and tried the blade lightly on the edge of the metal, then grunted, 'Gold, or I'm a liar,' and replaced the knife in his pocket.

Regardless of the drenching rain, he stood scrutinizing the octagonal object he held. 'Now what in the devil is this, some sort of prize Clayton won in horse-breeding, or training? And how did this dead hombre get it? What was his connection with Clayton? Or did he steal it? But from whom? Someone chased him to recover it, I figure, then shot him. 'Bout then I appeared on the scene to mess up matters.' He eyed the dead form on the earth. 'I sure wish you could have lived long enough to explain a few things. Why you were trying to throw away this medal — if you were. And why, with only one buck sixty cents in your pants, did you want to throw away gold? That doesn't explain, either, the scratchings on one side of the medal. Trying to make a medal of your own, mister? Did Clayton win something that should rightfully have been yours?'

He broke off. 'I'll go batty if I remain in this downpour, trying to solve the puzzle.' The sky was much darker now, the precipitation increasing. Glancing at the dead man at his feet, 'Not that you give a damn about getting wet, but I'd best get you to town before the coyotes do a job on you. Meanwhile,' — slipping the octagonal object into a pocket, — 'I'll just keep this until I see if anything can be learned about it.'

It was but a few minutes' work to catch up the dead man's horse and lash the lifeless body across the saddle. Then, taking up the reins, Quist mounted the buckskin and the horses moved on through the mesquite.

10

Grizzly Baldridge

It was after ten o'clock that evening when Quist led his grisly burden into Quivira City. The rain was still coming down, though not so hard as it had been a couple of hours before when Quist's mount and the other pony had more than once nearly gone down in the slippery, treacherous going. Quist's clothing was soaked; water dripped from his sombrero brim. He was hungry, chilly and thirsty; the very thought of steaming coffee and food had kept him going at a pace that he otherwise might not have tried to maintain, through the night.

There were only a few people to be seen on Main Street when he turned from Alamo, and these few were hurrying along with hats pulled low and collars turned up. Lights shone warmly from saloon windows and were reflected brightly in puddles of the muddy street.

A few ponies stood disconsolately at hitchracks along the way, heads down, wet tails drooping. A lamp shone in the window of the sheriff's office and it was there, Quist directed his wet buckskin pony.

As he neared the office and pulled his horse to a halt, he heard Todd Sargent's voice, 'Greg! You got here at last. I've been watching for you — ' He paused and stepped down from the porch. 'What you leading behind?'

'Another horse — or a crowbait,' Quist returned laconically, 'carrying a dead man.' He got down from the saddle and rounded the end of the hitchrack.

'T'hell you say!' the deputy exclaimed. 'Who is it?'

'You tell me and I'll tell you,' Quist grunted. 'Found him out on the range, a few miles this side of Clayton's house — ' He stopped, peering through the sheriff's window. 'Who's in there with Pike Wolcott?'

'Grizzly Baldridge. The two of 'em have been chewing the rag. Baldridge has been waiting for the rain to let up before starting for the Bee-Hive. Reckon he forgot time was slipping fast. I've been standing on the porch looking for you. 'Fraid something had happened.'

'It did. I got wet,' Quist said irritably.

'What about this dead man?'

'I don't know anything about him. I did my part when I brought him in. Now it's the sheriff 's problem.'

Sargent raised his voice and called to Pike Wolcott. The sheriff came out, followed by Grizzly Baldridge, a ponderous-shouldered individual in cowman's togs, with piercing dark eyes and iron-gray hair and bushy beard of the same color.

'What's this about a dead man, Todd?' Wolcott inquired, then catching sight of Quist, 'Oh, it's you,' — sourly. 'What you been messing in now?'

'Mud and wet weather,' Quist snapped.

'Where'd you shoot this feller?' The sheriff peered through the night toward the lifeless form across the bony pony.

'I didn't shoot him. I just brought him

in,' Quist said tersely. 'If you've got any sensible questions to ask, ask 'em now. I don't aim to stand here in wet clothing much longer.'

Todd Sargent introduced Quist to Grizzly Baldridge. Baldridge nodded shortly to Quist and received an equally curt acknowledgment. Neither man offered to shake hands. Pike Wolcott demanded, 'Quist, who's the dead man you brought in?'

'I haven't the least idea. And let's ask the rest of your questions in your office. If you get as wet as I am your fat belly might shrink — though I doubt it.'

'Now, now, Quist — that's no attitude to take. Don't forget I'm the law in Blackjack County, and I don't aim to have — '

'You'll have anything I feel like handing you,' Quist half snarled. 'I'm in no mood right now to listen to pompous stupidity — '

A sudden exclamation from Grizzly Baldridge interrupted Quist's words. Baldridge had rounded the hitchrack and, standing close to the bony horse, was examining the corpse.

Todd Sargent asked, 'What did you say, Grizzly?'

'This dead hombre,' Baldridge returned in his heavy tones, 'I'll be damned for a lousy sheepherdin' bustard, if it isn't old Hi-Johnny. Haven't seen hide nor hair of him in three, four years.'

'You know him, Grizzly Wolcott asked.

'Used to — knew him a long time.' Baldridge returned to the sidewalk. 'Let's go inside and do our talking.'

Wolcott nodded and spoke to Sargent: 'Todd, you take that corpse down to the undertaker's. Have him send word to Doc Twitchell, that I want the lead probed out for examination.'

'And, Todd,' Quist added, 'do you mind dropping my pony off at the livery? You'll likely take that other horse there too. Tell the livery man to give the poor beast a good feed. It's practically down to hide and bones now.'

'Glad to take care of it for you, Greg.'

The deputy moved out to the street and taking up the reins of the two ponies started off.

Quist followed Baldridge and Wolcott into the sheriff's office. Wolcott said grumpily, 'Now, Quist, I want you to tell me all about this dead hombre you — er, claim — you found shot out on the range.'

Quist eyed the sheriff a moment, removed his sombrero and whipped the rain from it, managing to scatter some of the drops in Wolcott's face during the procedure. Without waiting to be asked, he dropped into a chair and searched in one pocket for tobacco and cigarette papers, hoping to find them dry enough for a smoke. A sort of chilly shudder coursed down his spine.

'When I say I *found* that man, Wolcott,' Quist began grimly, while his fingers rolled a smoke, 'I mean just that — nothing less. So don't insinuate that I'm not speaking truth. I don't like it, and I like you less.'

'Now, you look here, Quist — '

'Hold it, Pike,' Baldridge grunted 'There's a time for everything, and this isn't your time to get proddy.' Reaching to a hip pocket, he produced a half-pint flask of bourbon, and proffered it to Quist. 'Something to take the wet chill off, Quist.'

Quist smiled, and extracted the cork. 'I'm not only much obliged, I'm plumb amazed, Baldridge.' He took a couple of deep swallows and was grateful for the warmth the liquor sent coursing through his veins. He handed back the bottle.

'Man needs a warm nip on a wet night,' Baldridge growled, seating himself near the sheriff's chair. 'Bought that liquor to fortify my own trip home. Quist, mebbe you are amazed. Sure, I'll admit that I don't — well, don't see any use of you being here. At the same time, I'd hate to see even a dog go cold on a night like this.'

Quist lighted his damp cigarette. 'Anyway,' he said tersely, 'I know where I stand with you, Baldridge. And I'm still much obliged.' He drew on the cigarette, and turned to the sheriff, 'You're waiting to hear about that body. I was — '

'I'd like to know what you were doing over there in the first place,' the sheriff interrupted. 'Todd tells me he let you have the key to Clayton's place. Don't know's I approve, but what's done is done. What were you looking for? What did you find?'

'Wolcott, you wouldn't understand what I was looking for, even if I told you,' Quist said coldly. 'What I found is my own business.'

'I got ways to make you tell, I'm betting,' Wolcott said testily.

'Don't try 'em — not any of 'em — not on me,' Quist snapped. 'You'll get your sit-spot in a sling if you do.' He held up a protesting hand to silence the sheriff's angry outburst and went on, 'So we've disposed of that part. Now, as to finding that dead man. I had turned back to head for Quivira City when I heard shots, though I couldn't see anybody — '

'Where exactly was this?' Baldridge broke in.

'I can't say — exactly — but I was a few miles south of Clayton's house.' Quist explained as near as possible where the shooting had taken place, then continued, 'I heard a horse crashing through the trees. Next, I came in sight of the horse and the rider. The rider was down, moving some, but before I could reach him he was dead. The shooting, I judge, was done with a rifle. Sounded like a .30-30 — but I can't be sure. You'll know when the bullets are probed out. Might even have been a .38-55 rifle. As I say, I can't be sure.'

'And you didn't take out after the feller what done the shooting', Wolcott asked skeptically.

'Would you have in that rain?' Quist evaded. 'Remember, the top of that hill was some distance off, and visibility was damn low.'

'And you didn't even see him?' Baldridge insisted.

'Remember,' Quist reminded caustically, 'I just said it was raining? Besides, it wasn't my fight.'

'And you say you don't know who the feller is?' Wolcott pursued. 'Didn't you even go through his pockets for identification, or anything?'

'Why should I go through his pockets?' Quist demanded coldly. 'It's nothing to me who he is. It's your job to find out, Wolcott.'

Wolcott sniffed. 'What did you do next ?'

'Got the body on the hunk of skin-and-bones he'd been riding and brought him in to you. Now, it's your problem.'

'Hmmph!' Wolcott snorted. 'I don't like your story, Quist.'

'What don't you like about it?'

'Well, er — well, a number of things,' Wolcott replied. 'In the first place, Quist, you got a rep for running down things. Don't seem like you wouldn't try to learn what was at the bottom of this business.'

Quist's topaz-colored eyes glinted angrily. 'I've told you what I know, Wolcott. If you don't like it, you know what you can do.'

Before the sheriff could answer, Todd

Sargent entered the office. 'The undertaker says he'll handle things for you, Pike,' the deputy said. He turned to Quist. 'I took care of the horses, Greg. Also, I dropped in at the Chink's restaurant. There'll be some hot food up in your room in about thirty minutes.'

'Now there's something I do appreciate,' Quist smiled. 'I'll be glad to get these wet togs off and some food in my stomach.'

Wolcott looked somewhat put out, but didn't say anything. Quist turned to Baldridge, 'Didn't I hear you say that you used to know the dead man?'

Baldridge nodded. 'He's been in this country for a number of years. We used to call him Hi-Johnny.'

'Any other name?' Quist asked.

'That's all I know of. His name was really Hadji Yanni' — Baldridge spelled out the letters — 'but we shortened it to Hi-Johnny. He was a Greek or a Turk or Armenian, or some sort of furren breed.' Baldridge chuckled. 'I 'mind one time after the War 'tween the States,

Hi-Johnny got hold of a pair of baggy red pants, like a Turk wears. I reckon it was a garment he got from some member of the Louisiana Zouave regiments. He was sure tickled with them baggy red pants. Wore 'em until they nigh dropped off.'

'How come,' Quist wondered, 'a hombre of that breed ever reached Texas?'

'He was a camel driver — ' Baldridge commenced.

'Camel driver?' Wolcott frowned.

'Camels in Texas?' from Todd Sargent, in an unbelieving voice.

Quist's forehead furrowed. 'Now that you mention it, Baldridge, I've heard of that business. Government brought 'em in, didn't it?'

Baldridge nodded, then turned to Wolcott, 'Pike, it's likely you never heard of those camels in your home up in Dakota, and I reckon Todd's not old enough to remember.' The deputy asked a question, and Baldridge continued, 'It was back before the War — Civil War, some calls it — that Jeff Davis got his idea — '

'You mean,' —Wolcott asked, 'Jefferson Davis, President of the Confederacy?'

'The same,' Baldridge answered, 'only at that time he was Secretary of War of the United States. Anyway, he got an idea that if a camel could be used to tote loads in the Sahara Desert and places like that, why wouldn't they be a good idea to work for the U.S. Army in our own southwestern desert country, as beasts of burden? So — '

Wolcott snorted skeptically. 'What could a camel do that a good horse couldn't do?'

Baldridge smiled dryly. 'Travel around thirty miles a day, or more, with a load of six hundred pounds on its back — or more. That was just average. Some could be loaded to nine hundred pounds — '

'T'hell you say!' Sargent exclaimed.

Baldridge nodded affirmation. 'Not only that, a camel can go without water for long stretches, due to one of its four stomachs being a sort of reservoir. On top of that, feeding wasn't too much of a problem. Camels can graze along the roadside as they travel, when there's a rush. They liked greasewood for instance. Unloaded, except for a driver, a camel can cover eighty — ninety miles a day — though not every day, of course.'

'I'll be damned,' Sargent said unbelievingly. 'But what happened? Didn't they work out in the Army?'

Baldridge shook his head. 'Not too well. The few drivers, like Hi-Johnny, who were imported, could handle 'em, but generally Americans didn't take to the beasts. Not only that, cattle, horses, mules, didn't like the smell of a camel. Sometimes that smell would start a stampede. 'Nother thing, the camel was used to sandy deserts. When it hit some of the flinty, harder soil of our desert country, its feet would get cut and split. They might have worked out in time, but about then the War came along, and the government turned most of the camels loose to shift for themselves. Once on their own they thrived in a wild state and multiplied. I saw a couple down in Mexico a few years back. Some of 'em were sold to circuses by the government, or to California companies who figured to start freight lines. But, shucks, after the War, the railroads came in fast and they could outdo even a camel.'

'And Hi-Johnny drove camels for the Army, then?' Quist asked.

Baldridge nodded. 'The government imported a dozen or so native drivers. Later, most of 'em returned to their own country. Hi-Johnny and a couple of others stayed. I don't know why. We used to say Hi-Johnny was crazy. He'd had a bad accident to his head one time, and it left him sort of queer — '

'But how did he live?' Sargent asked.

Baldridge shrugged his shoulders. 'You got me. Just hung around at any ranch that would feed him. He got so he liked horses better than camels. For a time he sort of helped out at the Bee-Hive, then he drifted on again — someplace.'

'I've heard of wild camels being seen over in the mountains of Arizona,' Quist put in.

'It's likely,' Baldridge said. ''Probably

scaring hell out of horses and cows whenever they appear.' He laughed shortly. 'I recollect, after the War, there was a gang of cow thieves caught a camel and used it to frighten trail-herds at night. The cattle would go scattering from hell to breakfast and the thieves would pick 'em up at their leisure. Back about twenty years ago a feller wrote a book about that gang. Called the book *Rustlers' Paradise* or *Cowthief Paradise* or some such fool name—'

There was a step at the open doorway of the sheriff's office, and old Lennie Plummer appeared. 'Howdy, gents—sheriff. Say, Pike, I hear tell Mister Quist brung in a dead body ternight.'

'Where'd you hear that?' Wolcott asked.

'Happen' I saw Doc Twitchell headin' fer the undertaker's. So I asked some questions. Figgered mebbe I could git a piece fer the *Blade*. George Nugent might pay me one or two dollars fer somethin' he could set up in print.'

'You'd better leave such matters to

George, Lennie,' Wolcott said shortly. 'Tell him to come around tomorrow and I'll tell him what I know. I ain't in no mood to repeat that story tonight.'

'Jes' you say, Pike.' The old man shrank back a little before Wolcott's brusque manner.

Quist noted the oldster's wet clothing and felt sorry for him. 'You'd better get along to your bed and get those wet togs off, Lennie. Still raining out, I expect.'

'Pract'ly stopped,' Plummer answered, his watery eyes lighting up at the attention Quist paid him. 'Mister, didn't she rain though! Now, if that had happened in my old home state of Montany, it 'ud have meant plenty inches of snow. I'm bettin' a pretty thet them bayous over in east Texas and Loosyana was flooded, if they caught sech a cloudbust.'

'Probably so,' Quist nodded. He got to his feet. 'Well, I'm going to drift along to the hotel. Sheriff, if you've any more questions to ask, I'll see you tomorrow — '

'Maybe you'll see me some more tonight,' Wolcott growled. 'I ain't sure but what I should throw you in a cell, Quist.'

'Quist stared hard at him. 'On what charge?'

'You haven't showed any proof you didn't kill that Hi-Johnny hombre yourself — '

'You've showed no proof that I did,' Quist snapped.

'Aside from that,' Wolcott said sourly, 'you've broke the law of this county.'

'And now you're sounding crazy as hell,' Quist said. 'In what way have I broken your blasted law?'

'Law states,' Wolcott replied, 'that a dead body ain't to be disturbed, until the sheriff, or his representative have had an opportunity to examine the body and surroundings.'

'Bosh!' Quist snorted. 'If Hi-Johnny's body had had to wait until you went out there, Wolcott, there'd been nothing but bones for you to see — and they'd been scattered by the coyotes. Use your head, man, if you have one! And,' — his voice rising — 'don't get any ideas about arresting me, either. You may be a big man in Blackjack County, but any time you try to push around a representative of the TN. & A.S. Railroad, you're biting off more than you can chew.'

'There ain't no railroad going to tell me my duty — ' Wolcott began wrathfully.

Baldridge interrupted wearily, 'Let be, Pike, let be. You're talking like you've growed too big for your breeches.'

'Well, just as you say, Grizzly,' the sheriff answered reluctantly. 'I just thought you wanted — '

'Let be,' Baldridge said sharply.

Quist started for the doorway with a curt good night, adding to the deputy, 'I'll see you in the morning, Todd.'

'Fine.' Sargent sent Quist a meaning glance. 'Anything that has to be said can wait until then.'

Grizzly Baldridge pushed up from his chair. 'Wait a minute, Quist. I'll drift along to the hotel with you. There's no use of me starting home tonight. My horse might slip and break his neck.'

He joined Quist on the sidewalk; the two men started toward the hotel in silence. It had ceased raining by this time. Here and there a star shone through broken clouds. Water dripped steadily from eaves along the way. Pools of water in the road caught up a few bright reflections from windows. Baldridge broke the silence at last:

'Sometimes I think,' he growled, 'that Pike Wolcott has outlived his job. Tonight he didn't show no more sense than a younker with a string of spools.'

'He seemed to shut up for you,' Quist observed.

'Meaning what?' Baldridge asked quickly.

'Nothing in particular.' Quist yawned. 'Except that you appear to show some control in that direction. Why do you allow Wolcott to stay in office? Todd Sargent's a far better man.'

'I wouldn't be surprised. But it's the voters who keep Pike in office.'

'No doubt. But don't the Baldridges throw a lot of weight in this county?'

'It ain't my place to say, Quist. Anyway,' — somewhat lamely — 'Pike's an old friend. Used to be a mighty sharp law-officer.'

Quist didn't reply. The two men crossed the street and walked on, past the Green Bottle Saloon with its lighted window, and the darkened Deming & Co. General Store. They were crossing Austin Street when Baldridge said abruptly, 'Laurinda tells me she had a talk with you.'

'Your daughter and I had some habla,' Quist returned noncommittally. He waited for Baldridge's next words.

'Laurinda tells me she doesn't like you.'

'I'm all broken up to hear that,' Quist said caustically. 'If she doesn't like me, maybe she has good reason.'

They had reached the steps leading up to the hotel porch by this time. Baldridge grasped Quist by the sleeve, detaining him a moment. 'Now don't get me wrong, Quist,' Baldridge said earnestly. 'I know that girl of mine and, from the very way she said it, I know she meant the opposite. It's just that you must have riled her about something.' He eyed Quist seriously in the lights from the hotel windows.

'That's possible,' Quist conceded. 'Sometimes a woman has to hear things she don't like, for her own good.'

'That could be,' Baldridge said heavily. 'Y'know, Quist, it might be that I judged you wrong too.'

'Is that why you handed me that bottle of liquor tonight, Baldridge?'

'I told you at the time why I gave it to you.' The big man sounded rather hurt.

Quist nodded. 'So you did. And it was a lifesaver and I'm much obliged. But you can kill a dog without choking him with butter.'

'What's that?' Baldridge frowned puzzledly.

'And,' Quist continued, 'I also know the old saying relative to honey catching more flies than vinegar. So, if this is an act, you might as well save your breath.'

'Well, I'll be everlastingly Gawd—' Baldridge checked the words, then, 'By the great horned steer, Quist! You're a damn hard man to get acquainted with.'

'Not when I'm approached the right way,' Quist laughed shortly. 'I just don't like to be pushed around, I don't like to be shot at, I won't be intimidated and I never could swallow slickery palaver. If you reach the point where you feel like telling me what actually happened at Clayton's killing, I'll be glad to listen. That's all. Good night, Baldridge.'

Brushing past the older man he moved lightly up the steps to the hotel porch, opened the door, got his key in the lobby, and proceeded upstairs to the warm food he knew awaited him, leaving behind a somewhat irritated Baldridge to negotiate with the clerk of the hotel for a room for the night. For some minutes, Baldridge stood in the lobby, apparently lost in thought, then, instead of making his way up to his room, he left the hotel and turned his steps back toward the sheriff's office.

11

Blind Canyon

Quist slept late the following morning. His rain-soaked clothing had been drying in the hotel kitchen, and when the garments were delivered, breakfast was also sent to his room. He ate slowly, meditating the various events of the previous day and trying to sort out the happenings in some sort of logical manner that would make sense, but every theory he evolved seemed to lead him into a blind canyon. Finally he finished dressing, donned his sombrero and left for the street. The sun was shining brightly when he stepped to the sidewalk. Overhead, a few drifting fleecy clouds chased each other across the turquoise blue sky. Vagrant puddles steamed in the roadway. Wagons and ponies waited at hitchracks; pedestrians passed on either side of the thoroughfare. Quist crossed Main Street at a diagonal and headed down Austin Street to the T.N. & A.S. Railroad depot. Here he sent off a telegram and after some short conversation with the telegraph operator, left the depot and set out on a course paralleling the railroad tracks until he turned north at Laredo Street, something less than a block's distance.

Arriving at the sheriff's office, he found it empty, though the door was open. Quist dropped into a chair and glanced around. Near the window was the sheriff's desk and chair. Directly opposite the entrance a closed door in the back wall opened onto a block of cells. Ranged along one wall was a cot with neatly folded blankets. Quist judged the cot to belong to Todd Sargent. A topographical map of Blackjack County and a couple of packing house calendars adorned the walls. Wooden pegs driven into the adobe walls held odd bits of clothing, handcuffs and an old cartridge belt and holster, weaponless. The floor of the office was of bare planks, swept clean; a cuspidor stood near the sheriff's desk which was littered with papers and held an oil lamp.

There was a step at the entrance and Todd Sargent entered, his gaze intent on some silver coins he picked over in one hand.

'I hope they didn't give you any counterfeit money,' Quist smiled.

The deputy's head jerked up. 'Oh, hello, Greg.' He slipped the silver into a pocket. 'You been waiting long?'

'Five minutes or so. Saw the door was open. Figured you or Wolcott would be in shortly.'

'Not Pike.' Sargent laughed. 'He never does get around very early. I reckon the mattress at his boarding house is too soft for his own good. I'd just slipped out for a minute to get some Durham.' He offered the sack to Quist and the two men rolled cigarettes. 'What's new?'

'I was just about to ask the same of you,' Quist replied. 'What sort of turnout was there for Clayton's funeral yesterday?'

'Didn't amount to much. I reckon there was nobody there that would interest you. About five minutes after it started from the undertaker's, it come on to rain. Gawd Almighty! How it did come down. And so, that whittled off the attendance. I was there — blast you for asking me to go out in that weather — and the undertaker. He had quite a job digging up enough pallbearers. That pastor from the east end of town officiated — short and to the point. That's about all, I reckon. Nobody cared to drive out in that rain. Grizzly Baldridge attended, of course.'

'I wonder why?' Quist frowned and blew cigarette smoke into the room.

'Grizzly told me that he felt sort of obligated, being as he'd stood the expense of burial and inasmuch as Clayton had been married to Laurinda. He thought somebody from the family should be on hand.'

'Grizzly Baldridge,' Quist said dryly, 'appears to be quite a stickler for appearances. It's a wonder he didn't want Laurinda and her brother there too.'

'From what Grizzly told me, I think that was discussed. Grizzly seemed to feel that if Laurinda or Chris showed up at the funeral, it would look like some sort of play for sympathy when the trial comes up.'

'I didn't figure he was worried too much about that trial. Don't the Baldridges sort of run things hereabouts?'

'Grizzly's word carries a heap of weight, no doubt about it,' the deputy replied, 'but that's no sign he'd try to fix a judge or jury. Say what you like about Baldridge, he's straight.'

'I hope so.' Quist sounded a trifle skeptical. 'He tried to hand me a line of palaver last night. I wasn't having any.' He told Sargent of the discussion he'd had with Baldridge.

Sargent frowned. 'I don't know, Greg. Maybe Grizzly was sincere. It could be he's realized that he can't ride roughshod over you, and he'd like to be friendly. Maybe he's afraid of what you may turn up. I know he told Pike, last night, it might be a good idea to tone down a mite where you're concerned.'

'When was this?'

'After you and he left for the hotel.'

Quist looked thoughtful. 'So he came back here? I wasn't aware of that. By the way, did Cobra Macaw ever ask you about his gun?'

Sargent nodded. 'He come in yesterday. I give him a right good talking to before I let him have it.'

'I hope you didn't hurt his feelings,' Quist said dryly. 'Hell! You can't even penetrate the hide of a Cobra Macaw. Say, Greg, did you tell Pike everything that happened yesterday about that Hi-Johnny shooting? Incidentally, Doc Twitchell probed out the slug. It was a .30-30 caliber that killed Hi-Johnny. That won't help much. There're plenty .30-30 rifles in this country.'

'No, it won't. And I didn't tell Wolcott everything. For instance I took out after that killer but he got away . . .' Quist related details, but made no mention of finding the octagonal gold object. When he had finished, Todd Sargent looked troubled.

'Damn! I don't like it, Greg,' the deputy frowned. 'Are you certain the hairpins and handkerchief you found belong to Laurinda?'

'I'm not *certain* of anything,' Quist growled, 'except that every way I turn, I head into a blind canyon. I don't even know if the shooting of Hi-Johnny had anything to do with the Clayton killing.'

'Look here, could whoever killed Hi-Johnny been shooting at you, and hit him by mistake?'

Quist considered. 'Might be,' he conceded. 'Coming through those mesquite trees I could have been visible from that hilltop, I suppose. The fact remains Hi-Johnny was struck twice. Until I got into the deal, no shots at all came my way.'

'That looks like somebody didn't want you messing around Hi-Johnny. Why ?'

'That,' Quist laughed shortly, 'is one prize question.'

'What did you find at Clayton's house?'

'About just what you told me to expect. Furniture knocked galley-west. Laurinda's holster and belt hanging on the wall — I suppose it was hers. I'm surprised you didn't bring that in for evidence, Todd.'

'To tell the truth,' the deputy admitted ruefully, 'I might have slipped there. But remember when I went out to investigate, all I had in mind was that *Chris* had killed Clayton. It wasn't until I returned that I learned of Laurinda's confession. And then you showed up, and — and — well, there you are.'

'I'm still wondering where we are. I looked over things at the house. It appeared to me that Laurinda had grabbed her clothes and left in a rush — '

'Yeah, but that was some time before the shooting that she left Clayton. Learn anything else?'

'I'm not sure, — and keep this under your hat like everything else I tell you — but I think Clayton was at one time known as Clay Whitney.'

'T'hell you say!' from Sargent. Quist explained about finding the Artexico Horse Breeders' Society card. Sargent shook his head in some exasperation, saying, 'That should teach me to make more thorough investigations. But suppose he used an alias? What does it mean to you?'

'I'm not sure yet. Todd, can you think of any reason Clayton — or anybody — would have for digging over near the entrance to Estrecho Pass.' He told of the excavations he'd noticed.

'Gripes! From the way you tell it, that digging must have been around Steeple Rock. No, I've never heard of any gold or silver being found in this country. I understand it's been prospected more or less too. 'Course, you don't know for sure it was Clayton did the digging, or how long ago.'

'You're right there, Todd,' Quist admitted. The deputy asked if he'd made any other discoveries. Quist said, 'Nothing I want to talk about now, until I've had a chance to mull things over. Say, Todd, did you check into why that carpet was being beaten at the particular time somebody choose to take a shot at me?'

'Yeah.' Sargent looked disgusted. 'I checked that whole neighborhood over on Lamar Street. I don't know whether it means much or not, but I finally learned that carpet-beating took place in the back yard of Lavinia Tinker's place — she runs a boarding house. That's where Pike Wolcott lives. Anyway, Lavinia was due to entertain her Shakespeare Club that night — '

'Her what?' Quist's jaw dropped. 'What's a Shakespeare Club?'

Todd Sargent grinned. 'I'll have you know,' he said pompously, 'that the Shakespeare Club is the high point of culture in Quivira City. Lavinia and some of her old-maid friends — married and unmarried — meet weekly from early fall until spring, to discuss the merits of Shakespeare's plays. I've a hunch that they settle Shakespeare at the first meeting and gobble gossip and tea the rest of the culture season — '

'What's this to do with carpet-beating?'

'Well, it seems that Lavinia has been nagging her henpecked husband, Staunch, to give that carpet a beating for three weeks, and he'd been sneaking out of the job. To aggravate matters, the day of the weekly meeting arrived and the carpet was still unbeaten. What is more, Staunch had arrived home that afternoon, with a skinfull of bourbon somebody had given him. To punish him, Lavinia made him get right at the carpet, late in the day as it was.'

'I imagine it sobered up as well as punished,' Quist commented.

'No doubt. Now here is something, Greg, that may or may not give you a lead. I looked up Staunch and talked to him, after I'd talked to Lavinia. I asked him if he'd heard a shot while he was beating the carpet. Staunch isn't sure, but he thinks he did. Says at the time he figured he must have been mistaken, because the sound seemed to have come from overhead — '

'From a tree?'

'It could be, Greg. There's a huge old cottonwood in the Tinker backyard. One big limb stretches right out of the yard, across the alley and hangs above the roof of the *Quivira Blade* building.'

'Sounds interesting,' Quist commented.

'Now here's something that may be even more interesting. Staunch Tinker claims that once when he stopped and turned around for a breathing spell, he was almost sure he saw a man move out across that big limb and drop to the *Quivira Blade* roof. After that, Staunch lost sight of him. Now bear in mind, there are lower branches and leaves there, and that Staunch's mind was still likely raddled with liquor. Maybe he knows what he's talking about; maybe it's all in his imagination. He didn't give the matter much thought. He was too anxious to get that carpet beaten and catch some shut-eye.'

Quist considered. 'It's something to think about anyway.' He ground out his cigarette under one booted toe and changed the subject: 'Todd, who all did Laurinda Clayton go around with before she was married — I mean, to dances and social doings and so on? '

Todd Sargent reddened a trifle. 'We-ell, I reckon most of the likely young fellows around here have tried to court Laurinda, one time or another. She was right popular.'

'All right,' — good-humoredly — let's put it this way. What men forged up toward the front in the race, up to the time Clayton married her. And no holding out on me, please.'

'Well, for a time it looked like either Gene Martinsen or Ownie Jordan might have a chance. Actually, though, Gene wasn't her type.'

'Martinsen you told me about. He's the hombre that owns the G-Bar-M — rough crew — has Cobra Macaw working for him. Now, who is Ownie Jordan?'

'Big quiet cuss — except when he's drinking, then he's got a hot temper. Ownie is a right nice fellow though. He owns the Box-J outfit. He'd been married young, his wife died. I guess that started him drinking. Then he started visiting at the Bee-Hive regular — '

'Where do you come in?'

Sargent's flush deepened. He laughed a little self-consciously. 'Just before Ownie got on the job. For a time there I thought I might be top dog. Laurinda seemed to like me, and — and then — well, what did I have to offer? I was only a deputy sheriff. Ownie Jordan has a right profitable spread — '

'Did Laurinda Clayton put it that way to you?'

'Cripes, no! I just figured I could read the handwriting on the wall. What did I have to offer?'

'You said that before. So you just dropped out. Todd, faint heart never won a horse race. Where did Martinsen come in?'

'He was calling on Laurinda before my time. Martinsen's got a smooth line of palaver, but I reckon Laurinda saw through him after a spell. Jeepers! It didn't make much difference. We all dropped out of the race after Whit Clayton finally decided it was Laurinda he wanted.'

'Finally decided?'

Todd Sargent nodded. 'Yeah. Clayton was giving a lot of girls a play in this town, when he first got here — though I won't say they were all the type a feller wants to marry. Still he enjoyed himself, I suppose.'

'Who'd Clayton give most attention to before he started with Laurinda?'

'Priscilla Kiernan. It was through Priscilla he met Laurinda, at which time he seemed to drop Priscilla flat. For a long time, everybody figured he'd marry Priscilla. Then, after Clayton and Laurinda were hitched, Clayton took to dropping in on Priscilla's shop pretty often. It got to sort of be the talk of the town until Priscilla told him to stay away.'

'Do you know for a fact she gave him the bum's rush?'

'Yeah, Ownie Jordan told me.'

Quist drew a long sigh. 'All right, Todd, let's have it,' he said resignedly. 'Do I have to pull every word out of you with a pair of pliers, like a dentist yanking teeth?'

'Well, that's the way it was,' the deputy

said. 'After Laurinda got married, Ownie Jordan started going with Priscilla.

When Clayton started coming around, Ownie objected. He took the matter up with Clayton, personally, and they had a fight — right on the corner of Alamo and Main — '

'And Clayton got licked?'

Sargent shook his head. 'Ownie was a mite lickered up at the time and he slipped and fell down. At that point, Clayton kicked him in the ribs and in the face, and lit out in a hurry. Ownie always swore he'd square matters for that, but nothing ever came of it, I guess.'

'You guess!' Quist swore. 'Here this Ownie Jordan had a reason for shooting Clayton and you never told me about it.'

'Blast it, Greg, I never thought — '

'Do some thinking, please, Todd. So after that, Priscilla Kiernan decided in favor of Ownie Jordan?'

'So Ownie told me. Ownie claimed that Priscilla never had wanted anything to do with Clayton, after he was married. And of course, Chris Baldridge has been sparking Priscilla too. He's got the edge on Ownie, if I'm not mistaken. It's common knowledge that Chris had various arguments with Clayton over his attentions to Priscilla —'

'I wonder if there's anybody left in this town who didn't have reason to hate Clayton's guts. First comes Laurinda, then Grizzly Baldridge and Chris. Now, Ownie Jordan. You're sure Gene Martinsen or the sheriff or Cobra Macaw didn't have a fight with him too?' The words were spoken sarcastically.

'I'm sure of nothing of the kind. They all had scraps, one time or another, with Clayton.'

'I'll be damned! What about?'

'Let me see — well, Gene Martinsen lost some money to Clayton matching cards. Later he claimed the cards were marked, but by that time Clayton had disposed of the cards. The two had some pretty hot talk about it, but it never came to blows. Next, there's Cobra Macaw. Clayton sold him a horse. It was a right good-looking horse too, but two days after Macaw had it, it sudden dropped dead on Main Street. Then the truth came out. Clayton had doctored the horse with some sort of narcotic, and used paint and varnish to cover certain blemishes on its body. It was a right slick-looking paint pony when Macaw bought it, but when it died it turned out to be nothing but something for the glue factory. Clayton never denied doctoring the horse. He said it was a big joke on Macaw. Macaw swore he'd get square some day, but folks laughed at him so much he decided to drop the matter, I reckon, and swallow his loss with his pride.'

'You said Clayton had a scrap with Pike Wolcott.'

Sargent nodded. 'That didn't amount to anything though. One day when Clayton was lickered up and acting quarrelsome, Pike started to arrest him. Well, Pike wasn't as young as he thought he was, and after he got the handcuffs on Clayton, Clayton started dragging Pike all over the street, which same was considerable humiliation for the sheriff.'

'What happened?'

'Pike lost his temper and was trying to get at his gun, while Clayton kept pushing and pulling him from one side to the other. I come along about that time and settled things.'

'How?'

'I gave Clayton a taste of my gun barrel over his head. It was either that or see Pike shoot him. Now I wish I'd let Pike shoot him.'

'Can't say I blame you, Todd.' Quist scowled. 'Damn it! Instead of clearing up, this case gets cloudier and cloudier.

Instead of less suspects, I get more every time I talk to you.'

'Aw, Greg, you don't suspect Pike — '

'T'hell I don't. I told you once I suspect everyone until he — or she — is cleared. First chance possible, I want to talk to this Priscilla Kiernan girl, and other men you've mentioned, as well.

'Well,' — dubiously — 'you probably know best.'

'I'm not sure if I do,' Quist growled moodily.

At that moment, Sheriff Wolcott entered the office and said good morning to both men. He didn't seem particularly pleased at seeing Quist, and quickly turning away asked Sargent in grumpy tones some question relative to the business of sheriff's office.

Sargent cut him short. 'I already took care of that, Pike. If you don't need me right now, I'm going to step out for a breath of air.'

'Step where you like, Todd,' Wolcott said sourly. 'Don't let me stop you. Maybe Mister Quist has some orders for you to take.'

'Not orders, 'sheriff, but maybe a request or two,' Quist said quietly. 'I can count on *Todd* to co-operate.'

The sheriff whirled around to his desk without replying.

12

Tip-Off

Quist and the deputy stepped out on Main Street. Quist said, 'Todd, if you feel that you should let me go my own way, without your help, it's all right with me.'

Sargent stared at him, 'What gave you that idea?'

'I don't think Wolcott likes your being with me so much. I don't want to hurt your job.'

'Forget it, Greg. Sure, I reckon Pike's a mite peevish, but it's just because he isn't in on everything with you. He resents your coming here. Feels it's an infringement on his authority. Cripes! Don't you worry about me. Fact is, I'm handling nigh everything for the sheriff now, and I don't figure he'd want to see me leave. Where we heading?'

'I'd like to take a look at that cottonwood tree your friend, Staunch Tinker mentioned.'

'Good. I'd sort of like to go into that matter deeper, myself .'

Sargent led the way toward Laredo Street, turning in at a narrow alley that ran between Main and Lamar streets. The rear façades of buildings facing on Main were on their left. On the right ran an almost unbroken length of board fences, enclosing the backyards of Lamar Street residents. Cottonwood trees grew in most of the yards, or in front of the houses. Half way along the alley Sargent stopped.

'Here we are,' the deputy said, nodding toward a mass of foliage and branches overhead. 'You'll note it's a right big tree.' He gestured toward his right. 'Tinker's backyard lies just over that board fence. That's where Staunch was beating the carpet. He was standing practically beneath that big cottonwood. You can see, Greg, how that one big limb stretches clean above the alley and overhangs the *Quivira Blade* roof.'

Quist nodded, eyeing the rear wall of

the newspaper building, of two-story rock-and-adobe construction. A goodly number of leaves had been falling from trees the past couple of days, and it wasn't difficult to discern the particular limb Sargent had indicated. Quist's gaze lifted to range along the alley toward the hotel. From this position it was impossible to see his window, which was cut from view by one corner of Deming's General Store, but he was quick to realize that a man stationed high in the big cottonwood would be on the approximate level of the second floor of the hotel, nearly opposite the window through which the shot had come.

'It all sort of dovetails, Todd,' he said.

'I thought you'd see it. That overhanging limb is plenty stout enough to support anyone making a getaway. It would be no job to work along its length, and then drop off on the *Blade* roof.'

'But where did the bustard go from there?' Quist frowned. ''It's my guess that he just dropped flat and lay still until he was certain there wouldn't be any search made through the alley. Later — after it got dark — he could hang from his hands from the edge of the roof and drop to the ground.'

Quist looked dubious. 'That's a pretty high two-stories to drop, Todd. A man could get a sprain or break an ankle.'

'It's possible. But for an active man that drop wouldn't be out of reason. The bustard might even have had a rope to lower himself on. Anyway you look at it, he had to take some sort of risk.'

'I somehow doubt,' Quist scowled, 'that he'd risk laming himself in a drop, anyhow. Let's go take a look at that building roof, if the owner will let us go up.'

'Sure. George Nugent will be glad to oblige. Nice hombre.'

A double-doored entrance stood open in the rear wall of the *Quivira Blade* building. Sargent led the way within. Quist found himself in a spacious room. At one side stood the big newspaper press, silent at the present time. A stack of newsprint stood nearby. A continual *clankety-clack-clank* came from a foot press across the room where a man in smudged overalls was printing some sort of handbills. The front of the room was partitioned off to form, Quist imagined, a sort of office, from which a door opened into the print shop. Near the center of the room, a man stood at a type case, composing stick in left hand, deftly setting type with his right. The wood flooring was smeared with spots of ink and grease, and an odor of printing ink pervaded the big room.

'There's George now,' Sargent said, indicating the man with the composing stick who had ceased in his labors a moment to consult a sheet of galley proof which lay on a table at his side. 'Hi-yuh, George. Looks like you're working for a change.'

George Nugent glanced up and put down his stick. 'Hello, Todd. What do you mean, 'working for a change'? Ever see anything but work around a newspaper?'

Nugent was a tall, pleasant-faced man of middle age, with graying hair and stooped shoulders. His eyes twinkled behind steel-rimmed spectacles and there was a daub of ink across one cheek. His long printer's apron was likewise stained with ink and grease, and his celluloid collar hadn't entirely escaped similar smudging. Todd Sargent introduced him to Quist. The two men shook hands.

'Mr. Quist,' Nugent said, 'I hope you don't believe what Todd says about my working. Fact is, I do nothing but work, what with gathering the news and writing it up, composing an editorial each week, and setting type, handle the financial end, run the presses — oh, jeepers, I sometimes wonder why I ever started this newspaper.'

'How often does it come out?' Quist asked.

'Just once a week, but that keeps us going. I'm getting Friday's edition ready now. Incidentally, Mr. Quist, you've made news with your arrival. Blackjack County will read quite a lot about you this week end. I've sort of written up a biography of your exploits — '

'Exploits?' Quist asked.

Nugent nodded. 'Folks like to know about a man like you. Of course, I'll have to admit that I've drawn pretty heavily on an article that appeared in *Karper's Weekly* sometime ago. I've been to the hotel twice to see you personally, but you weren't — '

'Don't put any faith in that *Karper's* piece,' Quist growled, his face reddening. 'That writer's imagination just went plain haywire — '

'It was a right entertaining article, Mr. Quist. You shouldn't be so modest. And then since you've arrived, there's that business of you being shot at, through your hotel window. Of course, Sheriff Wolcott tells me, in his opinion, that was just an accidental shot, and not intended for you. On top of that, you brought in a man you'd found dead out on the range someplace.' Nugent laughed. 'What with the fuss about the Clayton killing, this week's issue of the *Blade* won't lack for news — '

'Look here, George,' — Sargent had noticed signs of impatience growing in Quist's features — 'we'd like to look at your roof.'

'The roof of your building,' Quist put in. 'There's someway to get up there, isn't there?'

'Oh, certainly, but — ' Nugent appeared puzzled.

'Just keep it under your hat, though, George,' Sargent hurried on. 'It's part of Greg's investigating. If anything comes of the business, I'll see you learn about it for your paper.'

Nugent nodded and gestured toward a large rectangular opening in the ceiling, against one edge of which leaned a ladder. A steel chain-hoist hung through one side of the opening. 'You'll have to mount that ladder and go through my storeroom on the second floor,' Nugent said. 'Come on, I'll show you.'

He led the way to the ladder and climbed quickly to the second floor. The room here was in a sort of semi-gloom, lighted only by one small dusty window in the rear wall. Quist glanced around. Large cans of grease and printing inks stood against one wall. Stacked against another were bulkily wrapped bundles of newsprint. Loose piles of flat paper and a mound of cardboard sheets in varied colors stood beneath the single window. Various mechanical press parts — rollers, gears, nuts and bolts and so on — lay discarded at one side.

'This storeroom is a kind of catchall, as you can see,' Nugent smiled. 'Anything we don't know what to do with we store up here. It's a regular boar's-nest of junk and useful materials. It'd be worse than this, except that old Lennie Plummer tries to keep some order — '

'Somebody mention my name?' came in cracked tones from the gloomy front end of the storeroom.

Quist glanced around and saw the old man's form emerging from the semidarkness. He came chuckling toward the group. 'Howdy, Mister Quist — Todd. Be yer showin' these gents around, Mister Nugent?'

'Something like that, Lennie. I didn't even know you were up here or I'd left the job to you.'

'Glad to take on for you, Mister Nugent. I was jest catchin' me a mite of shut-eye up in the corner, when I heard yer voices. Anythin' I can do — '

'You might slip down and lend Tim a hand with those bills he's running off,' Nugent said. 'Check the count and don't let any smudged print go through.'

'Ye can count on me, Mister Nugent,' Plummer nodded. He bobbed his head in Quist's and Sargent's direction, went to the ladder and climbed to the floor below.

Quist smiled. 'I understand Lennie's your star reporter, Mr. Nugent.'

'Not quite, but you'd be surprised how much help he is,' Nugent laughed. 'Quite often he brings in small items. If he'd started younger he might have made a real newspaper man. I sometimes think he hates to leave this place. He's got a shack out where the Mexes live, but sometimes he stays here when we've been working late. I gave him an old cot to keep up at the far end of the room.'

'The night Hi-Johnny was brought in,' Todd said, 'old Lennie was right on the job, trying to get a story from the sheriff. Pike cut the old codger short, though. Said he'd give you the details.'

'Lennie's all right,' Nugent said. 'He keeps the place redded up and helps out with one thing or another. It'd surprise you how much interest he takes in the *Blade*. You'd think he was part owner of the paper. Always urging me to buy one of those new steam-power presses. Only a couple of days back, he was telling me I should discard my old fonts and get more modern type faces — '

'Is that where you get to the roof?' Quist cut in, motioning toward a ladder resting against a side wall.

'That's it,' Nugent replied. 'There's a trap door opening just above. Come on, we'll go up. Lennie mentioned there was a mite of a leak during that rain. I should check my roof.'

At the top of the ladder, Nugent paused to unhook the trap door and push it open. A few moments later, all three men stood on the roof which was of tarred gravel and nearly flat, with a high false front constructed at the Main Street end of the building. While Nugent paced about, inspecting his roof, Quist and Sargent glanced around. It was easier now to see the overhanging branch of the big cottonwood, only a foot or so above their heads. Quist moved nearer and studied the big limb, noting a couple of freshly-broken twigs, though *these* might have been damaged in some recent wind. Next, Quist turned his gaze toward the hotel, most of which was blocked from view by the interposed Deming General Store structure. Now Quist was more than ever sure that the shot which had entered his window, had been fired from among the branches of the cottonwood tree.

Sargent said, 'What do you think, Greg?'

Quist shrugged his shoulders without

replying, as Nugent approached saying, 'Well, I guess this roof will last out another season. Found one spot where leaves had blocked off a drain. Did you learn anything up here, Mr. Quist?'

'Don't know whether I did or not,' Quist evaded... "In my job you never know what you have until all the facts are in.'

A few minutes later, they descended to the lower floor. Lennie Plummer was helping the man at the hand press. Quist thanked Nugent for his help. Nugent laughed and said he guessed he hadn't been much help, then turned to Sargent, saying, 'Todd, while you're here, there's a couple of things I'd like to ask you about, regarding that Hi-Jonny man that was brought in last night. Was anything learned from the contents of his pockets . . .?'

To avoid being drawn into the discussion, Quist sauntered over to the alley entrance and leaning against the jamb stood gazing out while he rolled a cigarette. He was touching match to the smoke when he caught the sound of a shuffling step at his rear, as Lennie Plummer came sidling up. Quist blew smoke into the air and after breaking the the burnt match in two, tossed it to the earth.

Plummer said, ''I'll bet a pretty, ye were checking up on who shot at ye, that first day ye arrived at the hotel.'

Quist smiled. 'Ask me no questions, I'll tell you no lies.'

'Shore, I understand. A man has to keep his own confidence, in yore line of business. Still an' all, ye wouldn't refuse a tip-off, I'm bettin'.'

Quist stared into the alley. He said quietly, 'I'll be glad to listen, Lennie.'

Plummer glanced over his shoulder toward the other men, and lowered his voice. 'Cobra Macaw could be right mean if he took a notion.'

'I imagine.'

Plummer peered up at Quist, continuing, 'I'd shore hate to have him get mad at me. If he ever got a idea a man had talked outter turn 'bout him, Cobra might take strong measures.'

'Undoubtedly. Well, Lennie, you can depend on it, anything you tell me won't go any further. I protect my friends, as well as possible.'

'Thet's satisfactual to hear, Mister Quist. Well, here's somethin' thet might be of int'rest to yer. Thet day ye was shot at, I'd been right busy around here. Come five o'clock when Mister Nugent and Tim had stepped out, I climbed up above to rest my bones a few minutes while they was gone ter supper — y'know I got me a cot up at the front end of thet storeroom. It's sorter dark at thet end, and a man can rest peaceful.'

Quist asked, 'Did you hear the shot, or something like that?'

'I ain't sure. Mebbe I'd sorter dozed off, but somethin' waked me up. I could hear quick steps on the roof overhead, then thet trap door was opened and a man come down the ladder. He was movin' fast, but he'd tooken time to close the trap door again. Then he climbed on down to this floor, out of sight. Don't know where he went then.'

'You didn't follow to see?'

Plummer's old laugh sounded like a cackle. 'Not this coot, Mister Quist. I'm too old to tangle with Cobra Macaw — '

'Cobra Macaw was the man you saw descend from the roof?'

'Now I wouldn't go so far as to take an oath on it. My eyes ain't whut they uster be, and it's sort of dim — like up in thet storeroom, but I'm right certain, Mister Quist, it was Cobra Macaw. For gawsakes, don't never mention ter anybody thet I told ye, though.'

'Mum's the word, Lennie. And thanks.'

'I can count on ye, can't I?' Plummer anxiously studied Quist's face. 'I don't want thet Cobra Macaw a-gunnin' on my trail.'

'You can count on me. You're sure Macaw didn't see you?'

Again that thin cackling sound. 'Not this chicken, Mister Quist. I got enough sense ter freeze silent when Macaw comes 'round.'

'Well, thanks a lot, Lennie. Maybe

you'll prove to be a real help to me.'

'And don't forget anything you can give me for a story fer the *Blade* will be right welcome.'

'I'll not forget.'

At that moment, Nugent and Sargent approached and Lennie slipped back to help Tim at the hand press. Quist drew a couple of silver dollars from his pocket and handed them to Nugent, 'You might hand those to old Lennie, Mr. Plummer, after we've gone, and tell him I appreciate his help in showing us around.'

Nugent nodded and Quist and the deputy took their departure. Todd said, 'Don't tell me Plummer gave you a clue to something.'

'It could be, Todd, it could be. No, it's nothing I want to talk about yet. Fact is, I promised Lennie I'd keep my mouth shut. You'll know about it in good time.'

'It's up to you.' Sargent glanced at his watch as they emerged from the alley. 'Cripes! It's almost dinner time. Come on, I'll buy you a beer, then we'll eat at the hotel.

In the hotel bar a few minutes later, Quist noted that the deputy closely scrutinized the change he received from a dollar bill, after buying two bottles of beer.

13

'Don't Get Proddy!'

Emerging from the hotel dining room, after dinner, the first person Quist and Sargent encountered on Main Street, was Sheriff Pike Wolcott. Wolcott scowled as his eyes fell on Quist, and he detained his deputy with a harsh, 'Todd, I've been looking high and low for you.'

'Something gone wrong?' Sargent asked.

'Thievery. Pablo Ortego had his horse and saddle stolen yesterday — taken right from the *ramada*, back of his house.'

The deputy relaxed. 'When did Ortego report it stolen?'

'Hour or so back. Ortego said he hadn't noticed it was gone until after the rain started. Pro'bly he was drunk on tequila — '

'All right, Pike, I'll see what I can pick up. What kind of a pony was it?'

'How should I know? Instead of asking

me questions, you might drop out to Ortega's place and take a look at it.'

Sargent frowned. 'I thought you just said it was stolen.'

'So it was — but it was either returned, or drifted back of its own accord last night sometime.' Further discussion brought out the fact that the saddle, also sheltered beneath the *ramada*, was on the horse's back, when Ortego discovered the return of his property.

'So long's Ortego's got his pony back, do you want me to waste time on the case?' Sargent asked.

'Certainly, Todd. Ortego, as a voting citizen,' — smugly — 'has a right to the law's protection. Another time the horse might not return. No man has the right to take another's property without permission. If you can learn who took that horse, we'll make an example of the scoundrel — '

'All right, Pike,' Sargent interrupted, 'I'll see what I can do.' Wolcott nodded curtly and went off down the street. Sargent ruefully shook his head. 'Pike can sure be exasperating, at times.'

Quist chuckled. 'Don't tell me you don't know where to look for the man who borrowed one Mexican's horse.'

'What do you think? Somebody in the Mex section just needed a horse for a spell, that's all. Oh, well, I'll drift over there and look around when I've got a spare moment. But not now. Anything you'd like to do, Greg?'

'I can't think of anything right off. There's a few people I'd like to meet. Priscilla Kiernan, for instance.'

Sargent took a long breath, then repressed what he'd started to say. 'All right, but her place is back in the other direction.'

The two men turned around and started back. Now and then, passing pedestrians nodded to the deputy. Occasionally, Quist was included in the greeting. Quist wasn't certain who they were; probably men he'd met in Sargent's company somewhere the past couple of days. Quist realized, of course, he was by this time known to the majority of

Quivira City's citizens, as the railroad detective who had arrived to do some thing about the Clayton shooting. As to what he was to do, it was doubtful if anyone, including Quist at the moment, had any clear idea.

Sargent slowed pace as they approached the Green Bottle Saloon, running his eye along the hitchrack. 'Wait a minute, Greg. That looks like Gene Martinsen's horse at the rack. Several of those animals are branded G-Bar-M too. Looks like Gene and his crew are in town. He's a man you probably should see — '

'Anyway,' Quist chuckled, 'it will postpone a meeting with Miss Kiernan, won't it?'

'Oh, hell!' The deputy's features reddened. 'C'mon, we'll go see Priscilla — ' He started grumpily away.

'Hold it, son, hold it,' Quist laughed softly. 'I was only ribbing you a mite. You red-complected hombres sure keep your tempers at trigger tension most of the time. The Green Bottle it is. I could stand a drink.'

They pushed through the swinging doors into the Green Bottle. The bar was lined with men in cowpuncher togs, talking loudly and clinking glasses. At the opposite side of the room were a few round tables and straight-backed chairs. The walls were decorated with two stuffed deerheads and a number of framed pictures of race horses, burlesque actresses in tights, and prize fighters, all clipped from a certain pink-sheeted periodical of considerable popularity. Quist glanced quickly over the place. The mirror behind the bar was free of flyspecks and the pyramided glasses and bottles on the back bar looked neat and polished. Waves of cigar and cigarette smoke drifted close to the raftered ceiling.

As they moved toward the bar, Sargent said in an aside to Quist, 'Maybe this was the right place to come, Greg. Ownie Jordan's here too.'

They managed to make their way to a place at the bar. Quist's eyes flitted over the customers. Any favorable impression he might have formed on entering, vanished somewhat as he considered the customers. He'd already noticed Cobra Macaw; most of the others were fit companions for Macaw: hard-bitten men with unshaved faces, in worn cowman togs. All wore six-shooters. Two stood out, somewhat taller than the others, Ownie Jordan and Gene Martinsen. Sargent pointed them out, shortly after a white-aproned barkeep had taken their orders for bottled beer.

'. . . and that's Ownie Jordan,' the deputy was telling Quist, 'the big blond man, beginning to run to fat. He looks sort of liquored-up — which same isn't too unusual with Ownie. He drinks to forget, I suppose — '

'Forget what?' Quist asked quietly.

Sargent shrugged. 'Nearly any man has some disappointment to drown, one time or another. With Jordan — *quién sabe*? — who knows? I've already told you how he lost his wife — then he lost out with Laurinda. I feel sort of sorry for the cuss.'

'It's one thing for a man to drown his disappointments momentarily,' Quist stated. 'It's quite another, when he drowns his whole carcass with 'em. I noted Cobra Macaw spotted me the minute I came in. He's been talking an ear off that husky-shouldered hombre next to him — '

'That's Gene Martinsen. Martinsen laughs a lot, like he's doing now, but I don't know as it means much. I still can't forget that he keeps a pretty rough crew — '

'Any cow-stealing hereabouts?' Quist started to fill his glass with beer from the bottle. Sargent was doing the same.

The deputy shook his head. 'No more than you'd find on any range. If there was, I bet I'd know where to look first.'

'Don't jump to any conclusions, Todd. A man might have a crew that likes to raise hell now and then, and still have a bunch of damn good workers. That's what counts, with some owners. That kind doesn't give a damn about a crew's morals, so long as money isn't lost on herds. And don't forget, it takes a strong man to handle a crew of hard hombres.'

'I've thought about that too,' Sargent said moodily.

Ownie Jordan came weaving along the bar, blond hair straggling over his forehead from beneath the tilted-back sombrero. His eyes were a trifle bloodshot and he lurched into Todd Sargent. 'Well, if it ain't the law come to drink with us — two laws, if I hear right —'

'Ownie,' Sargent broke in, 'shake hands with Greg Quist.'

Jordan studied Quist with owlish eyes, then extended one hand. 'Glad to meet you, Quist — or am I?'

Quist took the man's hand, and laughed softly. 'That depends, Jordan.'

'On what?'

'On you, I should say.'

Jordan considered the question and then nodded gravely. 'Yep — s'pose it does. Well, now, I always believe in bring' things to frank c'clusion.' He swayed a trifle. 'Now, unnerstan', Quist — ain't nothing 'gainst you — personal. But what in hell you aiming — do — here, anyhow? Sure, Clayton was killed. Who's to say — did'n' — have it coming? You? Me? No — siree bob! Tell you what,' — moving one finger waggishly in Quist's face — 'it ain't — none — of — our — business. Two people — two, mind you — already confeshed killing. Wha' more you wan'?'

'Could be they didn't do it,' Quist said quietly.

'What?' Jordan's jaw dropped. 'Who else could — be?'

Quist shrugged noncommittally. 'There's plenty people around here hated Clayton's guts.'

'Mis-ter Quist,' — earnest dignity now — 'you sher — sher? cer'ainly spoke truth then. I'll tell you a secret. Didn' have no use — Clayton — m'shelf.'

'So I understand.'

'C'rect. Lesh have a drink — ' Jordan paused suddenly, thrusting his head forward, peering at Quist. 'Wazzat you said? Wha' gives you — *hic!* — cause unnerstan' a thing like that — 'bout me.'

'I heard Clayton kicked merry hell out of you in a fight. You swore to get even with him, didn't you? Maybe *you* killed Clayton, Jordan.'

Jordan gulped hard when the words penetrated his drunken consciousness. 'Now — look here — Quist,' he said earnestly, 'you can't mean a thing like that. My Gawd! — *hic!* — I wouldn't want to kill nobody. Sure, I was sore — but — got over that — '

'Where were you when Clayton was killed?' Quist snapped.

Jordan just stared at Quist, started to speak, then swallowed hard. One hand came up and scratched the back of his head, shoving his sombrero over his eyes. Nervously he shoved it back. 'Quist — ' he half whispered, 'surely you aren't suspecting me — not *me*.'

Quist said again in cold tones, 'Where were you when Clayton was killed?'

'Now, look here, Quist — ' Jordan began an indignant protest.

'I asked you a question,' Quist said sternly.

Jordan hesitated. His lips moved but no sound issued. Traces of drunkenness were rapidly disappearing from his eyes. All along the bar men were talking and drinking, though Macaw and Martinsen appeared more interested in watching Quist and Jordan, though they couldn't distinguish what was being said.

Jordan was staring at Quist like one mesmerized. Finally he mumbled, 'I — I reckon I was out to my ranch.'

'Don't you know for sure?'

'Yeah — yeah, sure I do. That's where I was — home.'

Quist said in sharp tones, 'You've got proof of that?'

Jordan scratched his head. 'I — I — sure, somebody must have seen me there — one of my crew — or — or — ' He started to back away from Quist. 'I'll have to check up and — and see — glad to met you, Mr. Quist — maybe we can have a drink together — sometime when I'm not in — in a hurry — '

He was still backing away while he

talked. Suddenly he turned and fled from the saloon. The swinging doors banged to behind him.

'Well,' Quist said softly, and again, 'Well.'

'Cripes A'mighty, Greg!' Sargent said, 'You sure do have a sobering influence on some people. But, look here, you don't really think Ownie killed — '

'What *I* think makes no difference — right now,' Quist scowled. 'It's what I'll think when all the facts are in that counts. Let's have another beer.'

'This is on me.' Fresh bottles were set before them, and as usual Sargent closely examined his change before putting it in his pocket. Quist eyed him curiously, while he was filling his glass, but didn't make any comment. Sargent drank deeply, put down his glass and said, 'Looks like Gene Martinsen is coming to get acquainted. Probably wants to get a line on you.'

'Yeah, it's my day for receiving,' Quist said sourly. He took another drink of beer.

Gene Martinsen came pushing up, a big man with a wide grin, bushy sand-colored hair and a rather florid complexion. He hadn't shaved in a couple of days and his woolen shirt was open at the throat. A well-worn Colt's six-shooter hung at his right leg, over the denim overalls; his spurs clanked across the board flooring. 'Sweet Jesus, Todd,' he guffawed. 'What did you do to Ownie Jordan? He left here like a bat out of hell and pale as a ghost.'

'*I* didn't do anything to Ownie,' Sargent protested. 'Gene, I'd like to make you acquainted with Greg Quist. You've probably heard about him —'

'Who in hell hasn't in this town?' Martinsen seized Quist's hand and pumped it vigorously. 'Somebody was telling me about an article in a magazine too —'

'Let's forget the magazine,' Quist grunted. 'I've already heard too much about it.'

'Just as you say,' Martinsen chuckled. 'I reckon in your place I'd feel the same. Why, that writer made you out to be a regular tin-god, Quist. Y'know, there ain't no man can be that good. Let's have a drink on me.'

'I've got a drink,' Quist said, gesturing toward his half filled beer bottle. 'And I'll agree with you about the article. So what comes next, Martinsen?'

'Huh?' The grin momentarily vanished, then returned. 'If it wasn't Todd that scared Ownie Jordan witless, it must have been you, Quist. What in hell you trying to do to us small-town hombres, with your big-city, slickery ways?'

'Well, if you must have it,' Quist said quietly, 'Jordan was inclined to be a mite belligerent about me being here. I just set him straight a little.' He added, 'I don't like to be pushed around.'

'I'll be damned!' Martinsen laughed. 'I'm curious as hell to know how you did it.'

Quist smiled. 'It was simple. I just asked him for an alibi for the time at which Clayton was killed.'

Martinsen looked a trifle startled. 'Ownie! Ownie Jordan! Oh, no, Quist, you can't imagine that Ownie — ' He broke off in a fit of laughter. 'That's the funniest thing I ever heard.'

'Go ahead, laugh your head off,' Quist suggested coldly, 'and when you get through, tell me about your alibi. It'll be entertaining listening.'

Martinsen stopped laughing then. His pale blue eyes searched Quist's face. 'Now *that* is the limit,' he snapped. 'In the first place, what reason would I have for killing Whit Clayton? Sure, I didn't like him, but — '

'Remember a little matter of a marked deck of cards, Martinsen? I understand Clayton got quite a chunk of money out of you. Didn't you swear that you'd get even for that deal? And so,' Quist concluded, 'I'm still waiting to hear your alibi.'

'This is the damnedest thing I ever heard of,' Martinsen swore. 'Two people have already confessed to the killing. What more do you want?'

'Facts,' Quist snapped. 'Maybe there were more than two people involved.

And don't get proddy with me, Martinsen. You came to us asking questions. If you don't like the answers, I'm worried sick over the whole business,' — caustically — 'but that don't change things any. And I'm still asking about your alibi.'

Martinsen's smile was almost a snarl. 'Any three or four of my crew can furnish that, Quist.'

Quist laughed scornfully. 'For me, that's no good. You have the name of hiring a pretty rough crew, Martinsen. I'm not sure I'd take their word for anything.'

'Aw, now, Quist, that's no attitude to take. Just because my boys come to town and raise a mite of hell on paydays, is no sign they're crooked. I like a crew that's full of spirits. They work better. Yau should understand that, Quist. You consider yourself a pretty hard man, don't you?'

Quist shook his head, smiled thinly. 'I *know* I'm a pretty hard man, Martinsen — too hard to be pushed around by a bunch of cheap gun-toters who like to shoot up bars. So if you can't offer any better alibi than the word of somebody in your crew, you'd better start thinking fast, Martinsen.'

Martinsen forced a smile. 'Yau still insist I'm under suspicion?'

'Along with a few others.'

Martinsen breathed deeply. 'Anyway,' he scoffed, 'you haven't yet any proof on me in connection with Clayton's killing — '

'That doesn't mean I won't have.'

'For jeez' sake, Quist, talk sense. Any fool would know that either Chris Baldridge or his sister — '

'I'm no fool. And now you start thinking straight, Martinsen.'

'All right, Quist, I'll not only think straight, I'll talk straight. I wanted to speak to you, anyway. You ran roughshod over one of my men, night before last.'

Quist nodded. 'Meaning Cobra Macaw. All right, so I ran roughshod over him. He needed running over. Anytime any man starts to jerk an iron on me, I'll manhandle him. Macaw's just lucky

I didn't gun him down. And so what if you don't like the way I handled him?'

'Take it easy, Quist, take it easy,' Martinsen said, 'I'm not threatening you. No sense you getting proddy with me, either. I just wanted to point out that you misjudged Macaw. He's not a bad young feller when you get to know him — '

'I don't want to know him any better than I do. And that's probably better than you know him, Martinsen. For your information, Macaw's a vicious little killer. If you had sense, you'd drop him from your payroll — '

Martinsen bridled. 'You're not telling me who I should fire.'

Quist shook his head. 'No. Just advising you — '

'You can't come in to this town and start pushing folks around, Quist, without encountering a heap of trouble.'

Quist laughed softly. 'Sure as hell you're right — for once.

Me, I like trouble, Martinsen. What do you think of that? You ready to shove some my way?'

Quist's topaz-colored eyes glinted savagely. Martinsen drew back a little. 'Now, look here, you've got me all wrong, Quist; I don't want trouble with you. Maybe we sort of got off on the wrong foot — '

'You did,' Quist snapped.

'All right,' — smiling again — ' I'll take the blame for that too, if it makes you feel any better. I shouldn't have contradicted, when you mentioned that Ownie Jordan was a suspect. Maybe Ownie had a lot of reason for hating Clayton. Ownie's hot-tempered. When he gets liquored up, he doesn't realize what he's doing. Just between you and me, a feller like Ownie could shoot a man when he's drunk, and not even remember what happened the next day.'

'You wouldn't be trying to point the hunt toward Jordan, would you, Martinsen?'

'Hell, no! Everybody in town knows that Ownie's that way. I'm not telling any secrets. Now, your bottle's empty. How about a drink on me, Quist?'

Quist shook his head. 'Thanks, no.

I've had enough for now.' He turned to Sargent. 'You about ready to shove off, Todd?' The deputy nodded.

'No hard feelings, I hope,' Martinsen said.

Quist laughed. 'Hard feeling I'll leave to you, Martinsen.' He started away from the bar.

At that moment, Cobra Macaw joined Martinsen. Quist paused a moment to smile sarcastically at Macaw, adding, 'Hello, sucker.'

Macaw's lips tightened a trifle, but he didn't reply. There didn't even seem to be any life in his flat opaque eyes.

'Anyway, Quist,' Martinsen put in, 'you surely can't suspect Cobra of having a hand in Clayton's death.'

'Why in hell shouldn't I?' Quist flashed. 'Macaw had reasons for squaring accounts with Clayton, too. Didn't Clayton sucker him into a deal for a sick horse? Hell's bells on a tom-cat! I'd suspect him as quick as anybody — likely quicker.'

And without giving Martinsen or

Macaw a chance to reply, Quist headed for the street, followed by Todd Sargent — as well as by looks of hate from Martinsen and Macaw.

14

Jail-Bird

'Whew!' Todd Sargent smiled wryly, when they stepped to the sidewalk. 'That was quite a session. You don't believe in handling folks with velvet gloves, do you, Greg?'

'Velvet gloves are for pussyfooters,' Quist said shortly. 'I like folks to know where I stand, right off.'

'You sure cut Martinsen and Jordan down before they had a chance to get started — not to mention Macaw.'

'All right,' Quist said irritably, 'so I acted the part of the hard hombre. But if I don't keep the jump on such men, they start climbing all over my frame. Don't forget, Todd, that I've been through this sort of thing before. It's the same old story,' — his voice sounded a bit weary now — 'you come into a town a stranger, and there's always certain people want to get the jump on you. Me, I aim to jump first.'

Sargent nodded understanding. He said, 'Do you actually think either Jordan or Martinsen had a part in Clayton's killing?'

'Put it this way: they both had reasons for killing Clayton — or arranging it. Maybe arranging it so they'd appear guiltless. Dammit, Todd, I just don't know — yet . . . . Where we heading for now?' They had started west on Main Street.

'You wanted to talk to Priscilla Kiernan, didn't you?'

Quist shot a quick glance at his companion. 'Well,' he smiled, 'no prompting, eh? You're improving, Todd.'

'I'm hoping to — but I've a long way to go before I ever master your methods.'

'Don't try to, Todd. You get like me and you'll find people just hate you. Friends are always few and far between, you're always riding a trail someplace, getting shot at or shooting — it's a hell of a life. If I had the sense God gave me to start with, I'd settle down and raise chickens — '

'Crack eggs instead of yeggs, eh?'

Quist chuckled. 'That one sure smelled bad, anyway.'

'Smelled, or shelled?'

Quist threw up his hands. 'All right, I surrender. You're taking my mind from my work.'

They crossed Austin Street and continued along Main. A couple of pedestrians nodded as they passed. Ponies and wagons drew in at hitchracks, or moved out to the roadway. Lennie Plummer came along and looked as though he'd like to stop and talk, but Quist and Sargent kept going. Sargent said, 'Lennie'll likely drop into the Green Bottle, and hear you had a few words there with some of the customers. I'll bet he'd be a hound for picking up news if he was younger.'

'Probably so,' Quist answered absentmindedly.

'Priscilla's place is just a couple of doors farther on,' Sargent was saying, when he stopped suddenly, then, 'See — ? Chris Baldridge is just leaving her place.'

'What's Baldridge doing in a novelty

store, I wonder?'

'It's not the novelty, it's the girl. Have you forgotten that Chris is pretty sweet on Priscilla Kiernan?'

'I didn't forget. I was wondering if love was all that took him there. Maybe Chris can tell us where she was yesterday.'

'Yesterday. What do you mean, Greg?'

'I had some notion of dropping in on Miss Kiernan without you along as sponsor — oh, sure, I'd located her shop. But the shade was drawn on her window and the door was locked. She didn't attend Clayton's funeral, did she, Todd?'

Todd Sargent shook his head. 'Do you know of any reason she should have?'

'Not a one. I was just doing some thinking.'

By this time they had come abreast of the novelty shop and paused. Chris Baldridge had turned back a moment at the doorway, and was speaking to someone within the shop. As he closed the door, he swung around to see Quist and the deputy facing him.

The smile quickly faded from

Baldridge's face. 'Where you two heading for?' he asked, appearing slightly uneasy.

Quist smiled. 'I'll trade information with you, Baldridge. What were you doing in this shop?'

Baldridge flushed. 'Why, I was — hell, I don't know as it is any of your business — '

'There's the answer to your question,' Quist interrupted. Baldridge bit his lower lip. 'All right, maybe I spoke sort of hasty. If you've got to know, I just dropped in a moment to pass the time of day with Miss Kiernan.'

'That's almost the answer to your question too,' Quist laughed. 'That's where we're heading.'

'Why?' Baldridge wanted to know.

Quist said reprovingly, 'Now, Baldridge, we didn't ask you why — '

'Cripes A'mighty! I had a reason.'

'Don't you think I have?' Quist asked.

'I know damn well you have,' Baldridge burst out wrathfully. 'Quist, why can't you leave people alone? Priscilla doesn't know one blasted thing about Clayton's killing.'

'She knew Clayton, though, didn't she?' Quist asked. 'Went around with him, quite considerable. Even saw him after he was married to your sister — '

'Why, damn you, Quist!' Baldridge took a quick step toward Quist.

'Take it easy, Chris.' Sargent stepped quickly between the two. 'Quist isn't meaning any harm to Priscilla — '

Baldridge hesitated. 'But he said — '

'He said what was true, as we both damn well know, Chris,' Sargent said. 'But that doesn't mean anything. I don't imagine Greg thinks it does, either.'

Baldridge relaxed, though his face still worked angrily. Quist said, 'All right, I'm a bustard, if you want it that way. Cripes, Baldridge, I don't like to hurt people's feelings, but there are certain things I've just got to learn. If I can't get co-operation, I have to do things my own way. Look here, which do you prefer — shall I talk to Miss Kiernan, direct, or learn about her from folks in town?'

Baldridge nodded reluctantly. 'All right, Quist, I can't stop you. Can I be present when you talk to Priscilla?'

Quist shook his head. 'No third party will be present. As soon as Todd's introduced me, he's heading for the Mexican section to do some checking on a stolen horse, aren't you, Todd?'

'Yeah, I guess I am,' the deputy answered in somewhat surprised tones. 'Come to think of it, Pike told me to do it, some time ago.'

Defeated, Baldridge shrugged his shoulders.

'All right, Quist, just don't get any wrong ideas, that's all.'

'Don't you give me any then,' Quist said shortly. He shot the next words with no hesitation: "Did you get wet in the rain, out near Clayton's house, yesterday?'

'Huh!" Baldridge's features assumed a blank expression.

'Who said I was out near Clayton's house ? What you trying to do, Quist ?'

'Nobody said you were out there,'

Quist replied mildly. 'It was just my way of asking if you were — '

'Look here, you trying to connect me with Hi-Johnny's killing?'

'Who told you about that?'

'Hell, the whole town knows about it, naturally.'

'Who told you ?' Quist repeated.

'My father — Grizzly Baldridge — this morning when he got to the ranch. He stayed at the hotel last night —'

'I know about that. Where were you yesterday afternoon ?'

'I was home — at the ranch.'

'You can furnish proof of that, of course ?'

'You're damn right I can. Laurinda will vouch for me. She was home from about noon on. She'd been in town to see you —'

Quist cut him short. 'Thanks' — dryly.

Baldridge flared, "Can't you believe us — take our word — ?'

'What do you think?' Quist asked. 'Have I said I didn't ?'

Baldridge stared at Quist, then with an

explosive, ‘Oh, hell!’ in disgusted tones, he whirled angrily away and kept going.

Quist chuckled as he eyed the rapidly departing figure. ‘Todd, I don’t think I’m one of Chris’s favorite companions. Well, let’s go inside this shop and get me introduced to Miss Kiernan.’

They entered the shop. A bell tinkled overhead as the door was closed. Quist glanced around. At either wall were shelves holding cardboard boxes of knitting yarns, embroidery rings, skeins of silk and various other feminine necessities. Two small showcases contained colorful rolls of ribbon, spools of thread, needles, buttons, darning cotton. The broad window, situated next to the entrance, held a display of various articles and a red geranium in a green pot. The rear of the shop was partitioned off with drapes of some rough material, behind which, Quist guessed, were Priscilla Kiernan’s living quarters. A small walnut table and a couple of chairs completed the furniture. A brown carpet with a figured design, covered the floor.

The drapes at the rear parted and Priscilla Kiernan entered the shop. 'Well, I declare! Todd! Men so rarely come into my shop.'

Sargent performed the introductions. Priscilla Kiernan was a rather small, shapely girl, with thick chestnut hair gathered closely about her head and a fringe of bangs trimmed evenly across her forehead. Her eyes were very blue and over speculated — showed considerable confidence. Her dress of some dark woolen material with bits of lace at her throat and wrists. She was, Quist decided, though widely separated from the Laurinda Baldridge type, a decidedly pretty girl. He found himself appreciating the warm handclasp she gave him, even as he mentally warned himself against feminine wiles. Priscilla Kiernan's full red lips parted in a soft laugh that showed white even teeth. 'I've been expecting you long before this, Mr. Quist.'

'You have?' Quist asked. 'Why, may I ask?'

'It'd be only natural. I knew Whit

Clayton. You'd want to know what I knew. Isn't that the way you detectives work?

At least, a piece I read about you in *Karper's Weekly* —'

'Please, let's not go into that fool article,' Quist begged. 'That whole story was a big mistake. I had nothing to do with it.' He felt himself floundering and growing red, then broke off, 'Todd, if you're going to see about that stolen horse, now might be a good time.'

'Right, Greg. See you later, Priscilla.' Sargent opened and closed the door, the overhead bell announcing his departure.

Priscilla Kiernan suggested that they sit down. Quist seated himself, twirling his hat between his knees, somewhat uncertain how to begin. The girl put him at his ease: 'You'll want to smoke, of course.' She rose, disappeared behind the drapes and returned with a saucer in lieu of an ash tray, which she placed on the table at Quist's side, then reseated herself. Quist rolled a cigarette in silence, then said, 'I'm congratulating myself.'

'On what?' the girl asked.

'Neatness. I don't think I dropped one grain of Durham on your carpet.'

Priscilla Kiernan laughed. 'Don't let that bother you.'

'I wasn't taking chances,' Quist smiled. 'Actually, it's rather difficult to roll a cigarette without spilling tobacco.'

'Shows steady hands,' the girl said.

'I hope so.' Quist lighted his smoke. 'To tell the truth, I'm not so sure.'

'Don't you like talking to women?'

'I love it,' Quist chuckled. 'But that doesn't make me anymore sure of myself.'

'Why?'

'Women are so much smarter than men,' Quist said seriously. 'If we're not careful they outfox us. Right now, you probably know exactly what questions I have in mind, even before I ask — '

'No, I didn't kill him,' the girl cut in.

Quist laughed. 'You see! All right, we're over that hump — '

' — and don't know who did, and even if I suspected anyone of killing Whit Clayton I'd hesitate to tell you. I wouldn't want to make a bad guess and make trouble for anyone. And, yes,'—Priscilla Kiernan hesitated briefly—'I did care quite a bit for Whit—at one time.'

'You're being very frank, Miss Kiernan.'

'If I had anything to cover, I probably shouldn't be. But I haven't, really, Mr. Quist. But I just think this way is better than fencing around, with you drawing out a bit of knowledge here and there, and wasting time getting to facts.'

'How long did you know Whit Clayton?'

'Long enough to learn he wasn't the man for me. Even before he married Laurinda Baldridge, I'd begun to see him for the shallow, untrustworthy man he was. But, yes, I'll admit it, he had a lot of girls' heads awhirl for a time—mine amongst them. He was good-looking, he had a ready tongue, he was even fun to be with at one time.'

'Had you ever considered marrying him?'

The girl considered. 'Let's put it this way. He never asked me to marry him. What my thoughts were at one time, isn't important.'

'But you did like him quite well,' Quist persisted.

Priscilla nodded. 'It was even more than a like, if you will. But my feeling for Whit Clayton isn't to be compared with what I feel for Chris Baldridge. I'm much smarter now than I was eighteen months ago. Chris and I are to be married you know.'

'So I've heard. Chris is luckier than he realizes. And you don't figure the present fix he is in will be any bar to marriage?'

'I'll wait until things are right,' the girl said quietly.

'Do you mind telling me what happened between you and Clayton, after he was married?'

'I mind — but I'll tell you. It was all very disagreeable. He kept hanging around the shop, dropping in quite frequently. He said he'd realized he'd made a mistake in marrying Laurinda. Offered to get a divorce from her eventually. I wouldn't have anything to do with that kind of thing, and I told him so. I finally had to tell him to keep away from here altogether.' The girl sighed. 'It didn't do much good. He kept coming in, every time he was in town. It — it was darn embarrassing. I'd started keeping company with Chris, by that time. Then, one night I'd returned with Chris from a housewarming at the Burtons'. Chris came in with me to see that everything was all right — I live at the back of this place, you know. Well, we found Clayton in my kitchen. He'd broken in the back way, probably not expecting that Chris would come in with me. Well — '

'I take it there was a whale of a fight.'

'Thanks for cutting this short. Yes, there was a fight. Chris knocked Whit down, out in the alley, when he was putting him out. Chris, already, had warned Whit to stay away from me. Finding him here just brought things to a head. Unfortunately, the noise drew some men into the alley, out back. Later, they talked. To save his own face, Whit gave out some stories about me. Pretty wild stories. This town was certainly full of clacking tongues for a time. It almost ruined my business. For days, no one entered the shop — '

She broke off as a woman and a small boy entered. The woman purchased some thread and needles, then departed. Priscilla resumed her chair, and continued, 'As I say, it was mighty embarrassing.'

'I can imagine. Where was Whit Clayton from, do you know?'

'He never talked much about his past life. I knew he was interested in horses. I think at one time he must have lived in Louisiana, from one or two small items he dropped. But when I asked about it, he said he didn't want to talk about his work in Louisiana. Said it was a sort of confining occupation that he didn't like at all, and that he preferred plenty of fresh air. I can remember him laughing about it, but I couldn't see the joke.'

'Did he know anyone when he first came here?'

'Not that I know of.'

'What's your opinion of Laurinda Baldridge?' Abruptly, Quist had changed the subject.

Priscilla smiled mockingly. 'I suppose I was meant to be caught off guard at that point. Probably 'jealous lights' should have shown in my eyes, as the books say. Actually, there are none to show.' Quist grinned sheepishly, and the girl continued, 'Whit Clayton had run his course with me, even before he asked Laurinda to marry him. I knew she was much too good for him. He gave her a bad time from the first. To sum up, she's one of the best friends I have. Laurinda felt terrible about that business when Whit kicked up so much trouble.'

Quist nodded. 'I suppose you go riding frequently with Chris.'

'Quite often, when I can borrow a pony. I don't happen to own one. Occasionally, Chris — or Laurinda — provides one from the ranch; When that happens, I just close up shop and take a holiday.'

'I noticed you were closed yesterday — but with that rain, yesterday was no day for riding.'

'And now you want to know where I was yesterday,' the girl laughed. 'All right, I'll make a clean breast of the crime. My closing up yesterday, Mr. Quist, was a matter of sheer defense.' Quist's yellow eyes asked a question. Priscilla explained, 'This town is full of gossips and busybodies. I knew, with Whit Clayton being buried, there'd be a continual procession of scandal-mongers coming in to learn if I attended the funeral, or to talk about Whit. I didn't want to be bothered with them, so I just closed up shop and spent the afternoon reading in my bedroom.'

'Sensible, I'd say. Oh, yes, did you happen to know Hi-Johnny?'

'That Greek, or whatever he was, who was killed? No, I didn't.'

Quist asked next, 'Of all the men who courted Laurinda Baldridge, who, aside from Clayton, did she care most for?' 'Knowing Laurinda as I do, I think that's easy to answer. While a number of men would have married her, I think Todd Sargent might have had the best chance. I know Laurinda liked him a lot. Trouble with Todd, he didn't push his case hard enough. Naturally, when he quit coming around, Laurinda took up with someone else.'

'That's as I understood it, too. Miss Kiernan, does this shop provide a living for you? I likely shouldn't ask, but — '

'It does not. I just about break even. But the shop occupies my time. I enjoy seeing people about town. Now, please don't start wondering what I live on. I don't want you to get arty wrong ideas. I happen to have a little money left me by my parents when they died. I wanted a change; I came here from Colorado. There, I think I've told you everything I know. And if you can put an end to all this trouble, so Chris and I can be married soon, I'll be eternally grateful to you.'

'I'm figuring to do my best.'

A few minutes later, Todd Sargent returned. After thanking Priscilla for her trouble, Quist accompanied the deputy out to the street.

After a few minutes, Sargent asked, 'Learn anything new?'

Quist frowned. 'I'm not sure yet. I'll have to sift my facts, first, before I decide anything. Priscilla sounds like a right loyal friend to have.'

'That's Pris, right from the start.'

'You learn anything about that stolen horse?'

'Did I learn who took it? No. It was in Ortega's *ramada*. Good-looking pony. Neither horse nor saddle had been harmed, though they'd been out in the rain. What had bothered Ortego was, he had promised to lend the horse to Lennie Plummer to ride to Clayton's funeral, and then when the horse disappeared, Ortego got worried about the business. As it turned out, Lennie didn't go to the funeral on account of the rain — Greg, are we heading any place in particular?'

Quist had led his companion in the direction of the railroad tracks. 'T.N. & A.S. depot. I'm looking for the answer to a telegram I sent. It might have come by this time.'

Five minutes later, Quist received from the telegraph operator the reply he'd been awaiting. A slight smile of satisfaction curved his lips as he read the telegram:

> CLAYTON WHITNEY NO LONGER MEMBER THIS ORGANIZATION. RESIGNATION DEMANDED WHEN CONVICTED FOR FRAUD LOUISIANA. EIGHTEEN MONTHS' SENTENCE NATCHIGOULA PENITENTIARY. LETTER FOLLOWS.
> ARTEXICO HORSE BREEDERS' SOCIETY.

'Well,' Quist said softly. 'Todd, maybe things are commencing to straighten out a mite.'

'In what way?' Sargent asked.

'You can read this while I get busy and

send some more telegrams,' — handing the Artexico message to the deputy. 'It looks like our friend Whit Clayton was a jailbird.'

15

'I Want Action!'

'It's not the fact that the horse was stolen that bothers me,' Quist was saying, 'but the fact that it was returned.'

'It could have come back of its own accord,' Todd Sargent pointed out. 'With all that rain, it might have wanted shelter.'

Quist frowned. 'You could be right, of course. But it's something that keeps sticking in my craw.'

'Why?'

'Damned if I know, Todd. I've just got a hunch there's a connection there, someplace, that might tie in with other things.'

Two days had passed since Quist had received the telegram from the Artexico Horse Breeders' Society. Since then, he'd had no further word from the association, nor had he received replies to other telegrams he had sent. Nothing in particular had happened, despite Quist's persistent efforts to uncover some sort of evidence through the medium of talking to various people who might have had some contact with Whitney Clayton in earlier days. However, nothing new had come to light, and a gnawing impatience grew in Quist.

'Blast it, I want action of some sort,' he growled. 'Something's got to break right soon. I don't like these cases that drag on and on.'

The deputy grinned. 'I seem to remember that you once told me that patience is a virtue to be cultivated.'

'Yeah, you're right,' Quist grunted. 'But this isn't my day to be virtuous.'

They were seated in the sheriff's office, with the hour approaching noontime. Quist put out a cigarette butt and commented, 'I see the G-Bar-M crew is in town today. For all Martinsen's talk of a hard-working outfit, those hombres seem to have plenty of time to waste.'

'Right now,' Sargent nodded. 'I was talking to Gene this morning. Beef roundup starts in ten days. Gene says he's letting his men take it easy before they go on roundup, as he intends to work the tails off 'em, once they begin. It sounds reasonable.'

'I reckon,' Quist replied noncommittally. 'Where's Wolcott today, Todd?'

Sargent shrugged his shoulders. 'Around town, some place. He came to the office — not too early as usual — and went right out again. I saw him talking to Gene Martinsen, on the corner of Laredo, a short spell before you dropped in. The sheriff was likely giving Gene one of his warnings. Talking serious, anyway — '

'Warnings?'

'Pike never overlooks a chance to warn Gene to make his crew behave while they're in town. It's got to be a standing joke. If the crew wants to get drunk and wreck a bar here and there, Pike's warning won't stop 'em. The crew knows if anyone gets thrown in the hoosegow, Gene will pay their fines without question. The Justice of the Peace collects quite a nice sum from Gene, in that way. Whether he takes it out of his men's pay, I can't say. Probably not. Martinsen's spread pays well, and he's not tight with money.'

Quist returned to the former subject. 'I want to talk to Ortego about that horse. Where do I find him?'

'Out in the Mex section, if he's home.' Sargent gave detailed directions. 'Or, I can go with you.'

'I'll find him alone,' Quist said.

'Think I might have overlooked something, Greg?'

'It's possible,' Quist said grumpily.

'Of course it is,' Sargent conceded. 'I'll be glad to have you check on the facts — such as they are.'

Quist nodded and got to his feet. He relented somewhat.

'No offense meant, Todd. Only, occasionally, two heads are better than one, as the saying goes. See you later.'

Warm sunshine poured along Main Street as Quist proceeded west, acknowledging a greeting now and then from passing men. He crossed Laredo, Austin, Alamo and Bowie streets in easy succession. After that the houses became more scattered. Most of them were blocky adobe Mexican huts, placed helter-skelter here and there, as though thrown down carelessly by some gigantic hand. Here there were no sidewalks, only well-beaten paths. Most of the houses were sheltered by cottonwood trees. Several had tall clumps of prickly pear standing against their whitewashed walls. Nearly all boasted small, neat flower beds.

'Queer how Mexes go for flowers,' Quist mused, as he strode in the direction of Ortega's house. 'They like color, I reckon. Maybe a lot of us would be better off if we thought more about flowers and less about money — or spilling blood.'

Five minutes later he had found Pablo Ortego and introduced himself. The two men stood talking in the shade of the Ortego *ramada* at the rear of the Mexican's home. Ortego was a roly-poly sort of individual with a smiling brown face and a mouthful of good teeth, dressed in shapeless white cotton clothing and a straw sombrero. They were standing at the side of the horse in question, a chunky bay animal with good lines.

'. . . an' ees all I can tell you, Señor Quist,' Ortego was saying. 'Firs', I'm discoveer the *caballo* is of the missing. I theenk the Señor Plummair 'as come to get heem, but,' — a dramatic gesture of hands — 'eet ees not yet of the time for the burial of Señor Clayton.'

'That's right, Lennie Plummer was going to borrow your horse to ride out to the cemetery.'

'*Segura!* Is correc'. For a time I am much of worry that I weel not be able to loan of my so fine *caballo*. The plan of the Señor Plummair will be of an entir-r-re upsetting. Always before when comes the funeral, the little ol' *señor* have depend on me for the horse. Now, he will be of much disappoint. *Es verdad, no?*'

'That's true,' Quist agreed. 'You wouldn't want to disappoint a regular customer.'

'Sodden, I have the thought which is of moch relief.' There was a wide flash of white teeth. 'The Señor Plummair have come early for the *caballo*. So-o! Then I am more easy of the mind. Is the only answer. The horse hav' already been borrow'.'

'Did Lennie usually take the horse without first telling you?'

Ortego shook his head. 'No, always before he hav' firs' come and tell me. And likewise when the horse is return'. But theese time no. The day pass'. Comes on the rain. Comes the night. My *caballa* is still of the missing. I go to the Señor Plummair's *casa*. All is dark. Is not home. I theenk to go in to speak weeth the Señor Sheriff. But eet is still rain like ten devils.' He shrugged his shoulders. 'I theenk I wait for the morneeng. Later, comes home the *caballo* — of a most wetness. Comes daylight. I speak to the Señor Plummer. No, he did not take my horse. Because of the rain, he did not ride to the funeral. All those hours he ees een town. He sugges' that I tell the Señor Sheriff, the *caballo* is gone weethout my pairmission. I do eet. Is all I know, Señor Quist.'

'*Gracias*, Señor Ortego. You have been of much help. Is Lennie Plummer a close neighbor?'

'*Si, si*'! Is of the nearest. See, I show you.'

The Mexican stepped out from the ramada and with pointing finger indicated Plummer's shack just beyond some branches of screening mesquite, standing beneath a tall cottonwood tree. 'Is ver' close, no?' Ortego said.

'Probably the closest neighbor you have,' Quist stated.

He studied the house which wasn't more than a hundred twenty-five feet away. On either side of it, set down at different angles, were other adobes — castles compared to Lennie Plummer's place: it was a shack all right, constructed partly of adobe-and-rock and partly of unplaned planks. Weeds grew tall beside the building's cracked walls. Shingles were missing from the roof and had been replaced with rusty flattened tin cans. The house had once boasted a brick chimney, but now less than half the bricks remained in place. The wall facing Quist showed a closed door, roughhewn, and a single window, one broken pane of which had been stuffed with ragged burlap. The closed door seemed to indicate that Lennie wasn't at home.

Even while Quist was looking at the shack, he saw a man approach from between the other buildings, walking swiftly. It was Cobra Macaw. Macaw hesitated only an instant, then shoved open the door of Lennie's house and stepped within. The door again closed.

'Now, I wonder — ' Quist began.

The words went unfinished. A second man had appeared from around the corner of an adobe. He glanced quickly, furtively, around, as though trying to avoid being seen. Then hugging the wall of Plummer's house, the man — who was Sheriff Pike Wolcott — made his way to the door.

'The Señor Plummair hav' the guests — no?' Ortego put in. 'He is not at home. Pairhaps I should go inform them of this.'

Quist cast a glance over his shoulder at the Mexican. 'I'll inform them for you,' he said shortly. 'I'd like to know what goes on myself.'

'Is ver' good, Señor Queest,' Ortego nodded, looking relieved. 'Is ver' strange to see the Senor Sheriff act in soch mannair — '

But Quist hadn't waited to hear the Mexican's words. He had turned back toward the house in time to see Sheriff Wolcott disappearing through the doorway, before the door was slammed shut. 'I might as well make it a third guest,' Quist snapped, as he started at a rapid gait toward the shack.

As he drew near, he could hear the sheriff and Macaw talking, but beyond catching an angry questioning tone in the sheriff's voice, Quist couldn't distinguish what was being said. He hesitated not a minute upon reaching the shack, but pushed back the door and stepped within.

At his entrance, both Macaw and Wolcott ceased talking, and their faces swung toward the entrance. Wolcott's jaw dropped in surprise. Macaw's face presented his usual deadpan features, with their flat, seemingly lifeless eyes.

Quist took in the whole scene at a glance. A rough bunk with tumbled blankets stood against one wall. A couple of empty boxes took the place of chairs. A rusty stove and stovepipe stood at the back wall in which there was no door, but a small window. In the center of the room stood a rickety table on which lay a Winchester rifle. The hands of both Wolcott and Macaw had been reaching toward the rifle — or had they been drawing away from the weapon — when Quist interrupted them.

'Looks rather interestin',' Quist said softly. 'Would that be a .30-30, by any chance?'

An angry oath was torn from Wolcott's

throat. 'Damn you, Quist, what do you want here?'

'I might ask you the same,' Quist replied.

'It's none of your business,' Wolcott said angrily. 'Why can't you leave law-enforcement to the proper officers? I'm sick of your snooping around. Now you can just turn around and get out. This is my affair — '

'Not so fast, Wolcott. And I'm not getting out on your say-so. What are you and Macaw doing here?'

'I've told you it's none of your business. I'll say nothing more —'

'You'll say plenty more before I'm through with you,' Quist cut in. 'Now talk fast. Whose rifle is that?'

The sheriff opened his mouth to speak, then tightly compressed his lips. Finally he said, 'I've told you I'd say nothing more.'

'All right, make it tough for yourself,' Quist growled. He turned to Macaw. 'What do you know about the gun, Cobra?'

'I don't know nothing,' Macaw said sullenly.

'Is that the gun that shot Hi-Johnny?'

Neither man replied. Quist stood studying the two, feet wide spread, just within the open door. Finally the sheriff spoke, 'Look here, Quist, you have your methods and I have mine. I don't like mine interfered with any more than you do. Now, get out and stop sticking your nose in where you're not wanted. I'll explain things to you at a later date.' His voice trembled angrily.

Quist shook his head. 'You don't get rid of me — or dispose of that rifle — that easy.'

Macaw spoke unexpectedly, 'Pike, why don't you tell him you brought the gun here and be done with it — '

'What do you mean, Macaw?' The sheriff whirled furiously on Macaw. 'You know damn well — '

'You're in for it, Pike,' Macaw said in his flat tones. 'You might be better off if you — '

'Of all the outrageous lies!' Wolcott

stormed. 'Macaw, you had that gun, as you damn well know. Quist, I swear to you —'

'Don't pay Pike no attention, Quist,' Macaw interrupted. 'Just make him talk. I'll leave you two gents to scrap things out. I got some business with Martinsen, so I got to leave now.'

He started around Quist to reach the door. Quist lifted one hand and pushed him back. 'You're not going any place, Cobra, until I've talked to you.'

'I ain't got nothing to tell you,' Macaw said flatly.

'You'll answer some questions or go to the clink. Maybe both.'

'You can't arrest me for anything, Quist. I'm clean.'

'Yeah, like a sewer,' Quist snapped. 'Macaw, the day I arrived here, somebody shot at me. What do you know about that?'

'Well, *what* do you know about that?' Macaw repeated, his sneer giving the words an insulting inflection. 'Too bad the feller missed.'

'The shot was fired from a tree back of the newspaper building,' Quist continued. 'Can you alibi yourself — ?'

Wolcott, from the other side of the table at Quist's left, interrupted. 'Is that true, Macaw? Did you fire on Quist that day?'

Macaw swore. 'Ask this law-man, Wolcott. He knows everything.'

'That's not far wrong where you're concerned, Macaw,' Quist said sternly. 'A man was seen leaving that tree to make a getaway through the *Blade* building. That man, Cobra, was you. Do you deny you were up in that tree when the shot was fired?'

Macaw's cold flat eyes studied Quist. 'You wouldn't believe me if I denied it, railroad dick. Lemme think a minute, what was I doin' in that tree? Could I have been robbin' bird's nests? Nope. That wa'n't it. Oh, yeah, now I remember. Y'see, I'd been flyin' my kite and it got hung up in the branches,' he said insolently. 'I'd dumb up to wrangle it loose. That satisfy you, Quist?'

Now, Quist knew what to expect. It was a showdown. He took two quick steps toward Macaw and whipped the back of his hand across Macaw's lips. 'I don't take that sort of talk from rats,' he said grimly.

Macaw staggered back under the blow, but even as he righted himself he was reaching for his gun. Wolcott screeched something about forbidding fighting in the name of the law, as he started toward Quist, but Quist was moving too fast to give heed, even had he felt so inclined. His left hand was already jerking back his coat lapel, while his right darted to his underarm holster.

The two guns thundered almost simultaneously, with Quist's weapon enough in the lead to divert Macaw's aim. Dust spurted from Macaw's vest, and he was smashed back by the savage impact of Quist's .44 slug. Even as Macaw went to the floor, his six-shooter crashed out again, but the bullet, like his first, came nowhere near Quist.

Powder smoke swirled through the

small room. Quist held his .44 ready for a second shot, but lowered it when Macaw rolled on his face and lay quiet. A sort of strangled gasp came from Pike Wolcott. The sheriff, eyes rolling in his head, was clutching the table for support. Blood seeped through his shirt-front. Even as Quist started toward him, Wolcott groaned and slumped to the floor.

Quist swore angrily. 'Macaw sure played hell this time.'

Plugging out his spent shell, he reloaded, holstered the .44 and knelt at Wolcott's side. He realized almost instantly that the sheriff had been hard hit. The man was already unconscious.

Quist strode to the door, jerked it open. Twenty feet away he saw Ortego cautiously approaching the house. Other Mexican faces appeared at a safer distance. Quist called swift orders, and Ortego turned to get his horse and bring the doctor. It was some time later that Quist noticed a small crowd outside, peering fearfully through the open door.

He was still working over Wolcott's

unconscious body, when drumming hoofs were heard, then squeaking saddle leather as Todd Sargent dismounted and entered the house. He stopped just within the entrance. 'Good lord, what's happened, Greg?'

Quist spoke in jerky tones as he knelt by Wolcott's side: 'I had Macaw cornered. He took the only way out he knew. His slugs flew wild. Wolcott caught one of 'em.' Sargent asked a question. Quist replied, 'No, I don't know what they were doing here. Tell you about it, later. Something to do with that Winchester. Take a look at it. Cripes A'mighty! Where's that doctor? What? How the devil do I know if Wolcott will live or not. I'll be surprised if he does.' He paused and ripped up another bandanna. 'Don't like the sound of his breathing — what's left of it — by a long shot.'

Sometime later he rose wearily from Wolcott's side. 'That's the best I can do. Send one of those Mexes for some water, will you, Todd?'

Sargent went to the doorway and

spoke a request in Spanish. Then he came back. 'I was looking over Macaw, Greg. Your one shot must have got him instanter.'

'I was lucky,' Quist scowled. 'Lord, he was fast.' He repeated, 'I was lucky.'

'What was it you said this morning,' Sargent said, 'some thing about wanting action? Brother, you got it.'

'And I don't want any more of the same.'

Lennie Plummer came pushing through the crowd at the doorway. 'What in tarnation's gain' on here?' he demanded querulously. 'Heard there was some trouble here — '

'Where'd you hear it, Lennie?' Quist cut in.

'That Mex — Ortego — he yelled at me as he rid past. Said somethin' about gittin' a doctor. I come right along — ' He paused, eyes widening, as he saw the two forms on the floor. Then, in a shaking half-whisper, 'Goddlemighty! Macaw and Pike Wolcott. Whut's been a-happenin'?'

Quist said, 'Trouble, like you said, Lennie. You any idea what brought those two here?'

'Reckon I have, mebbe,' Plummer replied. 'Can't say's I know whut caused the trouble, though. All's I know, Pike Wolcott come ter me a spell back and asks could he use my house for a time.'

'Did he say what for?' Quist asked.

Lennie shook his head. 'Jest said he had some business to talk over with a friend and he wanted to talk private where nobody would see him. Never said who the friend was. Now I see it was Macaw, I can't say I blame Pike for not wantin' to be seen makin' *habla* with a rattler like that.'

'And that's all you know?'

'Cross my heart, Mister Quist. That's all I know 'bout it.' The watery eyes looked puzzled.

Sargent said, 'What do you make of it, Greg? Pike wasn't the kind to have underhand dealings — '

'Damn it, Todd,' Quist said irritably, 'I don't make any thing of it yet. And get it through your head, you never know, nowdays, who'll have underhand dealings and who won't. Not until they've been thoroughly tested to your own standards. And then, keep your fingers crossed.' At that moment, someone in the crowd outside called that the doctor had arrived. Quist half snarled, 'For cripes sake! Get him in here, quick!'

16

A Matter of Coinage

Following the shooting of Cobra Macaw, three days of almost complete inactivity passed for Quist, and, as he expressed it, he 'was about ready to gnaw his fingernails down to the knuckles.' A coroner's inquest had been called over Macaw's body, and Quist exonerated of all blame in the man's death. Summed up, the verdict had merely stated that Quist had been forced to fire in self-defense, and that he should be held entirely blameless in the death of Macaw. The verdict hadn't set well with Gene Martinsen and his G-Bar-M hands, and they had sworn — it was rumored — to even the score for the death of their comrade, once he'd been decently buried. So far, however, no move had been made in this direction, beyond the wide circulation of some dark hints to the effect that Quist and Sheriff Pike Wolcott had ganged up on Macaw, and that while Macaw had been occupied with the sheriff, Quist had triggered the fatal shot that finished Macaw. What the Winchester rifle had had to do with the affair, no one seemed to have the least idea. The presence of the weapon on the table, in Lennie Plummer's shack, didn't figure largely in any testimony given.

Wolcott had been taken to Dr. Twitchell's house where he lay still unconscious, very close to death. The doctor wasn't holding out a great deal of hope for him, though he had promised Quist that when and if Wolcott regained consciousness and was strong enough to do so, he would allow the patient to talk for a brief few minutes. Since that time, Quist had moved about town like a caged tiger, seething with frustration.

The fourth day following the shooting at Plummer's place, Quist emerged from the hotel dining room, after having eaten a breakfast of pancakes, fried barn and hot biscuits, the whole washed down with copious draughts of black coffee. It wasn't yet eight o'clock when he stepped out to the hotel porch, gaze running swiftly in both directions along the street. People, horses, wagons, moved past, stirring dust motes under the bright morning sun. The sky had never seemed bluer, but Quist was in no mood to appreciate pleasant weather. His very soul rebelled in black exasperation.

A movement at his right caught his eye and he turned to see Todd Sargent, booted feet propped against the railing, in one of the row of chairs the hotel ranged along the porch for the convenience of its guests, where time could be idled away as life flowed along Quivira City's Main Street. Quist said grumpily, 'Mornin', Todd,' and settled into a chair at the deputy's side. There was no one else on the hotel porch.

Quist rolled a cigarette and passed the 'makin's' to Sargent. The two men smoked in silence for a few moments. Sargent said, 'You look like you were attending the funeral of a dear friend.'

Quist scowled. 'Can you think of

anything to make me feel cheerful? It's enough to drive a man crazy, stalling around, waiting for the sheriff to be able to talk — if he ever is. I want to know what was doing that day —'

'I may have a mite of good news for you.'

'I doubt it,' Quist grunted moodily.

'I went around to see Doc Twitchell this morning. He tells me Pike had the best night yet — that his pulse is a heap stronger.' Quist was half out of his chair, when Sargent drew him back. 'Take it easy, Greg. Pike is still unconscious. He can't talk yet. I asked Twitchell definitely on that point.' Quist swore an oath and sank back. Sargent went on, 'Maybe it might be better for Pike if he never talked. I hate to see a good man go wrong.'

'What do you mean?' Quist asked.

'It should be plain. You've told me that Macaw stated that Wolcott brought that rifle to Lennie's shack.'

'Which same Wolcott denied — vehemently.'

'Did you believe him?'

'Todd, I don't know what to think. While that Winchester is a .30-30, there's no proof — yet — that it's the gun used in killing Hi-Johnny. And if it was, you said yourself Wolcott was in town all that day. I've been thinking the whole matter over. It could be that Macaw realized he and I were due for a showdown. Maybe he lied when he said the sheriff brought that gun there, hoping to embroil me in an argument with Wolcott, and while we were busy, he'd slip off. He had started out of the place, when I shoved him back and he went for his gun. That started things with a bang — three bangs in fact. And I didn't like any of it.'

'I noted you didn't play up that rifle to any extent in your testimony to the coroner's jury.'

'Why should I have? I've no actual facts to go on. The evidence was enough tangled, with that jury wondering what had taken Wolcott to Lennie's place to see Macaw. And that same point is still unexplained to me too. Oh, damn the luck! If I could just dovetail a few of the facts I have, but all I seem able to do is shove square pegs against round holes — and they don't fit.'

Todd chuckled. 'I'm glad this business is your problem. I'd be nigh insane myself if I had the job of figuring things out.'

Quist swore bitterly. 'Blast it! It is your problem, and you'd better start thinking fast. You're sheriff now, you know.'

'For the time being. Look, Greg, if I bought you a drink would it make you feel any better? Or is it too early to — ?'

'It's not only too early to drink, but it wouldn't make me feel any better, either,' Quist grouched. 'You only add to my exasperation — '

'Me!' Sargent's eyes widened. 'Me? What did I do?'

'It's this way, Todd,' Quist said uncomfortably, 'I don't like to pry into any man's business without I've got a good reason, and if I appear to be — '

'Hell, Greg! Spit it out. There's not a damn thing in my life I wouldn't tell *you*.'

'All right,' Quist said irritably, 'here it

is. Ever since I've known you, I've seen you buy drinks, and when you get your change you look it over like you expect to be cheated. Never saw you get any coins yet, that you didn't scrutinize 'em as if you had been shortchanged. It's all right to be careful, but by cripes! you act like it was an obsession with you. Some times I wonder if you aren't a mite cracked on the subject — '

A whoop of laughter from Sargent interrupted the words. 'All right, go ahead and laugh,' Quist said peevishly, 'but it bothers me to see any hombre act the way you do about his chicken feed — '

'Greg, you're all wrong. You just don't understand — '

'What is there to understand?'

'I've got a good reason for looking over my money the way I do. I'm what some folks call a noomismatick — that is —'

'You're a what?' Quist exclaimed.

Sargent spelled it out: 'N-u-m-i-s-m-a-t-i-c. That's not quite right for what I'm called, or what they call a feller who collects coins — '

'Jeepers!' Quist's brow cleared and he commenced to smile. 'Now I get it — you're a numismatologist. You collect old coins —'

'Old money, medals and so on. Just in a small way. But there are certain old coins worth more than their face value. Sometimes they get into currency and I'm always on the outlook for 'em. I don't make a regular business of it, of course. Two months ago I found a quarter-dollar, dated 1804. That's worth about two dollars now.'

Quist shook his head. 'I'll be damned! How'd you ever get into anything like that?'

'My father had quite a collection of ancient coins when I was a kid. Then he got sick, and had to sell most of the collection. Still had some of it left when we moved out here for his health. He didn't last long, but he left me some coins that he claimed would some day be worth quite a bit, and he gave me a general idea of what to watch for.'

'Sold any of 'em yet?'

Sargent shook his head. 'Never had to. I've always had a job. But I always think if I ever go broke, I might find I have something to fall back on. Not that the coins I have represent any great sum — except maybe two or three. Actually, I never paid too much attention to the business, but I have fallen into the habit of saving any coins bearing old dates, that I pick up — '

'Look here,' — Quist was struck with a sudden idea — 'you said, a minute or so back, that numismatologists collect medals as well as coins.'

'That's right. I haven't any medals right now, though. Dad sold what he had in that line, before he died. Why, have you got a medal of some sort?'

'Could be.' Quist fished in his pocket and produced the octagonal piece of flat gold he had taken from Hi-Johnny's dead hand. 'Got any idea what this might be?'

Sargent's face lighted with interest as he took the piece.

'Cripes, Greg! Where'd you find the

Humbert?'

'Humbert? What do you — ?'

'Humbert — name of the man who turned these out. Some folks call 'em California slugs. Darn scarce now days — '

'Humbert? California slugs? I don't understand — '

'Hey! What's this?' Sargent had turned over the piece and was studying the ground-down surface with its various figures and scratchings. 'Somebody didn't give a damn how much money he threw away, when he scraped this smooth enough for his hen-scratchings. Or has some kid been at it?'

'That I can't tell you.'

'Where did you get it, Greg?'

'Took it from Hi-Johnny's hand that day . . . ' Quist related details, ending, 'From the position of his arm I gained an impression he'd been trying to throw it away, rather than let the hombre who shot him get it. That's just guesswork on my part, y'understand.'

'You never mentioned this before?'

'No, I didn't. When I brought

Hi-Johnny in, I wasn't ready to tell Wolcott any more than necessary. It wasn't just Wolcott, either. I got an idea from Grizzly Baldridge's manner that he knew more about Hi-Johnny than he was letting on.' Quist broke off, 'But what sort of medal is it?'

'It's not a medal at all. It is — or was — a fifty-dollar gold piece — '

'T'hell you say! In that shape? Eight-sided? And here I had it figured out for some sort of medal Whit Clayton had won.'

'Money hasn't always been round in form. I happen to have three of these old Humberts. Right now I could get seventy or eighty bucks for each one. They're what is known as collectors' items — '

'You mean the government turned out money in that form, at one time?'

'They were turned out for the government, or with governmental approval, whatever you like. Back in the California gold-rush days, there got to be a shortage of gold money. At that time the government refused to accept gold-dust in payment of taxes, God only knows why. Anyway, gold coins were quick used up. It got to a point where speculators sold gold coins at a premium. Something had to be done, so a number of various companies started coining gold money — fifteen or twenty companies, anyway — and among them Humbert issued this octagonal piece, in various denominations, right down to one-dollar, fifty-cent pieces and two-bit coins, in gold.'

'I'll be blasted! You say you have three of these pieces? I'd like to see 'em.'

Sargent got to his feet. 'Come along to the office and I'll satisfy your curiosity, Greg. I always keep my collection with me, wherever I live.'

A few minutes later, in the sheriff's office, Sargent dragged from beneath his cot with its folded blankets, a large metal box. 'Dad used to keep the coins in trays, laid out separate on velvet,' Sargent said, getting a small key from his pocket, 'but living the way I do, I can't be bothered with a cabinet to hold trays.'

He threw back the cover of the box and Quist saw within a number of small packages wrapped in newspaper. Sargent frowned, 'I'm not sure which of these packages the Humberts are in, but it won't take more than a little spell to ferret 'em out.'

Lifting the box to a chair near the desk, he commenced unwrapping the small bundles. Various old coins were placed on the desk for Quist's inspection — an ancient English guinea piece, a Florentine florin, a couple of Greek drachmas, a Bombay rupee, an ancient Roman coin, various pieces of United States money. Sargent handed up a small silver coin. 'Here's one that might interest you. It was put out at a time when the English king wouldn't allow our colonies to mint money, but they did it anyway. It's what they call a three-pence, known as Pine Tree money.' A pine tree and the date 1686 showed on the coin.

'Must be rare,' Quist commented.

Sargent shrugged. 'Not particularly. Curious, though.' He unwrapped another package, then chuckled, 'This might give you a laugh, Greg. This is one of the first copper cents issued by the United States of America — in fact, this cent was the first coin of any value issued when we got a Congress.'

Quist took the old disc of copper in his hand. On one side, surrounded by thirteen connected links to represent the thirteen original states, were the words, 'United States' and 'We are One.' He turned the coin over and read at one side the word 'Fugio.' Opposite was the date '1787.' At the top of the coin was a representation of a rising sun beaming down on a sundial, and below the sundial were the words, 'Mind Your Business.'

Quist laughed. 'Mighty appropriate, I'd say, for today as well as those old times.'

'You're correct as — ' The Deputy broke off. 'Here's those Humberts.' He rose from the box and placed the three coins on the desk before Quist, reverse sides up. 'Y'see, one of these is just like your coin — on this side. Then, this next one doesn't have the pattern of fine lines on its back. Now, this third fifty-dollar piece has the figures '50' in a center circle, with spreading out from the circle a sort of flower-petal design.' He turned over the three Humberts. 'There's some slight difference on these sides, but they're practically the same.'

Quist scrutinized the three coins. One of them had a sort of raised, slightly curving, border, with an American eagle design within. The other two coins lacked the raised border, which was flat. Quist lifted one of the coins to study it. Running completely around the outside border of the coin were the words, 'Augustus Humbert United States Assayer of Gold California 1851.' Within was a design showing an eagle with spread wings, bearing in its beak a scroll inscribed 'Liberty.' Above the eagle's head a second scroll read '887 Thous.,' denoting the fineness of gold in the coin. Just within the border and curving neatly around the eagle were the words 'United States of America,' and below, 'Fifty Dolls.'

Quist replaced the coin on the desk. 'Mighty interesting,' he commented.

'Want to see some more old coins?'

'Not right now, Todd. I've got to figure out the meaning of the Humbert I found in Hi-Johnny's hand, before I'll have time for further entertainment.'

'Jeepers! You don't figure that has any connection with Clayton's killing, do you? How could it, Greg?'

'That's what I want to know,' Quist growled. 'My brain is nothing but a mess of muddled soup swimming with words like gold, California, camels, Humberts — oh, hell, you know what I mean. I probably sound crazy as hell, but what Baldridge said about camels, a few nights back, and now this chunk of gold from California, — well, I just feel sure there's some sort of connection. I just can't seem to tie it altogether though.'

'Maybe you're following the wrong trail, Greg.'

'Dammit, I've got a hunch I'm on the right trail. Trouble is, people won't tell me what I want to know. They clam up. Folks are afraid to talk for fear of getting into something unpleasant.'

'I've told you everything I know.' Todd was rewrapping his coins and stowing them away.

'Todd, you've been just fine. But there are others — Grizzly Baldridge, for instance. He might hold the key to this whole business — if he'd talk. Could be it's my fault. Likely I irritate folks. But, by cripes! I didn't start out that way — oh, hell, what I want is some action.'

'Remember what happened the last time you said that.'

'I haven't forgotten,' Quist said grimly. 'But even that kind of action I'd welcome.' He turned toward the doorway. 'I'll see you later, Todd. Thanks for squaring me off on that coin business.'

'*Por nada*, Greg. Glad to do it. Where you going?'

'Crazy,' Quist snapped. 'Anyway, I'll be headed that way, if something doesn't break soon.' At the doorway he turned back, a wry grin on his face, 'You'll note

I didn't ask you to go along.'

'In other words,' — Sargent continued his rewrapping of coins — 'you've got something in mind you want to work out by yourself.'

'Could be,' Quist nodded. 'Right now I'm heading for Grizzly Baldridge's place. Maybe I'll learn something — or at least sweep away some deadwood. *Adios, compadre!*'

17

Evidence

On the sidewalk, outside Sargent's office, Quist consulted his watch. It wasn't yet ten o'clock. He turned toward the Lone Star Livery Stables and a few minutes later he emerged riding the buckskin gelding. There were more people on the street by this time. A woman passed carrying a sun parasol and bearing a market basket. Horses and vehicles moved along the road.

Before guiding his pony into the stream of traffic, Quist pulled up a moment to let a buckboard pass. Then as he touched the horse lightly with his spurs, he noticed that Ownie Jordan and Gene Martinsen were standing, talking, before the hitchrail of the Green Bottle Saloon. Jordan appeared sober and very much in earnest. There was something scornful in Martinsen's laughing tones. Quist couldn't hear what was being said, but he slowed pace and directed the pony toward the hitchrack.

At that moment Ownie Jordan glanced away from Martinsen and saw Quist. 'Howdy, Quist,' he called genially enough, 'figurin' to exercise your pony while we got good weather?'

'Something like that,' Quist replied.

Martinsen scowled, then forced a sneering laugh. 'Too bad you haven't got the sheriff with you, Quist. Then you could plug some other poor sucker, like Macaw, while the sheriff keeps him busy.'

Quist didn't reply to that — not at once. He pulled the pony to a complete halt, then deliberately climbed down from the saddle. He strolled just as deliberately around the end of the tierail, and stepped to the sidewalk to approach Martinsen. Martinsen wasn't laughing now. He had sobered abruptly when he saw Quist coming, and much of the belligerency died from his eyes. He lifted one protesting hand, 'Now, look here, Quist, I was just hoorawin' you a mite. You don't want to take it serious — '

And that was as far as he got. Quist's left fist, clenched to a hard knot of bone and muscle, smashed solidly into Martinsen's middle. An explosive 'Ooof — f!' was ripped from Martinsen's throat, and the big man bent nearly double. As his head came forward, Quist connected with a violent right to the point of the jaw. The blow straightened Martinsen to full height. For a brief moment he stood erect, eyes already glassy, tottering a little. Then, quite suddenly, his knees gave way and he crumpled to the sidewalk to lay motionless.

'My — my Gawd, Quist!' Ownie Jordan gasped. 'You shouldn't have done that — '

Laughing savagely, Quist whirled on Jordan. 'You're telling *me* what I should do?'

Jordan backed away, arms raised protectively. He stuttered, 'B-B-But you didn't g-g-give Martinsen any w-warning — '

'He had his warning, when he saw me climb down from my horse,' Quist snapped. 'After what he said, he should have been expecting trouble. Well, he got it!'

Excited cries moved along the street. Several of the G-Bar-M cowhands came rushing from the Green Bottle.

Quist had backed against the hitchrack, alert for further action, his topaz-colored eyes glinting sparks of angry fire.

'Cripes A'mighty!' a G-Bar-M hand shouted. 'It's Gene! Knocked colder'n a dead catfish!'

The punchers braked to a sudden stop, seemingly stunned by the downfall of their boss. They stood around gazing down in some bewilderment at their stricken leader, as though unable to comprehend exactly what had happened. Gunplay they could have understood and any one of several men would have been ready, nay, eager, to take up the fight against Quist in retaliation, but this was something different, not quite within their orb.

A crowd gathered. Todd Sargent came galloping diagonally across the street from the sheriff's office. He pushed through the thick cluster of men and a sudden exclamation left his lips. 'Cripes A'mighty, Greg! What happened?'

Quist said grimly, 'Martinsen made a remark that brought on an accident. Or maybe it wasn't an accident. Come to think of it, I hit him deliberately — '

'He's not dead?'

'I don't hit that hard. Dead to the world, perhaps. He'll come round in a minute or so. I'm on my way. Tell him he can have more satisfaction, any time he likes and it won't necessarily have to be with fists. See you later, Todd.'

Quist shouldered his way through the crowd and back to his horse. On his way he encountered Ownie Jordan. Jordan backed off when he saw Quist coming. 'Just a minute, Jordan,' Quist said. 'I'd like to know what you and Martinsen were talking about when I showed up.'

'Nothing much.' Jordan's teeth chattered a little. 'I'd just been telling Gene that we should all throw in to help you in any way we knew how, rather than hinder —'

'Do you expect me to believe that?' Quist snapped.

'Probably not,' Jordan conceded, 'but can you prove different?'

'And in what way did you figure Martinsen — or you — could help me?'

'That I don't know, for sure,' — earnestly — 'but I was just trying to make Gene see, that maybe if we were a mite friendly, it could work out better all around.'

'That's a nice speech anyway,' Quist said dryly. 'Thanks for your Christian sentiments. And I suppose by this time you've thought up an alibi for your whereabouts at the time Whit Clayton was killed.'

'I — I think I have. My cook, out to the Box-J, remembers that I didn't leave the ranch all that day.'

'I'll have to talk to your cookie one of these days.'

Another interested group had started to form around Quist and Jordan, so Quist prepared to leave. As he climbed into his saddle, he heard Todd Sargent ordering someone to get a pail of water to throw in Martinsen's face.

By the time Quist had reached the trail running to the Bee-Hive Ranch, he was in considerably better humor. 'Nothing like blowing off a mite of steam now and then,' he mused, as the buckskin carried him along at a swift lope, 'to keep the boiler from exploding. And if I wasn't mighty nigh the exploding point, I don't know why.'

* * *

It was just about noon when Quist, topping a gentle rise, found himself looking down a long slope toward the Bee-Hive outfit. From his saddle he could see the low rambling ranch house constructed of rock and adobe; the whitewashed bunkhouse, barns, corrals and blacksmith shop. The vanes of a windmill turned easily in the fresh breeze, with a steady *clank-clank*. Looking down through the big live oak trees that dotted the landscape, Quist spied some cowhands bending a fresh tire on a chuckwagon. There seemed an unusually large number of horses in the corrals. Off to one side, a bronc-peeler was straightening a few kinks out of a bucking pony. It was about that time that Quist remembered that beef-roundup time was drawing near. He urged the pony down the long grassy slope and as he drew near, saw that Grizzly Baldridge and Laurinda were seated on the long gallery that fronted the house.

A moment later he drew the buckskin to a halt at the edge of the gallery, feeling the hostility that rose from the two seated before him. Quist spoke greetings and added something about it being a nice day for a ride. He noticed they both had tall glasses in their hands.

Neither invited him to alight. Grizzly Baldridge said bluntly, 'What brings you out here, Quist?'

'I'd hoped to have a chance to talk to Mrs. Clayton. There are one or two things I think we should get straight.'

Laurinda's chin came up a trifle. She

didn't reply at once. Quist noticed that her dark hair was parted in the center and drawn to a knob at her nape. She wore some sort of Mexican peasant costume, cut low across the shoulders, the skirt being rather full. Her legs were bare; she wore sandals on her feet. At that moment Quist thought, Laurinda Clayton was the most beautiful woman he had ever seen.

Before the girl had an opportunity to reply, Baldridge growled, 'What things you think we should get straight?'

'As a matter of fact,' Quist said, 'it seems to me there are various aspects of the — er — trouble hereabouts, that might be straightened out through a bit of *habla*. It may be asking a great deal, but I'd like to have Mrs. Clayton take a ride with me, to visit that house where her husband was killed.'

'I forbid it!' Baldridge boomed in his heavy voice. He sat back in his chair, glowering at Quist, his thick iron-gray beard fairly bristling with resentment.

Laurinda cast a quick glance at her

father, then said, 'Wait a minute, Dad. Mr. Quist has his reasons, I imagine. Perhaps, we might be a bit co-operative. At any rate it won't hurt to try.'

Baldridge cast a glance of angry surprise at his daughter. 'You mean you're willing to go riding with Quist?'

'I don't know why not,' Laurinda replied. 'At least the time will pass faster in a saddle than on this gallery. Besides,' — caustically — 'when the law commands, it may be best to comply.'

Quist winced. He said quietly, 'It was a request — humbly made if you will — definitely not a command. Let's forget it.' He moved as though to turn his pony away from the gallery.

Laurinda cried, 'Wait, Mr. Quist. I'll go with you — '

'If you're going, I'm going along,' Baldridge snapped, rising from his chair.

'I prefer not,' Laurinda stated firmly. 'Please, Dad, let me be the best judge of this. Mr. Quist, I'll be with you as soon as I can get into riding things. Dad, will you get my horse saddled?'

'I ain't nobody's saddle-boy,' Baldridge said peevishly, 'but I'll have Chris do it. He's down to the corral. You ain't had any dinner yet, neither, girl — '

But Laurinda had already disappeared within the house. Baldridge looked through the open doorway after her, then swore. 'If ary man can ever figure out what's in a woman's mind, I just don't know. One minute she hates you, the next — by the seven horned steers of Moses!' He broke off, then grudgingly, 'Light and sit, Quist. I'll be back pronto.' And again grudgingly, holding up his glass, 'Can I accommodate you with one of these?'

Quist replied in the negative with thanks. Baldridge didn't know whether to like the reply or not. Finally he shrugged his shoulders, stepped down from the gallery and made his way around the house.

Quist dismounted and settled into one of the chairs on the gallery. He rolled and lighted a cigarette. About the time he had crushed the butt under foot,

Laurinda appeared, in spurred boots, riding togs and sombrero. 'Where's Dad?'

Quist got to his feet. 'Far's I know he went after your horse.'

The girl bit her lip. 'Probably holding some sort of conference with Chris. If Dad sends someone to follow us — ' She left the words uncompleted, as Grizzly Baldridge appeared, leading Laurinda's saddled bay pony. Quist made a move to help the girl into the saddle, but she ignored the gesture and mounted without his help.

Baldridge handed Quist a newspaper-wrapped parcel when he was mounted. 'Here's some sandwiches I had cookie mess up. Y'ain't neither of you had your dinner. Wouldn't send a dawg off hungry. And, Quist, if you make any trouble — '

'Let's not go into that, Dad,' Laurinda cut in stiffly. 'Mr. Quist may be hard and ruthless, as I've heard, but I feel quite safe with him.'

'I'm also kind to children and dumb animals,' Quist said dryly.

Laurinda tossed her head and turned her pony away from the house. Baldridge looked steadily at Quist. 'I'd like to be friendly with you, mister,' he said hard-voiced, 'but I'm not sure what you're up to. Just mind what I say, that's all. We Baldridges — '

'There's a lot of things I don't like either,' Quist snapped, 'but I don't jump to conclusions. It would be a lot better for you, Baldridge, if you'd tell all you know instead of keeping back facts.'

'What facts?' Baldridge bristled.

Quist tried a shot in the dark. "I'd like to know what you know about Hi-Johnny. You didn't tell me everything.'

The shot in the dark found a target. Baldridge stiffened, eyes narrowing. 'Anything I happen to know about Hi-Johnny doesn't concern you, Quist, and has nothing to do with the business at hand.'

'I'm not so sure of that,' Quist said coldly. 'Maybe you'd best think things over, Baldridge.' He tried another shot, and drew from his pocket the Humbert gold-piece he had taken from Hi-Johnny's dead hand. 'You might think this over too.'

Baldridge's eyes bulged. 'Cripes A'rnighty, Quist! Where'd you get that California slug?' He stepped nearer the horse, reaching up one hand, fingers shaking a little. 'Let me have a look at that.'

Quist slipped the gold piece back in his pocket. 'I'll explain that Humbert, when you tell me what you know about it, Baldridge. We might even get together and exchange a few ideas. Think it over. Meanwhile, *adios!*'

Giving Baldridge no time to answer, he wheeled the buckskin and went loping after Laurinda who, by this time, was some short distance off. Closing in at her side, Quist started in the direction of the tumbled range of Montañosas etched sharply against the turquoise blue sky. They rode steadily for a time, neither speaking, only swerving the ponies, now and then to avoid a clump of prickly pear or an occasional tall pecan tree. Gradually, the rolling hill country lifted before them. After a time the horses were slowed to an easier gait.

Quist reined closer to the girl's side, but still maintained silence. Finally Laurinda could stand it no longer: 'I don't suppose there is any law that says we can't talk.'

'None at all,' Quist said quietly. 'What do you want to talk about?'

The girl looked at him a moment, her lustrous dark eyes with their unbelievably long lashes steady under his keen penetration. 'I'd rather that the subject would be of your choosing, Mr. Quist. Aren't you wanting to ask some questions?'

Quist shrugged. 'A couple, perhaps. What were you wearing the day your husband was — was — ?'

'The day I shot Whit, you mean,' the girl said steady voiced. 'That's an easy question. The same outfit I have on at present — corduroy riding skirt, divided. This sombrero. Light flannel shirt — of the type that is called mannish. Riding boots. Spurs. Do you want further details?'

'That'll be enough to start with,' Quist said dryly. 'I don't want to get in over my depth. Same pair of spurs, I suppose. Same shirt and bandanna?'

'Same spurs,' the girl nodded, then frowned. After a moment: 'I can't be sure about the bandanna at my throat. It was probably different — at any rate, it has been washed, if that makes any difference. So has the shirt — wait, this isn't the shirt I wore that day.' Quist noticed the color was gray. 'The shirt I wore that day was a sort of plum-color — something between plum and maroon. Anything else you want to know?'

'Yes, tell me exactly what happened that day?'

It was again as though the girl were relating a well-rehearsed speech, but without any particular feeling — or perhaps she was striving to prevent all emotion from entering her voice. The words were flat, almost toneless. When she had concluded, Quist was silent. Finally she said, a trifle defiantly, 'Well, what do you think?'

Quist studied her, smiling a little. 'I think that you have too lovely a voice to distort it in that manner,' he replied quietly. 'You're defeating your own purpose, in trying to convince me in such fashion. In short, Mrs. Clayton, you've just wasted time.'

Laurinda flushed. 'You're saying I'm not telling the truth?'

'I don't know how I can make it any plainer. You've told virtually the same story you tried to make me believe at the hotel. Why not quit stalling and let me have facts, for a change?'

The girl's eyes blazed. Abruptly, she jabbed spurs to the bay pony's ribs and darted ahead of him a few rods. Quist increased speed to catch up, and they again proceeded in silence, the girl's chin high, her lips compressed. In time they reached the shallow-flowing Montañosa Creek and moved down the low banks. Moving hoofs stirred the bottom of the creek, which quickly cleared as they passed. Emerging on the opposite side, they pushed through high brush, willows and cottonwoods to reach more open country. Before long they came to the stand of blackjack oaks and made their way through the trees. Then, topping the hill that rose before the house, they loped down the slope.

Laurinda didn't speak until they'd dismounted before the building. Then she said in a compressed voice, 'I haven't a key. How — ?'

'I still have the key Todd gave me.' Quist went ahead and opened the door, stepping aside to let the girl enter. Now he watched her closely every minute. Stepping across the room, he reached for her cartridge belt and empty holster. 'You might as well take this with you.'

'Probably so.' Laurinda's hand was steady as she strapped on the belt, with cool composure; her breathing was easy and regular.

Quist led the way through the jumble of overturned furniture, pausing now and then to let his eyes rest on the girl. Her gaze passed across the brownish stain on the floor as though it hadn't existed.

They passed through, then entered the kitchen and continued on into the bedroom. The girl's lips were tight, but there was no evidence of strain in her manner. Leaving the bedroom, Quist went to the back door of the kitchen, unlocked it, and they stepped outside.

The rear of the house looked as it had on Quist's previous visit, except that rain and wind had disposed of the faint footprints he'd seen on that occasion. The clump of prickly pear rose high at the corner of the house, and nearby, against the back wall, stood the old packing case. The broken-off pad of prickly pear on the earth, looked a trifle drier than before. Perhaps the rust had deepened on the tin cans scattered about.

Laurinda said mockingly, 'I suppose that slow silent procession through the house was supposed to have broken me down in some way.'

'You're mistaken, Mrs. Clayton. What I'm trying to do is build you up, if you'd only let me.' Abruptly, he changed the subject. 'Ever been up on this roof? You can get quite a view of the surrounding country from up there. Come on, I'll show you.'

'I don't believe I'm interested,' the girl said coldly.

A sarcastic smile curved Quist's lips. 'I understand. You don't think it would be ladylike for a Baldridge to climb up on roofs. You can't even conceive of anything so undignified.'

He turned away, mounted to the packing case against the wall, and an instant later had hoisted himself to the roof. Glancing down, he saw that Laurinda's eyes were blazing furiously. 'Mr. Quist,' she snapped, 'I must say you have a damn queer idea of us Baldridges.'

'That's likely,' Quist conceded, 'but it could be your actions planted that idea in my mind. And now you're just angry enough to climb up here — providing I lend you a hand, as a gentleman should.'

'Keep your hands to yourself,' Laurinda snapped angrily. 'I don't need your help.' Stepping to the packing case she placed her hands on the roof and vaulted easily up, then rose to face Quist, her dark eyes pools of raging fire. 'Now, I hope you're satisfied.'

Quist said mildly, 'More so than you'd ever dream, Mrs. Clayton. Actually, you've no reason to get riled at me.'

The girl checked the hot retort that rose to her lips, and turned away. Her gaze roved around the horizon. 'I can't say that the view's improved much,' she stated icily. 'How could it be from this low roof?'

'On the contrary,' Quist smiled. 'I find the view vastly better, now that you're also up here. Perhaps a change of position might help your viewpoint.' He lightly touched her arm, guiding her across the peak of the roof and toward the front of the house where it slanted down. Laurinda's tall, slim form moved lightly, if reluctantly, at Quist's side. Finally she said shortly, 'For me, the view isn't good anywhere in the vicinity of this house.'

'That I can well imagine,' Quist acknowledged. He laughed softly, 'After all, it is your roof, though. I should think you'd notice its condition. It was cheaply built. A great many shingles have become loosened. Even walking as carefully as I could, I couldn't help dislodging two or three. I doubt some of them have been properly nailed in place. Perhaps I should compliment you on your light step. Not one single shingle have you disturbed — '

'Just what is this foolishness all about?' Laurinda asked irritably.

Quist turned away. He didn't reply until they'd once more descended to the earth. This time he extended a hand to help her, but she jerked angrily away and got down without his aid. Quist said, 'Perhaps it's not foolishness, Mrs. Clayton. You see, I was just picking up a bit of evidence.'

The girl's dark eyes widened. 'What sort of evidence?'

'The sort that makes it unnecessary for you to tell me any more untruths,' Quist replied. 'Neither you nor your brother, Chris, killed Whit Clayton. I'm certain of that now. What do you say we talk it over?'

18

Laurinda's Story

'I must say,' Quist commented, biting another chunk from his sandwich, 'that Grizzly Baldridge raises a prime grade of beef. I was hungry.'

He and Laurinda were seated on the earth, at the foot of the tall pecan tree that grew about thirty feet southwest of the house, munching on the lunch the Bee-Hive cook had wrapped. Quist sat cross-legged, taking a drink now and then from the canteen of water he had brought from his saddle. The girl's knees were drawn nearly to her chin as she sat facing him, her manner uncertain now, and only occasionally did she bite into the sandwich in her hand. So far Quist had forestalled her questions regarding the evidence he had found at the house, with the remark that he would explain things, when she had decided to give him the true facts 'with no more of your fairy tales, lady. I just can't believe 'em.'

Quist's eyes roved around the landscape. A short distance to his left was the empty horse corral, a couple of bars of which had already fallen. The gate hung loosely to one side. Farther over were the tall trees and brush bordering Montañosa Creek. At his rear the rugged hills lifted against the sky. Quist started to roll a cigarette. The scratching of his match seemed to bring the girl's thoughts back to the present.

She said suddenly, 'Mr. Quist, can I believe you weren't telling fairy tales, when you said you knew Chris hadn't killed my husband.'

'Cross my heart,' Quist smiled, 'nor you either.'

'You — you aren't pulling a trick of some sort to — to get me to admit things?' She sounded very earnest.

'You must admit, Mrs. Clayton,' Quist said quietly, 'that I'm not the one that has been pulling tricks around here. Are you finally ready to tell me what you know?'

The girl's dark eyes searched his face

and found there nothing but confidence. She considered the matter a moment while a small frown creased her forehead. Impulsively she said, 'I — I believe I am. What do you want to know, Mr. Quist?'

Quist exhaled a cloud of gray smoke. 'Tell me exactly what happened, so far as you know the facts, the day your husband was shot.'

Laurinda drew a long breath, then, 'There's no use relating the events leading up to the time I left Whit. Let's just say I was definitely through with him — or thought I was at the time. Some months passed while I stayed at the Bee-Hive. There were arguments with Dad, at first. He's pretty hardboiled in some ways, but underneath he's old-fashioned; he hates the thought of broken marriages. There was always the thought in his mind that Whit would come to his senses and act like a man, and that we'd get things straightened out. Chris had been all for me quitting Whit for some time, and that caused a lot of wrangling between him and Dad.' She paused a moment.

'Family scraps are never pleasant,' Quist said sympathetically.

'Finally,' Laurinda went on, 'I decided I'd make one more try at getting along with Whit. I thought if I talked to him — made him see how we all felt, he might make a fresh start. I didn't want to do it, but on Dad's account I was willing to try. Chris was against the idea and for the first time in our lives he and I had some bitter arguments. He and I have always been very close, and that hurt too. But figuring that Dad's feelings came first in the matter I saddled up one morning and started to see Whit. I wasn't riding fast. I wanted to think over what arguments I could employ with my husband.'

'What direction did you take going to the house?' Quist asked.

'I followed the north bank of Montañosa Creek, intending to cross when I'd reached a point about opposite here. As a matter of fact, I was so lost in thought that I rode a trifle too far. Then I had to turn back for the crossing and push through the trees and brush, before I emerged through there, approximately — ' gesturing to a place in the trees that lined the stream.

Quist nodded. 'That's as I figured it — but go on, I'm interrupting.'

'As I approached the house, I saw Whit's pony in the corral, so knew he was at home. I entered at the back way, and then called to him. When he didn't answer, I went on through to the front room — ' The girl paused, her lips trembling.

'And found Clayton dead,' Quist put in, 'and the room pretty much wrecked. There, we're over that rough spot.' The girl looked gratefully at him, and Quist went on, 'Did you have any idea, at the moment, as to who might have done it?'

'Not the slightest. You see, I wasn't actually sure, at first, that it was Whit. The — the body was covered with a blanket. I — I lifted the edge of the blanket to make sure. Then I saw the six-shooter on the floor. I recognized it as Chris's gun, of course, and jumped to the conclusion he'd — he'd done the killing. I was terrified. It had been bad enough for me to wreck my life, but I didn't want Chris ruined on my account. I knew he and Priscilla Kiernan planned to get married. Whit had been making himself obnoxious, one way and another, with Priscilla, too. Feeling as Chris did about the whole business, I could see where he had plenty of reason for killing my husband. Also, I was excited, flustered. I wasn't thinking straight.'

'That's understandable,' Quist said quietly, his topaz eyes steady on the girl.

'In fact, I was downright stampeded. My first thought was to save Chris. His gun, on the floor, was evidence against him. I figured if I took it away with me, the killing would be considered just another mystery, and Chris wouldn't be suspected.'

'You did take it away with you, then?'

Laurinda nodded. 'How my own gun — the .38 — happened to be found near the body, I've not the slightest idea.'

'Was it in the holster, hanging on the

wall, at the time you discovered your husband's body?'

'I didn't notice — never gave *my* gun a thought. I rode on home. Later, when I learned Chris had confessed to the killing, I told Dad I killed Whit, then rode into town, with Dad, and told Sheriff Wolcott my story.'

'Where is Chris' six-shooter now?'

'I gave it to him only a couple of nights ago, when we finally got together and compared stories. He'd been angry with me for contradicting his confession and had refused, at first, to listen to my story of how I found Whit dead. It required time to make him believe me, and he kept insisting that I let him go through with his story.' The girl smiled ruefully. 'Oh, Chris and I had some lovely wrangles, until we both got straightened out. Now he insists he found my gun on the floor near the body and threw it into the brush near the stream — '

'Ah!' Quist said suddenly. 'Now details are dovetailing.'

Laurinda frowned questioningly.

Quist said he'd explain later. The girl continued, 'There's little more to tell. Last night, Chris and I told Dad what we knew. He'd been insisting we retract our confessions, then if and when the case came to trial he felt certain the jury would disagree — '

Quist interrupted to say that neither Laurinda or Chris were coming to trial. She asked if he knew the identity of the killer. Quist replied, 'Right now, let's just say there was a third person present that morning, the person who killed Clayton. Yes, I mean while both you and Chris were at the house — '

'But I don't understand. Where could this person have been?'

'On the roof,' Quist replied. 'Mrs. Clayton, I wasn't sure for a time that *you* hadn't been up on that roof, while Chris was there, if you'd actually killed Clayton. Now, perhaps you understand my actions to get you up there. I wanted to make you mad enough to climb up alone, with no help from me.'

Laurinda was bewildered. 'But I only

proved I could get up there.'

'But not in the same manner as the murderer. You made it easily. The murderer lacked your agility, and was forced to step on one of the branches of that prickly pear, at the corner of the house, to boost himself up. In his haste he broke off one of the pads, and damaged another. Scratches prove that. Not only that, the killer loosened shingles while on the roof. You didn't —'

'Good grief. Now I'm more puzzled than ever.'

'Listen, this is how it appears to me. The person who killed Clayton came to the house that morning. The overturned furniture shows there was a tussle. That person seized your gun from its holster on the wall, killed Clayton with it, then dropped the gun near the body. Clear so far? Good. About that time, the killer spied Chris riding toward the house. There's no place to hide in the house, and not enough time to reach the brush near the stream without being seen by Chris. My guess is that the killer slipped out the rear door, scrambled up to the roof and hid there until Chris rode away. Chris entered the house, found Clayton dead. Seeing your gun near the body he jumped to wrong conclusions too. To save you, he left his own gun in its place and when leaving tossed your gun into the brush — '

'But, in that case, how did — ?'

'I'll explain. Give me time. Remember, there's enough pitch either way from the peak of that roof, for a person to hide on either side, and thus be hidden from a person approaching from either direction. The killer is about to descend when he sees you approaching, so it is necessary to hide longer. You came into the house, discovered the body, and shortly departed, taking with you Chris's six-shooter. Once you were out of sight, the killer descended from the roof, retrieved your .38 from the brush and once more placed it near the body. And that is where Todd Sargent found it, when he came to investigate.'

Quist manufactured a cigarette and

continued, 'Chris's actions after his confession as much as told me he hadn't done the killing. He hadn't dreamed the doctor would probe out the .38 slug, after he'd claimed to have done the shooting with a .45. When he met Todd Sargent, returning from the investigation, he didn't even know the .38 had been found near the body. All that cleared Chris in my mind. And that fairy tale you tried to make me swallow at my hotel showed you didn't know the facts of the killing. You were almost clear in my mind then. It required only your climbing to that roof to convince me — '

'But are you certain of all this — about the third man — ?'

'About as sure as I can be there was a third person present. You see, I searched through the brush near the river. I found sign where a horse had been tethered. At another place I picked up sign where somebody had entered the brush — presumably to retrieve the weapon, your .38, which Chris had thrown there. And in still a third spot, sign showed where a horse and rider had passed, leaving caught on a thorny branch a few shreds of a maroon shirt, such as you wore the day of the killing. So your story stands up, Mrs. Clayton. Now are you satisfied?'

'Ye-es,' — frowning — 'but I can't understand why the killer was so anxious to leave my gun near the body?'

'To avert suspicion. It was known that you had left Clayton — that you didn't get along. You were simply to be made the victim of another person's crime. You see, you seemed most logical. Your confession only built up the case against yourself. You — '

'Mr. Quist — ' Laurinda's voice broke and Quist saw her dark eyes were moist. 'You — you don't know what a load — ' Again she paused.

'My friends call me Greg,' Quist said gruffly.

'Gr — Greg, you — oh, lord, I've been so wrong about you — ' Laurinda's shoulders shook. She tried to go on, but failed.

'Darn it,' Quist growled, 'I've done

nothing. And let's have no tears, please. You know women just look foolish when they cry — Laurinda, stop it!' There was another sob. Quist pulled the Humbert gold piece from his pocket. 'Look here, what can you tell me about this?' But that didn't work either. Laurinda reached for a handkerchief, eyed the gold piece a moment, said she'd never seen it before, and put her head down on her knees.

Quist heaved a long sigh and got to his feet. 'All right, get it out of your system,' he said irritably. 'I'm going to take a walk. I'll be back when the showers are over.' Swearing softly under his breath, he went striding off in the direction of the house.

He was gone quite some time. When he returned the sun was dropping fast toward the Montañosas. The girl was on her feet now, approaching him, all sign of tears gone. 'I'm sorry I was such a fool, Greg. It won't happen again — '

'Everyone has the right to act foolish now and then,' he said shortly. 'Look here, have you any idea why Whit Clayton built the house in that particular spot?'

'Er — no — not exactly. He said he wanted to be near Estrecho Pass. That's not far from here. Probably what counted most was, there was a good deal of flat loose rock scattered about at that point, which the builders could use for the foundation. It saved time and money hauling rock.

Why, have you discovered something else?'

'I dont know,' Quist said slowly. 'I've got to think it over. Certainly it doesn't help me in establishing the killer's identity. Come on, we'd best get headed back. The afternoon has slipped away from us.' Side by side, they started for the house to pick up the horses.

It was dark by the time they reached the Bee-Hive. Lights shone from bunkhouse and ranch house. Quist unsaddled for the girl and turned her pony into the corral, then led his horse behind as he walked with her to the house. At the edge of the gallery they paused. Laurinda asked him to come in, but Quist refused. 'I want to get back to town, soon's possible,' he explained. 'You can tell your Dad and Chris what's happened today, but tell 'em both to keep it under their hats. And tell Grizzly I want to talk to him when he gets some time.' He started toward his horse.

'Greg. Wait a minute. I haven't thanked you decently yet for — for the load you've lifted from my mind — '

'No thanks necessary, Laurinda.'

Again he turned away, but the girl caught at his sleeve. In the lights from the house windows he saw her eyes were wet. She swayed toward him and then she was in his arms, holding her tall slim form close to his own. Her head lifted to meet his and her lips were warm against his mouth. 'Greg,' she whispered, 'You've been so decent — that's not for thanks — I can never thank you enough . . .'

They heard someone at the house door and moved apart. A broad rectangle of yellow light shone across the gallery and Grizzly Baldridge said, 'That you, Laurinda — Quist?'

'It's us,' Quist replied. 'I'm just taking off.'

Reluctantly, Grizzly said, 'Care to come in and sit a spell?' 'Thanks, no,' Quist replied, climbing into his saddle. 'I've got to get back. I'll let Laurinda tell you what we discovered. And, Grizzly, you might be surprised.'

Without giving Baldridge a chance to answer, he turned the horse and went loping off through the darkness.

19

Ancient History

The morning sun was warm on Quist's face as he sauntered along Main Street on his way to the hotel, after stopping off at the sheriff's office and finding Todd Sargent not there. A pedestrian nodded to Quist and received a pleasant greeting in reply. A few horses and wagons stood at hitchracks along the way. Clouds drifted lazily across the blue sky, and there was a bit of a nip in the clear air. As he mounted the steps to the hotel porch, Quist spotted Sargent seated in one of the chairs ranged along the verandah railing. 'So this is how you collect your salary from the county,' Quist laughed. 'I looked for you at the office.'

'And I was looking for you. The hotel clerk said you'd left early.'

Quist nodded. 'I got word from Doc Twitchell that Sheriff Wolcott would be able to talk to me a couple of minutes.

Naturally, I hurried right over to Doc's office. Haven't even had breakfast, yet.'

'T'hell you say! What did Pike have to offer? Learn why he was at Plummer's place with Macaw, that day? How is Pike?'

'Pretty damn weak. He answered a few questions — '

'About what?' Sargent interrupted interestedly.

'One thing and another,' Quist evaded. 'I'll tell it later, Todd, when I've had a chance to think things over. Yes, Doc thinks that Wolcott will recover eventually, but I've a hunch you'll be sheriff here for a long time to come, Todd.' He changed the subject. 'They said at the post office that you'd picked up my mail.'

'Yeah. You were out. I thought I might save you a bit of time.' He passed over a couple of bulky envelopes. 'I talked the telegraph operator out of a pair of telegrams for you too. He insisted on putting 'em in envelopes, though, so I couldn't snoop into 'em.' The telegrams were handed to Quist. 'Looks like you got some action when you fired off requests.'

'We T.N. & A.S. operatives co-operate pretty well. I wanted to dig up a mite more information on our jailbird friend, Clayton Whitney — or Whit Clayton, if you like aliases.'

'What's an alias to a dead man?' Sargent shrugged his shoulders. 'What I want to know is who killed the bustard. After what you told me last night when you got to town? Well, my brain's been going round and round. I'm sure glad to have Laurinda — and Chris — cleared though —'

'Just keep it under your hat for a while, Todd. What's on your mind this morning? Your face was clouded up like a thunderstorm when I first spotted you. Anything wrong?'

'Not wrong, exactly. I'm just puzzled,' Sargent replied.

Quist asked a question. Sargent continued, 'No, it has nothing to do with Clayton's killing — so far as I know. It's just that Gene Martinsen has — '

'What about Martinsenin?' Quist

asked quickly. 'Sore at the way I manhandled him yesterday, I suppose, and looking for trouble.'

'That's not it, Greg. 'Course, like I told you last night, he did a heap of talking about squaring matters, while he was still groggy from your knockout. But a man is li'ble to say anything wild under such conditions. No, what has me wondering is why he states he's not going to throw in with the other outfits, this fall, for the beef roundup. Says he and his crew will do their own rounding up of beef cattle.'

'How is beef roundup usually handled in this section?'

'All the outfits throw in and work together. They start in 'way over on the east range and work gradually west. First, they comb through the Star-Cross holdings, then the Pot-Hook; next comes the Laxy-N. There's a couple of small outfits before Jordan's Box-J is reached. Following that, they work across Martinsen's G-Bar-M and finish up with the Baldridge Bee-Hive, farthest to the west.'

'And what does Martinsen plan this year?'

'Says he's going to wait a spell before rounding up. Any cows in other brands that he finds, he claims he'll throw over on their rightful range, and he expects other owners to do the same by him.'

Quist frowned. 'I shouldn't think that would set well with the other outfits.'

'It won't. But you know that G-Bar-M outfit. It always did think it was a law unto itself, and nobody can make a man work his cows if he don't feel like it. But it will make for hard feelings, I'm afraid, and might lead to trouble. Queer part is, that Martinsen needs money too.'

'How do you know that?' Quist asked.

'I was talking to Jared Whittaker in the hotel bar last night. Whittaker owns the bank, you know. He holds a right heavy mortgage on the G-Bar-M and is about ready to foreclose. Martinsen hasn't even tried to keep up the interest. Well, Gene always was a pretty wild spender. Whittaker told me Gene had put a lot of money in some mining stock that failed.

All this was told me in confidence, you understand. But the idea has me stopped. Here's a man who needs money, postponing his roundup that would bring in money. How do you figure it?'

'I don't,' Quist frowned. 'Right now I'm not going to try, either. I'm still short one breakfast for today and that's my first problem. Then I'll go through these envelopes and other messages. You've had your breakfast, I suppose? How about a cup of coffee?'

'Thanks, no, Greg.' Sargent got to his feet. 'I'll mosey around town and see what I can pick up — if anything. See you later.' Sargent descended the porch steps and strode off down the street, while a fragrant odor of ham and eggs drew Quist's steps toward the hotel dining room.

It was nearly three hours later when Quist was seated on the bed in his hotel room, looking over the papers and photographs that had been mailed to him from other T.N. & A.S. operatives, that a knock sounded at his door. Quist raised his head and called 'Come on in,' while he quickly shuffled together the papers on the bed.

The door was shoved back. Grizzly Baldridge, followed by Chris, pushed his way into the room, then closed the door behind him. Quist got to his feet, smiling, 'Well, Baldridge and Son! What brings you two to town?'

Grizzly Baldridge advanced, hand outstretched. 'Curiosity,' he boomed in his heavy voice. 'We just wanted to learn if you'd be willing to shake the hands of a couple of damn fools and accept apologies. Laurinda's told us how you cleared things up yesterday—'

'No apologies necessary,' Quist laughed, shaking hands with the two men. 'Let's just say we had a misunderstanding. Here, you men take those chairs. I'll sit on the bed.'

Cigarettes were rolled and lighted. Grizzly said, 'Misunderstanding is c'rect! With us, as well as you.'

'We can see now,' Chris put in, 'that we'd been better off to work with you from the first, Greg — er — Mr. Quist.'

'It's always Greg to my friends,' Quist said.

'Trouble was,' Grizzly growled genially, 'I was too much of a damn fool to see the light. I figured my way was right and that I could work it to get either Laurinda or Chris off, if nobody meddled. Y'see, Clayton didn't get no more'n he deserved, t'my way of thinking. Then you arrived and I was afraid you'd make some blunder that could really tie my kids into trouble. So, like damn fools, we fought you. I don't mind sayin', though, it went against my grain to act that way. I sort of took to you from the first, Greg.'

'At least,' Quist said dryly, 'I'll not have you two to buck from now on.'

Chris said, 'Make it three. Have you forgotten Laurinda?'

Quist shook his head. 'A girl like your sister isn't easily forgotten,' he said quietly.

'Have you discovered yet who killed Clayton?' Grizzly asked.

Quist evaded that, and gestured

toward the papers on his bed. 'I've been running down a few facts on Clayton. I don't suppose you knew he was an ex-convict. Todd Sargent told me he had a washed-out look when he first came here. I suspected prison pallor, at the time.'

'T'hell you say!' Grizzly exploded. A similar remark came from Chris. 'What was Clayton put away for?'

'Fraud,' Quist replied. 'Under the name of Clayton Whitney he accepted payment for ten blooded horses from a horse fancier in Louisiana, then tried to slip out of the state without making delivery of the animals. He was caught, most of the money was recovered, and he served eighteen months in the Natchigoula Penitentiary. It wasn't too long after his release that he showed up in Quivira City. When he was tried and found guilty, the Artexico Horse Breeders' Society demanded his resignation from the organization.'

'I'll be blasted!' Grizzly exclaimed. 'The skunk pro'bly never had the horses to deliver to his customer. That sounds like Whit. To give the devil his due though, he sure knew horseflesh. Always boasting of Arab barbs and *grullas* he'd formerly owned — '

Chris put in, 'I remember him telling me one time that all dun horses came originally from the wild Mongolian ponies.' Quist changed the subject. 'Tell me, do you know of any reason why Clayton should have done a lot of digging over near Steeple Rock, not far from Estrecho Pass?'

Father and son eyed each other blankly. Both shook their heads. Grizzly said, 'None of us get over that way often. Didn't know there'd been digging done there. You sure Whit did it?'

Quist shook his head. 'No, I'm not sure. Could there be any precious minerals to be found there?'

Grizzly looked dubious. 'It's possible, I reckon. But all that country was prospected years back, 'thout any success.'

Quist frowned. 'Clayton must have had some special reason for buying that particular piece of property from you —'

'Speaking of that property,' Grizzly interrupted, 'your railroad can have its right-of-way whenever it pleases, Greg, and it's not going to cost your company a cent.'

'Thanks, Grizzly. That's right decent of you — '

'Decent be blasted,' Chris said. 'After what you've done —'

'Forget it,' Quist cut in. 'Grizzly, there's one point I would like to clear up. You had an argument with Clayton, near the depot, one day, and disarmed him. What caused the trouble?'

'Certainly I disarmed the buzzard,' Grizzly snorted. He hesitated, then, 'He had the nerve to pull a gun on me. He was drunk. I'd been trying to talk some sense into him, tell him to straighten up. He resented it and we quarreled. That's all there was to it.'

Quist nodded. 'Now, something else. I want to learn what you know about Hi-Johnny and that California slug I showed you yesterday.'

Grizzly's face fell. 'Pshaw! That's all ancient history, now. I figured you were going to ask something regardin' Clayton. I haven't the least idea who killed Hi-Johnny, or why he was killed.'

'Can you tell me anything about that Humbert gold piece?'

'Ain't sure I know anything about that particular slug. I've seen quite a few in my time, though not of recent years. My father once had a good number of 'em in his possession. He's dead now. Anything I know is mostly from hearsay — events that happened during the War 'tween the States. I got the story from my father, Virgil Baldridge, who served as a colonel, and got wounded, and then was shipped home the first year of the War. A Minie ball smashed his hip and he couldn't make to ride well. Crippled him for life. Infection set in, and he died only a few months after Lee surrendered. I'd been fighting the War with Terry's Rangers. B'Gawd we'd been hanging on to Sherman's heels all that long march through Georgia, hinderin' him as much as possible. I mind the time a handful of us — '

'Dad,' Chris grinned, 'Greg didn't ask for a history of the Civil War.' Then, turning to Greg, 'Dad's hard to stop once he starts on the fighting the Confederacy did.'

Grizzly looked sheepish. 'All right, I'll stick to facts. Like I say, my father, Virgil Baldridge, was shipped home wounded, the first year of the War. He couldn't be used at the front, but he was determined to do all possible to help the Confederacy win. Due to the Federal blockade, the Southern states couldn't ship their cotton to England. England needed that cotton to keep their mills from shutting down. We Baldridges raised some cotton, along with cattle, but most of the cotton came from the east part of Texas. My father started in buying cotton — he was fairly wealthy at the time the war broke out — and shipping it down through Mexico where English ships loaded it at Mexican ports. Eventually payment for the cotton came though, and father donated the money to the Confederate cause.

'To play safe, such payments were made by England to banks in California, and thence to Confederate agents out there who saw to it that the money got to Texas. I've already told you how Hi-Johnny used to drive camels in this country. When that was done with, he got in the habit of hanging around our ranch. He'd do some work for the meals we gave him and so on. When war broke out, he managed to get hold of a camel someplace, and started driving it between California and Texas. He was right trustworthy and brought in plenty money for the Confederate cause. That camel'd outpace a horse any day.'

'Funny thing,' Chris said, 'I can remember hearing about all this when I was a kid, but it had slipped my mind. But, go on, Dad, I'm interrupting.'

Grizzly continued, 'The war dragged through all those dreary years until 'sixty-five, but every so often a payment for cotton would come through, and usually it was Hi-Johnny who brought it on his camel. Sometimes, payment for more than one shipment would be made at a time, when there were delays. Confederate secret agents in California would be finished off by the Feds, and then the South would lose time getting fresh men to work for the cause. But the whole South was being gradually bled to death. Cattle ran wild and unbranded through Texas, and father had only a couple of horses left. All the hands had gone into the ranks except one, feller named Luke Damson. My mother had died, and only my father and Damson were left at the ranch to keep things going.'

Quist asked, 'How come this Luke Damson wasn't fighting?'

'He hadn't been called. Father, crippled like he was, had to have help around the place to keep things running, so Damson was deferred as they call it.'

'Was he one of your regular hands?' Quist asked.

Grizzly shook his head. 'He'd come to work for us Baldridges just a coupla weeks before I joined Terry's Rangers. I suppose in a way he was a regular hand, considering how long he stayed with father, but I never considered him as such. Don't know where he come from originally. So, like I say, it was just him and father at the ranch during the closing years of the war, with things getting worse all the time, and father holding out stubborn hope of an eventual Confederate victory. And then, one day in April of 'sixty-five, Hi-Johnny came driving in with his camel carrying twenty-thousand dollars in gold, packed in a little leather trunk contraption. A couple of delayed payments had been made and it was the most money Hi-Johnny had ever brought in at one time. And that time he had run into trouble. Federal men in California had grown suspicious of him. A trap was laid. He was shot at, but managed to escape. The camel was hit in the leg though and that slowed it up considerable. By the time Hi-Johnny and his load reached our place, that camel was in bad shape, and not traveling anywhere near it's usual speed.'

Grizzly drew on his cigarette, then went on, 'Father examined the gold. I remember him telling me there were a great many California slugs in the trunk, along with the usual round twenty-dollar gold pieces, as well as some smaller coins. The amount came to slightly over twenty thousand. He and Hi-Johnny held a council and decided to send the gold up to the State Treasury at Austin, the following day. Hi-Johnny felt the camel could make the trip, providing it had a night's rest and care given its wounded leg. Austin was only around seventy miles distant, and it was felt the camel would be more reliable than the two old crowbaits of horses that were left. So the following day, Hi-Johnny set out with his lamed camel and the load of gold, and not able to travel as fast as one of the crowbaits. But gold is heavy, and the camel at least could be counted on to carry it. Hi-Johnny had been gone only an hour when a rider came by and told father that Lee had surrendered to

Grant and the war was over. I suppose it took a time for father to digest that bad news. Then he got to thinking that the Feds would come down and raid the Texas Treasury. He didn't want that gold to fall into Federal hands. Crippled like he was, he couldn't ride after Hi-Johnny. There was nothing left to do but put Luke Damson on one of the crowbaits with directions to catch up and bring Hi-Johnny back. And that was the last ever seen of the gold or Luke Damson.'

'But what happened?' Quist asked.

Grizzly shrugged his ponderous shoulders. 'You got me, Greg. Days afterward, Hi-Johnny was found wandering around, out on the range, out of his head. He'd been shot in the head. The bullet had lodged against his brain. My father had him taken care of by the best doctor within reach. The doctor said he couldn't understand why the shot hadn't killed Hi-Johnny. He got the bullet out, but there was some sort of pressure had been made in the skull. At no time, though, did Hi-Johnny come near dying.

He was just crazy as a loon, from then on. We questioned him as to what had happened, but he couldn't seem to understand. He stayed around the ranch a year. Finally, he wandered away. Later he came back, then wandered off again. Folks in this country got to know about him. They fed him if he showed up. Now and then he would mutter something about gold, but it didn't make sense to us.'

'Sounds to me like Luke Damson and Hi-Johnny might have been jumped by outlaws,' Chris suggested.

'We thought of that,' Grizzly replied, 'but nobody ever did run across Luke Damson's body. Nor did we find what happened to the camel.'

'If the camel had been run off the trail and shot,' Quist speculated, 'the coyotes would have taken care of it in pretty short order. The flesh would have been eaten and the bones scattered, after a time.'

Quist asked, 'How old was Luke Damson? Could he have been in league with some outlaws?'

'That I don't know,' Grizzly answered. 'As to his age, I'd judge offhand he was a year or so younger than I am. But there's the story, Greg. Hi-Johnny used to show up at the ranch now and then, and ask for my father. By that time father had died, but we couldn't make Hi-Johnny understand somehow. And he'd never say what he wanted father for. It got so Hi-Johnny's visits to the ranch grew fewer and fewer.'

'Perhaps, back in his crazy mind,' Quist said, 'he retained some knowledge of what had happened to the gold.'

'If so, we never learned what it was,' Grizzly answered. 'Probably it was just as well the gold didn't get to the Treasury at Austin. Two months after the gold disappeared, outlaws raided the treasury and made off with seventeen thousand dollars. Could be they were the same crowd that got Damson, Hi-Johnny and our gold. We offered rewards for the return of the gold, even up to half the amount of the missing money, but no one came up with any information.

Anyway, you can see, Greg, Hi-Johnny's death has nothing to do with Clayton's killing —'

Quist interrupted to ask, 'Do those rewards still stand?'

Grizzly looked surprised. 'Why, er, yes, I reckon they do.'

'Good,' Quist said. 'If you ever find that gold, pay the reward to Todd Sargent. He's been a lot of help to me on this case — '

'Greg!' Baldridge exclaimed. 'You're not telling me that you know something about that money? How could that business be mixed into Clayton's case? That's all ancient history — '

Quist asked another question: 'Have you any idea why Clayton built his house in the particular spot he did?'

'That,' Chris put in, 'might have been my idea. Clayton didn't seem too particular about the location, so long as it was in that vicinity. I noticed that there was a quantity of flat rock at that point which could be used for the foundation for the house. With the rock at hand, money could be saved hauling rock from some other point.'

Quist frowned, saying half to himself, 'It could be chance, I suppose — '

'What are you talking about, Greg?' Grizzly asked. 'What's the location of that house got to do with — with — ?'

'Look here,' Quist cut in, displaying the octagonal Humbert gold piece he'd taken from Hi-Johnny's dead hand, 'Hi-Johnny was clutching this at the time he was shot. Grizzly, you didn't get a good look at this yesterday. There's some lines and figures scratched on one side of it.' The other two gathered close while Quist's forefinger traced the markings. 'There's this wavy line paralleling one of the flat edges. Running from that is one arm of a Y which stands on a sort of curving line below. The three arms of the Y carry the figures, one hundred fifty-two, forty-six and thirty-one. At one end of the thirty-one line, is a short straight line with scratches, at right angles, across it. See what I mean?'

Grizzly studied Quist's face. 'Sure,

Chris and I see it,' he said blankly, 'but what do those scratches mean?'

Quist smiled a bit sheepishly. 'Maybe I'm aiming wide of the mark, but since hearing about that missing gold, I got a sort of wild idea. You'll probably think I'm crazy — no, wait — ' at the sudden exclamations — 'let me explain a mite. Yesterday, when I was out to that house with Laurinda, she started to turn on the weeps, so I took a walk while she got over 'em. I had been showing her this Humbert and still had it in my hand. It suddenly occurred to me that the wavy line scratched on the coin could represent Montañosa Creek. There's a W at one end of it which could represent the direction, west, though the stream runs slightly southwest. But that was near enough to start me off. The short straight line with the scratches across it, could stand for the pecan tree beneath which we'd been sitting. The circular line below could designate the top of the hill fronting the house. It all seemed to fit in, so I measured off, in paces, the three lines, one hundred fifty-two, forty-six, and thirty-one.' He paused and looked at the interested faces of the other two, then, 'Damned if each measurement didn't bring me directly to the house, where they joined to form the Y. Now, let's assume that — '

'Cripes A'mighty, Greg!' Grizzly's eyes bulged and his bushy beard seemed to bristle. 'Are you figurin' that missing gold could be buried beneath the house?'

'Isn't it a possibility it's buried somewhere and that someone knows it was buried? A lot of digging has been done near Steeple Rock, but the digger perhaps didn't know exactly where to look. It could be *he* guessed wrong. Maybe *I'm* wrong in my surmises. Maybe the gold was never buried, but I'm working on a strong hunch — and I learned long ago never to disregard my hunches.'

'Let's hear about it,' Chris said.

Quist laughed a bit self-consciously. 'I'm about to stretch hell out of your imagination, gentlemen, and if you believe me, maybe we're all three of us crazier'n Hi-Johnny. I haven't yet got facts to fit my guesses, but here's what I think might have happened. Remember, I took this gold piece from Hi-Johnny's hand. That sort of ties him to the missing gold in my mind. Now, let's go back a bit to the time he started for Austin with the gold on his camel. Let's pretend he was held up and forced to drive the camel someplace else. Maybe the outlaw or outlaws even made him dig a hole to bury the gold.' 'That's possible,' Grizzly put in. 'Hi-Johnny was pretty tough and strong in his younger days.'

'Once the hole is dug and the gold buried, the outlaw shoots Hi-Johnny, leaves him for dead and then skips until things quiet down. But Hi-Johnny doesn't die, we'll say. The bullet has affected his mind more than his body. He regains consciousness, and while his mind has been tipped widely off its beam, he still retains enough sense to want to save that gold for Virgil Baldridge. It's well known that a crazy person often has more strength than a sane one. Anyway, we'll say that he digs up the gold, transports it to another place, and reburies it. Just through chance he happens to pick the same place that Clayton picked to build his house. Or maybe it wasn't chance on Hi-Johnny's part. There was a lot of rock scattered there, that was used in the house's foundation. Isn't it reasonable to assume that Hi-Johnny might have buried the gold among the rocks, where there'd be less likelihood of the earth being washed away in case of a cloudburst, or if the stream overflowed its banks?'

'That could be,' Chris conceded. 'Hi-Johnny could have had streaks of sanity mixed in with his crazy periods. But that map — ?'

Quist had an explanation for that too. 'It could be he realized his mind wasn't so good, and he wanted to record the burying place of the gold. It's doubtful he had paper and pencil or he'd have used 'em. So he grinds off the surface of one of the gold pieces on a flat rock, then with the point of his knife he scratches his map.

Later, he is picked up, out on the range, out of his head. Later, he hangs around your ranch, unable to realize Virgil Baldridge is dead, but back in his crazy mind is a drive to tell Baldridge, and no one else, what he knows. Eventually his mind grows weaker and weaker. Maybe in time he forgot all about the gold, but through force of habit hung on to the gold piece with the map on it. Does any of this make sense?'

'By Gawd, by Gawd, by Gawd,' Grizzly Baldridge was muttering excitedly. 'It's hard to believe, but maybe you've hit on it, Greg.'

'I've a strong hunch in that direction,' Quist smiled. 'Why not take a bunch of your hands out to that house, rip up the flooring and start digging. Only don't blame me if I've made a bad guess. I just think it's worth a try.'

'Good Lord, I should think so!' Chris exclaimed.

There ensued a few more minutes of discussion before the two Baldridges departed. Quist handed the Humbert map to Grizzly. 'If you do find that gold,' Quist warned, 'keep the news secret until I give you the word. Have your hands keep quiet too.' The two men promised and went hurrying down the stairway. Quist turned back to his room, chuckling and shaking his head, 'It's queer as the devil what the thought of gold will do to a man.'

20

Showdown

'So that,' Quist concluded, 'is the story of the Humberts, Todd — and if you ask me, that gold is the key to all the skulduggery that's been taking place around here.'

Todd Sargent's amazement had been growing. 'But — but, cripes a'mighty, Greg, do you suppose Grizzly will really find that gold under the house? It doesn't seem possible.'

The two men were seated in the sheriff's office, while Quist talked. Late afternoon sunlight streamed through the window; dust motes danced in the sunshine. Along Main Street, men were preparing to go home to their suppers. The hitchracks commenced to look deserted. Glancing obliquely across the street, Quist saw that most of the G-Bar-M ponies had left the Green Bottle tierail, to head homeward, though he recognized Gene Martinsen's and Ownie Jordan's ponies, still waiting, heads down and tails drooping.

Quist's eyes came back to Sargent. 'Yes, it's possible, Todd. I'd even convinced myself it was probable, but now I've started to wonder. I've kept putting off telling you, until Grizzly could bring some news, but, jeepers! it seems like I should have heard from him long ago. After the way he and Chris tore out of town, yesterday, I expected prompt action. But, dammit! I haven't had a word.'

Sargent looked disappointed. 'Maybe your hunch was wrong.'

'I'm not sure,' — Quist frowned —' but that the delay in hearing from Baldridge might prove I'm right. Maybe they're still searching. I'm still holding out a mite of hope —'

Quick, heavy steps sounded beyond the open doorway, then Grizzly Baldridge came barging in, beard bristling and eyes bright with excitement. The instant his gaze fell on Quist he opened his mouth in a wild rebel yell, '*Yip-yip-yipee-e-e!* Greg, we found 'er!'

People passing on the street looked toward the sheriff's office. Sargent and Quist were on their feet now. Quist, laughing, strove to quiet Baldridge. 'Let's not tell all of Quivira City about it, Grizzly. Remember, we've got to keep things quiet for a spell.'

Baldridge looked sheepish and toned down. The three men dropped into chairs, all talking animatedly. '. . . and you needn't to worry, Greg,' Baldridge was saying. 'My hands won't utter a peep about it, until I say the word. By Gawd, that was a job you set us, Greg! We worked all night. Took tools and most of the crew with us. Damn nigh wrecked that house. Ripped out the floors. Dug all over under 'em. No luck, right up to the foundation stone on all sides. Then Chris got the idea of diggin' under the foundations, too — and we hit 'er! Only about a foot down, round eleven this mornin'.'

Both Quist and Sargent asked questions. Baldridge supplied answers. 'Sure, I counted it. Few hundred short, but what th' hell! About a tenth of that money was in California slugs too — '

Sargent cut in, 'Probably the outlaws who stuck up that gold shipment took some for handy cash before buryin' it. Anyway, the present value of those Humberts should make it up — '

'That little old leather trunk was rotted all to hell,' Baldridge interrupted. 'We found the lock. It looked like it had been smashed loose with a bullet from a cap-and-ball — ' He broke off, 'Look here, Greg, seems like you should get a reward — '

'We've already decided about that reward, Grizzly,' Quist replied. 'And let's not talk about it now. I draw a good salary for doing my job. I'm satisfied.'

'Tell you what we are going to do,' Baldridge rushed on, 'we're going to hold a celebration t'night. Now, wait, nothing will be said about gold. I've given it out that I'm celebrating my birthday with a supper at the hotel. Six-thirty sharp.

There'll be Chris and Priscilla, you and Laurinda, and Todd and me. I already arranged with the hotel. Ran across Ownie Jordan and Gene Martinsen on my way here. Even invited them to help me celebrate my birthday. Ownie said he'd come, but he was already staggerin' drunk. I doubt he'll sober up in time. Somebody at the Green Bottle will likely pour him into his saddle and start him home. Martinsen allowed he wouldn't set at the same table with you, Greg. I don't think he likes you.'

'I'm deeply hurt,' Quist observed caustically. 'I guess no harm will be done if Jordan and Martinsen don't learn the cause for your celebration until later — birthday or gold, whatever.'

'Promised my crew I'd give 'em a bang-up celebration, too, in a few days,' Baldridge boomed. 'I'm just dang regretful that Pike Wolcott can't be with us.'

'That's too bad too,' Quist said shortly. 'Howsomever, he can learn the details later.'

'The only thing that bothers

me,' — Baldridge sobered — 'is that we don't yet know who killed Clayton and Hi-Johnny.'

'Could be you'll learn, tonight, at supper,' Quist stated cryptically. 'The time's about due for a showdown.'

'Greg!' Sargent started excitedly. 'You mean you already know.'

Quist laughed. 'Ask me no questions, I'll tell you no lies.'

'Anyway,' Baldridge chuckled, 'if I asked you to come out and have a drink, you'd answer that, wouldn't you?'

'Hell's bells on a tomcat!' Quist chuckled, 'I've been wondering how long it would take you to remember I get thirsty at regular intervals. Let's go!'

At six-thirty that evening, the four men were awaiting the arrival of Laurinda and Priscilla Kiernan in the hotel lobby, Laurinda at the moment being engaged in changing from riding things, in Priscilla's shop. The faces of the four men shone from recent shaving. Only Quist and Grizzly wore their usual togs. Chris and Todd Sargent had donned their Sunday best, and Todd had already deposited his six-shooter and cartridge belt with the hotel clerk, for politeness' sake, until supper was concluded. Men, and a few women, passed continually through the hotel lobby, which had never been constructed to hold much of a crowd in the first place.

'Beats all hell how long it takes that girl of mine to get a few fixin's on,' Grizzly grumbled. 'We'd had time for a couple of drinks at the hotel bar — ' He broke off to speak to a passing acquaintance. Laurinda and Priscilla put in an appearance eventually, their hair done smoothly and eyes sparkling. Laurinda wore a dress of some soft dark-green material, with a great deal of lace at the throat and cuffs. Priscilla was in pale blue, tightly bodiced. Quist envied the fond look she gave Chris when they met, but the feeling was quickly forgotten when he felt Laurinda's long warm fingers clasped in his own. 'Well, come on, come on,' Grizzly urged, 'let's get into the dining room. That cook will be fit to be tied, should all the fixin's I've ordered get cold.'

An hour and a half later, Grizzly and his guests sat back to relax. Priscilla vowed she had never eaten such a supper in all her born days. Most of the dishes had been cleared from the long table at which they sat, the only one occupied by this time. A waitress hovered near the door to the kitchen; a second girl was engaged in tidying up other tables and turning low some of the oil lamps. A box of cigars was passed. The conversation during supper had been light, with a good deal of laughing and joking. Finally, Sargent and Grizzly looked expectantly at Quist, Sargent saying, 'Greg, you sort of gave us to understand you had things to tell after supper.' Quist nodded. 'I wouldn't be at all surprised, Todd, if you had some arresting to do before the night passes.' He drained the remainder of the coffee in his cup and put down his cigar. 'Suppose we start like this,' — taking from one pocket three hairpins and a handkerchief which he placed on the table before Laurinda who sat next to him. 'Laurinda, I take it these belong to you. Now don't spoil the story I've built in my mind by denying it.'

Laurinda frowned, picked up the handkerchief and examined it; she held it to her nostrils a moment. Next, she inspected the hairpins. Turning questioningly to Quist: 'The handkerchief is mine. I recognize it. It still holds a slight trace of my scent. I'm not sure about the hairpins. They could be mine; they're the sort I use. Greg, where in the world did you get these things?'

Quist glanced around the table. Across from him, Priscilla Kiernan's pretty features were questioning. The others looked puzzled. Quist turned back to Laurinda. 'I found the handkerchief and hairpins the day Hi-Johnny was killed. They'd been dropped in the brush where the killer who finished him, and shot at me, was hidden.'

Laurinda's eyes widened. 'Good grief, Greg! You don't suspect *me!* But I don't understand — I must have left this handkerchief —'

'At the house where your husband was killed,' Quist finished, 'the day you cleared out. You left plenty trace of your residence there when you pulled out, Laurinda — ribbons, beads, and so on.'

'But I still don't understand how these things — '

'They were picked up by the killer and dropped purposely to throw me off the trail. I wasn't fooled for a minute. Any person smart enough to pick up his expended rifle shells doesn't drop clues so carelessly. Did I say dropped? These things were carefully placed on the grass, so I'd be certain to see 'em. Had they been dropped, the hairpins, at least, would have disappeared from sight.'

'Whew!' Laurinda laughed nervously. 'For a moment there I thought I was in for something again — '

Her words were interrupted by the arrival of the hotel clerk with a sealed envelope which bore Quist's name. 'I just now found this on my desk, Mr. Quist,' the clerk was saying. 'I don't know how long it was there, but not long I'm sure.'

Quist examined the envelope. 'Who left it on the desk?'

'I've no idea, Mr. Quist. There were a number of people in the lobby sometime back. I was quite busy. Nearly anyone might have dropped it —'

'Thanks,' Quist cut in. 'I'll take care of it.' The clerk departed and Quist, after excusing himself, ripped open the envelope. Within, written with lead pencil, on a single folded sheet, were the words:

If you want real proof that Grizzly Baldridge killed Whit Clayton, come to the newspaper building right away. Don't mention this to anyone.

The note was unsigned. Quist glanced toward Grizzly and the others, then back to the note again. He muttered half to himself, 'This complicates matters.'

Sargent, seated on his left, said, 'Anything wrong, Greg?'

'Nothing to worry about right now,' Quist smiled. He glanced around the table, getting to his feet, 'Sorry, but I have to leave for a short spell. I hope it won't take too long.' Shoving the note back in the envelope, he placed it on the table, partly under Sargent's saucer, gave Sargent a meaning glance and, nodding to the rest quickly made his way from the dining room.

Less than five minutes later he had proceeded along Main Street and reached the *Quivira Blade* building. The windows were dark. There was no sign of life about the place. Quist hesitated, then made his way around to the alley back of the newspaper building. Glancing up, he saw light through the dusty window on the second floor. Moving to the wall of the building, he tried the wide double-doors. They proved to be unlocked and, opening one, he quickly slipped inside and shut the door after him. In the gloom an odor of damp printing ink assailed his nostrils.

Some light shone from an opening in the ceiling overhead, where a ladder rested against one edge. Quist lifted his voice, 'Anybody up there?'

There was a moment's hesitation, then, 'Thet you, Mister Quist? Come right on up. Keerful ye don't slip on thet ladder. Them rungs git sorta greasy now and then.'

Quist mounted to the upper floor and stepped through the opening. Almost immediately he saw Lennie Plummer seated on a wooden box across the room. On the floor, at Lennie's side, was a kerosene oil lamp with a badly smudged chimney. It didn't give forth too much light, and Lennie sat half in shadow. The far end of the building, toward the front, was in gloom. There were the usual objects cluttered about that Quist had noticed on his former visit: large metal containers of printing inks and grease; loose piles of flat paper; tall mounds of cardboard sheets; bulkily-wrapped packages of newsprint. Nothing seemed to have been disturbed since last time: there were the same discarded mechanical parts for presses scattered here and there.

'Why don't ye sit on thet can yonderly

and be comfortable?' Lennie indicated with a gnarled forefinger a five-gallon container of printer's ink, as yet unopened, which was placed against the wall, directly across the room from Lennie. 'I should've stirred muh stumps a mite and cleaned up for a visitor,' he continued, as Quist sat down, 'but my rheumaticks has got me feelin' porely o' late. Jest kick them old gears and nuts an' bolts an' sech outten yer way, should they get under foot. Make yorself easy, Mister Quist.'

'I'll do that, Lennie. Was it you that left that note for me, at the hotel?'

'A friend done it fer me,' Lennie replied. 'Ye didn't speak ter nobody 'bout it, did ye?'

'Didn't mention it to a soul,' Quist replied. Plummer started to ask what he'd done with the note, but Quist cut in, 'Look here, Lennie, why all the secrecy?'

Plummer's short laugh was more like a snort. 'I ain't no fool. Gotter watch out fer my own hide, ain't I? If it got to be knowed thet I give ye vital information, muh life wouldn't be wuth terbaccer spit on a hot stove. So I'm askin' thet ye keep yer trap closed.'

Quist smiled. 'So far you don't sound unreasonable. All right, you claim you have proof that Grizzly Baldridge killed Whit Clayton — '

'Proof thet can't be denied, Mister Quist. I'll trade it to ye for other information.'

'What information is that?'

Plummer explained, 'Ye've spent a heap o'time a-snoopin' 'round. Like's not ye learned a heap of stuff. If ye'll tell me whut ye know, might be I could make up a piece for the Blade and sell it ter George Nugent. So let me have yer information, then I'll tell ye how I know Grizzly Baldridge rubbed out Whit Clayton.'

Quist considered the matter. A small steel gear lay near his left foot. He picked it up and abstractedly kept tossing it in the air and catching it while he considered Plummer's proposal. Finally, he shook his head. 'I can get your slant, all right, Lennie,' he said quietly, 'but after all you didn't mention any such deal in your note. You offered information to me if I came here. I'm keeping my part of the bargain. You tell me what you know. You can count on me to see that you're included in anything I do, later.'

'I dunno.' Plummer frowned and shifted uneasily on his seat, the movement making tall shadows against his surroundings, thrown by the lamp near his feet. The circle of light didn't extend far beyond him and Quist. The rest of the room was in deep shadow. To Quist's left was the large rectangular opening to the floor below, with the top of the ladder showing above the edge. Plummer reached a sudden decision. 'All right, I'll play fair with ye, Mister Quist. I'll give you my information first. Grizzly Baldridge killed Whit Clayton.'

'How do you know? What makes you so certain?' Quist asked eagerly.

'I got the story from a friend who saw the hull dirty business,' Plummer replied. 'While Baldridge's daughter and his son was there, Baldridge was hid up on the roof of that house. There was a switchin' of guns took place. Chris Baldridge had left his .45 in place of the .38 he found thar, nigh the body. Later, old Baldridge got the .38 whut had been thrun in the brush and replaced it by the body.'

'Damn interestin',' Quist said softly, tossing the gear idly in his right hand. 'I want details, though, Lennie.'

Plummer gave details while Quist listened intently. Finally, 'Thet suit yer, Mister Quist. Are ye convinced?'

'I'm plenty convinced,' Quist nodded. 'Matter of fact, that's exactly as I figured things out, except for the killer being Baldridge.'

'Ye did?' Plummer looked surprised. 'Smart, ain't ye?'

Quist shook his head. 'I'm not so smart. Dumb crooks just make me look that way. There's just one thing I want to know. This friend that told you all this, where was he that he could see the guns being switched? He must have been inside the house.'

Plummer hesitated, frowning. 'I reckon he likely was. We can ask him later.'

'But where could he have been hidden?' Quist persisted. 'He couldn't have been in that same room. If he'd been under the bed, he couldn't have seen the switching of guns — '

'Ye'll have to ask my friend, all thet.' Plummer sounded a trifle irritable. 'I've given ye my facts. Now, you tell me all ye've l'arned since ye been on the case. Thet's only fair and square. I've give ye enough evidence to arrest th' murderer.'

'You sure have, Lennie,' Quist acknowledged. 'You've just convicted hell out of yourself. You know too much about the killing. No one but the killer could have told me that much — '

'Whut ye aimin' at, Mister Quist?' Plummer sounded somewhat alarmed. 'Ye sound like ye was suspectin' *me*.'

Quist laughed shortly. 'Have I got to make it clearer? All right, I'll do just that. You killed Whit Clayton, Plummer.'

21

Conclusion

Plummer stiffened. His pale blue eyes searched Quist's face. Quist continued carelessly tossing the small gear in his hand. Then Quist asked quietly, 'Or should I call you Damson — Luke Damson?'

'Whut in hell ye talkin' erbout, Mister Quist? I ain't never heerd of no Luke Damson — '

Quist cut in, 'You can't lie your way out. I've been on to you for a long time, Damson. This business of blaming Grizzly Baldridge for Clayton's death, was just an excuse to bring me here and find out what I know. I figure you've been getting nervous about me, Damson. Hell! I've had your number since the first day I met you. You never did manage to discard that dragging shuflling walk a convict acquires after long years in the pen, did you? You've given yourself away in other ways too.'

'Ye're crazy!' Plummer — Damson said hoarsely. 'Whut other ways ye talkin' 'bout? I don't understand, Mister Quist.'

Quist smiled grimly. 'You mentioned once that your home state was Montana, but that night it rained so hard I remember your saying you'd bet the bayous, over east, would be flooded. Most people from up north would pronounce it 'bay-oo.' You pronounced it correctly, 'buy-oo.' So I figured you were acquainted with Louisiana speech. Another time, you spoke to Nugent about getting new type faces. That didn't fit in with the old beggar-tramp act you'd been staging. Worked in the prison printing shop at Natchigoula, didn't you, Damson? Know a heap about printing, don't you? Worked right alongside your pal, Clayton Whitney. Another thing — the night it rained, your clothing looked pretty wet. I knew you'd been out that day, instead of staying under cover, like a tramp would have done.'

'Goddam you, Quist, ye can't bluff me — '

'You might's well drop that old man act, too. I know prison ages a man in looks, but you're no older than Grizzly Baldridge in actual years — and a heap more active than you've been pretending.'

'Correct, Quist,' Damson acknowledged harshly. 'But you realize now you'll never leave here alive.' He sat straighter on his box; his head came up. Years seem to slough from his frame, and as he moved, light from the oil lamp on the floor near his feet, cast a metallic highlight on the barrel of the gun he'd been holding, leveled at Quist, in the shadow of his right leg. 'You know just too damn much,' Damson concluded nastily.

Quist laughed softly. 'I figured you might be keeping me covered, Damson, when you had me sit over here — away from you. But I'm not worried. You won't bump me off for a spell.'

'Why in hell won't I?' Damson snapped.

'You want to learn first what happened when Hi-Johnny was shot; oh, sure you shot him. Where'd you get that rifle?'

'From Clayton. He'd had a scrap with Baldridge one day, and Baldridge warned him never to carry a gun again. Clayton was scared. He passed the .30-30 on to me. One day I was out on the range and I sent a shot drifting toward that law-sharp, Dowd, too. I didn't want him nosing around — ' Damson broke off. For the moment he had seemed rather confused. 'What in hell business is it of yours, anyway?'

'Now you know better than to ask a fool question like that,' Quist chided. 'My business — y'know. And I've had you right worried since I came here. You knew I had a certain rep. You feared what I might uncover. And, Damson, I've uncovered plenty!'

Damson hesitated a moment, then gave a slight shrug. 'All right, it don't matter if you know. Sure, I killed Hi-Johnny. He had something I wanted. Quist, did he give you something that looked like an eight-sided piece of gold?'

'Gold?' Quist asked innocently.

'Cripes! He was dead when I reached him. One arm was stretched out like he'd thrown something. Maybe he threw that gold piece away to keep you from getting it — '

'By God, I'll find it then — ' Damson paused, eyes narrowing. 'What do you know about gold, Quist?'

'I got a story from Grizzly Baldridge about some gold his father started to Austin, on a camel, in Hi-Johnny's care. During Civil War days. Baldridge sent you to recall Hi-Johnny. None of you were seen again — until recently. The gold disappeared. Where'd you bury it, Damson?'

'That's none of your business — who said I buried — ?'

'All right, so you've admitted something unintentionally. So long as you've got me trapped anyway, you might as well tell me what happened. I'll be frank with you, Damson. There's things I don't know — for sure. Maybe we can trade a mite of information. There's things you'd like from me, too.' Damson hesitated, scowling. Quite suddenly his face cleared. 'Sure. Why not? That was a slick job, Quist, only I ran into a mite of trouble in Louisiana. Yeah, old Virgil Baldridge sent me after Hi-Johnny to bring him back. I knew that was my chance. I sneaked a shovel away when I left the ranch. Caught up to Hi-Johnny and that limping camel critter sooner'n I expected. Instead of bringing him back to the ranch, I told him Baldridge wanted us to bury the money near Steeple Rock. Hi-Johnny believed me. He even dug the hole, after I'd loosened the lock on the little leather trunk holding the gold, with a shot from my cap-and-ball. I figured I'd need some cash for my plan. Hi-Johnny thought I was getting the money for Virgil Baldridge. About the time Hi-Johnny give the burying place the last pat with his shovel, I worked around behind him and pulled trigger. He went down like a poleaxed steer.'

Damson stopped, the gun always held steady on Quist. 'Y'know, I'm damned if I understand it. I left him for dead.

Jesus! I could see the wound where the bullet struck his head. He must have recovered, later —'

'That's one explanation, anyway,' Quist said dryly.

'Yeah, it is,' Damson said thoughtfully. 'That damn camel was skittery of shots and went hightailing it away. Took a shot at it, but missed. Don't know what became of it. Then I lit out for Louisiana, figuring to lay low until things quieted and I got a chance to sneak back and dig up that gold. I got across the Mississippi, all right, and then I ran into trouble. The Feds were in charge, there. A guard challenged me when I was heading through some brush. When I didn't stop he fired. I fired back. Killed the lousy buzzard. Trouble was, he had some of his pals near. They closed in and caught me. I was held for trial before the provost marshal. Convicted and sentenced to be shot. Later the sentence was changed to life imprisonment.'

'And by that time, you had no friends you could appeal to in Texas,' Quist said.

'Later you were transferred to Natchigoula Penitentiary. The life sentence still held good. What? Sure, I know about that. I've got your records at the hotel. Photographs taken at different times. I learned who you were chummiest with in prison. Fellow named Clayton Whitney. By that time you were considered incorrigible, Damson. Three times you'd tried to escape. Once you'd almost made good, too, when you stabbed a guard with a knife made from a kitchen utensil — '

Damson growled, 'All right. I'll grant you're smart, Quist. Sure I knew Clayton in the pen. Just before he was released, I told him about the gold. Promised to cut him in on it. He was to dig it up, and hire a good lawyer to get me out of the pen. He promised faithful. I waited. The months piled up. I figured he'd got the gold and double-crossed me. Finally I managed to escape under a load of garbage that was being carted off. I arrived here, pretending to seek a lost sister. My looks had changed. I steered clear of Baldridge who might have recognized me. My beard grew long. When I located Clayton he had got married and built a house — '

'So as not to be hindered in his digging near Steeple Rock, he had to have land in that vicinity. He married Baldridge's daughter to get it.'

'Clayton swore he'd been unable to find the gold, showed me where he'd been digging. Still I distrusted him. Figured he'd cached it away someplace. One morning early I borrowed Ortego's horse and rode to Clayton's place, intending to sneak in and force the truth from him at gunpoint. But he spied me coming. Hid behind the door. When I went in, he jumped me. Took my gun away from me. I rushed him and we battled all over the room, with me hangin' like death to his gun arm. That .38 Colt was hanging on the wall. I grabbed it as we went struggling near, shot Clayton, and got my gun back. That .38 tied the killing to Mrs. Clayton. I rummaged through the house looking for gold. No luck. But I found some of her doodads, ribbons, hairpins, a handkerchief. Took 'em with me, figurin' to sprinkle some clues, should an investigation get too close to me. About then I spied Chris Baldridge riding in. I scooted out the back way. Climbed to the roof. I could hear him moving around below. Then he fired a shot. Later, after he left I understood why. He'd left his forty-five to draw suspicion to himself and save his sister. He didn't have a gun when he rode off, and I saw him throw that .38 in the brush. Then Mrs. Clayton showed up, and I see her ride off carrying his gun. Later I got the .38 Chris had thrun in the brush and replaced it beside the body. Then I dug outten there fast. Reckon I was smart, eh?'

'Dumb as hell,' Quist scoffed. He tossed the gear in his hand a couple of times. 'I climbed to that roof myself. You left clues.' Anxiously, Damson asked where he'd slipped. Quist laughed at him. 'The sooner I tell you, the sooner you'll shoot me, Damson. Let's trade further information. What was your tie-up with

Cobra Macaw?'

'That stupid buzzard,' Damson growled. 'When I heard you were headed for Quivira City, I didn't like it. Didn't want you snooping around. But I needed help. I went to Gene Martinsen, promised him a share in the gold — told him the whole story, in fact. We decided you had to be got rid of, so we gave the job to Macaw. He shot from the tree and missed — '

'And that's where you tied yourself to Macaw. The previous time I came here, I noticed that George Nugent unhooked that trap door to the roof, from the inside. So I knew someone must have unhooked it so Macaw could come down through here and escape. What better suspect than you, Damson?'

Damson scowled. 'All right, maybe I slipped on that point. But it makes no difference in the long run. You're done, Quist.'

Quist shrugged carelessly. 'Risks in my job are what are known as an occupational hazard. Death is sure to come sometime.'

'You're taking it too damn cool, Quist. If you're holding some idea of jerking your gun, forget it. I could plug you at the first move. Just keep your hands in plain sight. And quit tossing that gear up and down. It makes me jumpy.'

'Nerves, Damson, just nerves,' Quist laughed softly. 'Your nerves were making you jumpy when Macaw failed to down me too. You come to me with your tip-off about him being the man on the roof. You figured I'd go after him, and kill him, so he couldn't tell what he knew about you. Or he'd kill me, which would be much better. Either way you stood to win, Damson. So now we come to Hi-Johnny.'

Damson had been glaring angrily at Quist. 'What about Hi-Johnny? You know so damn much, you should know that — oh, hell! it won't hurt to tell you. He come begging food that day, over in the Mex district where I got my shack. I happened to notice he looked sort of familiar. Then, by Gawd, when he come past my door I recognized him. You could have knocked me down with a feather. Here all those years I'd figured him dead. I coaxed him inside the house. 'T'wan't hard to do. It was raining. Then I see he was crazy as a bedbug, when I tried to talk sense to him. He even sort of seemed to recognize me — anyway he mumbled something about gold and burying it and digging it up. Didn't seem mad at me or nothing. Just cuckoo as all hell. Finally he draws out a California slug and gives a sly laugh. I see some scratches on it. Figured it could be a map he drawed. I grabbed at it, but he jerked away. Then he got mad and run out of the house, jumped on a skin-and-bones horse and took out — '

'And without asking leave you borrowed Ortego's horse again and took after him, first grabbing your .30-30.'

'That's right. But he had a right good start. I didn't last attract notice by ridin' hell-bent through town. Had to take it easy, until I got clear of Quivira City. The son-of-a-buzzard led me a long chase, before I could get within rifle range. Then I let him have it. Tried to get you too, when you sudden appeared — Quist, you sure you didn't get that gold piece from Hi-Johnny before he died?'

'Cripes! I told you he was dead when I reached him. So you, not wanting to tangle with me, sprinkled some hairpins and a handkerchief around, and lit out for home. But you were afraid someone might discover that rifle at your house, so you sent Macaw to get it — '

'How in hell do you know that?' Damson looked surprised.

'I've talked to Sheriff Wolcott. He spied you talking damn serious to Macaw and Martinsen one day. It looked like you were giving orders. That struck Wolcott as queer, so he trailed Macaw to your place and stopped Macaw just as he was leaving with the rifle. About that time I stepped into the picture — '

'You damn snooping buzzard,' Damson said bitterly.

'Let's just call it investigating,' Quist

suggested quietly.

'It's something that pays dividends. For instance, when I learned Clayton had been in the Natchigoula Penitentiary, I sent for information. I got prison photos and records of a lot of men he'd known there. To tell the truth I didn't recognize you at first, Damson. I was looking for a man named Plummer. And then I happened to remember there's a variety of plum known as a damson. So I examined the photos more carefully. And there you were.'

Damson sneered grudgingly, 'Jesus! You do work it smart.'

'I have to in my job. And now you still think you and Martinsen are going to find that gold, don't you? During roundup time. I understand Martinsen isn't going to throw in with the other outfits to work the herds. Oh, no, he's going to wait until the other outfits are 'way over on the east range. Then while the Bee-Hive range is deserted, the G-Bar-M crew will feel free to dig all over the place.'

'I still think you might have got that

California slug from Hi-Johnny.'

'Think what you like, Damson.' Then Quist raised his voice, 'Todd, did you get all of it?'

The reply came almost at Quist's feet as Todd Sargent, six-shooter in hand, emerged from the floor opening and stepped off the ladder. 'I got it, Greg. Heard it all — '

'Damn it!' Quist's angry exclamation interrupted Damson's cry of surprise. 'Why the devil didn't you stay below?

Now we're — '

'I'll handle it, Greg.' Sargent stepped farther into the room. 'Drop your gun, Lennie — Damson — '

There came a swift movement at Sargent's rear, and Gene Martinsen emerged from the shadows beyond a stack of newsprint. 'Drop your own gun, Sargent,' he grated savagely. 'Make it pronto! Get your paws high! Damson, keep Quist covered.'

Sargent swore bitterly. 'You were right, Greg,' he fumed, dropping the weapon and raising his arms. 'I should have kept out of here, and not muddled your —'

At that moment the steel gear sped from Quist's hand, striking the lamp, and the fingers that had thrown it darted to the .44 six-shooter in the underarm holster. Even as he fired, Quist had left his seat, hurling his body toward Sargent's legs. He fired a second time, the explosion blending with other shots, as Sargent went toppling to the floor in the instant darkness brought about by the smashing of the oil lamp.

Streaks of orange fire crisscrossed through the room; heavy detonations shook dust from the rafters. Sargent was down on hands and knees, swearing, scrabbling about in search of his weapon. A man went crashing to the floor. Quist fired again. Waited, tense. Fired a fourth time, changing position after each shot from the .44. Someone groaned. Then quite suddenly silence descended on the ebony gloom. Abruptly, sounds of movement ceased. Powder smoke swirled through the darkness. Quist waited tense, crouched low near the floor.

Listening. From the street came faintly the sounds of excited yells. Quist's left hand moved a trifle and encountered something small and hard. A loose bolt from the discarded press parts. Moving easily, he tossed the bolt through the gloom toward the front of the building. It landed on some paper, bounced to the floor.

Instantly, the thundering detonation of a .45 shook the rafters. A red flash momentarily lighted the room, as the leaden slug struck something near the front of the building. Again, silence.

The acrid odor of powder smoke stung Quist's nostrils. In the pitch-black quiet he laughed softly. 'Sounds like you're all right, Todd — '

'Greg! You safe?'

'Not a scratch. You?' Quist started reloading the .44.

'I was lucky, I guess. Never did locate my gun to get into the scrap until just now. What did you crash into me for?'

'Martinsen could have fired at you. He knew Damson had me covered. I was hoping to get you below his fire.'

'Thanks. Hell, I hadn't thought of that — '

'Let's see about some light.' Quist scratched a match as he got to his feet. Sargent was just rising. Guns in hands, they examined the prone bodies sprawled on the floor. Martinsen was dead. Damson was still alive, but unconscious, breathing with difficulty. His gun lay on the floor in a pool of blood. Quist moved over and righted the lamp. Some oil still remained in the base. The chimney was shattered. He touched a lighted match to the wick and a sort of smoky torch-like flame sprang into being.

A crowd was creating a noise in front of the building by this time. Down in the alley, someone was pounding on the double-doors.

Sargent stood looking down at Damson. 'Cripes A'mighty! Who'd have believed old Lennie Plummer — '

'I'm just glad,' Quist was saying, 'you had sense enough to read that note and follow me — '

'Hell, and I damn near spoiled everything by coming up here,' Sargent said ruefully. 'Thought I could help — '

'Forget it. You've helped plenty, Todd.'

'Did you know Martinsen was hidden back there?'

'I suspected somebody was. Caught a sound of breathing a couple of times. Damson acted too confident to be alone, too. But they were both so damn anxious to learn what I knew, that Damson kept talking. They didn't figure I'd leave alive.'

'Did you notice you'd hit Martinsen twice?'

Quist nodded. 'I got Damson with my first shot, then concentrated on Martinsen.'

The noise below had increased. Then there came the sound of one of the rear doors opening, and Grizzly Baldridge's voice demanding, 'What in hell is going on up there?'

They called to him to come up. Shortly after his head appeared in the floor opening, followed by Chris. 'Good

God!' they exclaimed simultaneously. More men swarmed up the ladder and into the room. Todd was explaining what had happened. 'We got all the evidence we need,' he was saying, then broke off to send someone for a doctor to attend Damson. 'He might live long enough to make a full confession.' He started to clear the room, once more.

Quist asked, 'What happened to the girls? '

'They're at Priscilla's place. Look, Greg, this isn't all clear to me yet. How does it happen — ?' Baldridge started.

'You're slow catching up, Grizzly,' Quist said dryly. 'Take a good look at that Plummer hombre. It might be someone you used to know.' And as Grizzly turned away, Quist said to Sargent, 'Todd, you're sheriff. I'll leave things to you. See you later.' He turned and descended the ladder. Pushing through the crowd in the alley, ignoring questions, he made his way around to Main Street. In the open doorway of Priscilla's shop he saw Laurinda waiting. As he came near she recognized him and caught at his arm. 'Greg! What in heaven's name happened?' He asked where Priscilla was. Laurinda said she was at the back of the store and would be out presently, then asked again, 'What happened?'

He gave her brief details, concluding, 'You can get the full story from Todd, later.'

'Good grief! Lennie Plummer! I can't believe it — but, Greg, what happens next?'

'I leave Quivira City and move on to some other job.'

The girl came closer, both hands clutching at his arms. 'Greg, you can't go away and leave us. What in heaven would we do without you now? You've simply got to stay here.'

A wistful smile touched Quist's lips. He shook his head. 'You'll get along all right.'

'But I want you to stay. Would it help if I asked you not to go away — to stay here for my sake?'

'Laurinda,' — his voice wasn't quite

steady — 'that means more to me than you'll ever realize. I've got to leave. My work's done here. There'll be other jobs.'

'But what will I do?' Her voice was almost a wail.

'That, I'll leave to Todd,' Quist said. 'He's a good man, Laurinda, none better.'

'I know that, Greg, but — ' Slowly she shook her head, her eyes filling. There was no one immediately near. She swayed toward Quist and he folded her within his arms, holding her close. 'Greg, we owe you so much.'

'Even if you were right,' he said quietly, 'this moment would more than pay me.'

A noise at the rear of the shop brought their minds back to Priscilla. Again, Quist's lips brushed against Laurinda's. They lingered a few seconds, then Quist stepped back, releasing the girl, just as Priscilla emerged from her back room. She called to Quist, inviting him to come in.

'Thanks. no. I was just about to say

adios, anyway. Maybe I'll see you both tomorrow. Laurinda can explain what has happened. Good night.'

Turning, he walked swiftly in the direction of his hotel.

Laurinda lifted one arm as though to call him back, then dropped it again, and stood gazing after him, seeing through her blurred vision his fast retreating form walking swiftly out of her life. She was remembering a tall confident man with tawny hair and topaz eyes and strong arms and . . . and

. . . Then she turned reluctantly and started to reply to Priscilla's persistent questioning . . .

We do hope that you have enjoyed reading this large print book.

Did you know that all of our titles are available for purchase?

We publish a wide range of high quality large print books including:
Romances, Mysteries, Classics
General Fiction
Non Fiction and Westerns

Special interest titles available in large print are:
The Little Oxford Dictionary
Music Book, Song Book
Hymn Book, Service Book

Also available from us courtesy of Oxford University Press:
Young Readers' Dictionary
(large print edition)
Young Readers' Thesaurus
(large print edition)

Other titles in the Linford Western Library:

MATCH RACE

Fred Grove

Quarter horse racing presents a thrill few men in the Old West can resist. Dude McQuinn, Coyote Walking, and Billy Lockhart are no exception, riding from town to town, matching and trading racehorses. Dude is the straight-talking front man, Coyote the jockey, and Billy the doctor, concocting potions that can cure a horse of anything — at least temporarily. But Billy is being watched by a strange man in a black bowler hat — a man who knows a secret about his past . . .

LAW AND OUTLAW

William E. Vance

The old woman was dying. That meant a lot of things to Will Titus. It meant sorrow, for she'd raised him from a pup. It meant one fewer good person in a world where they were rare enough already. But mostly, it meant the eventual arrival of Bart Laney. Bart was almost a brother to Will — but a brother gone wrong. While Will had chosen a U.S. Marshal's badge, Bart had gone down the outlaw trail . . .

BAD MAN'S RETURN

Willian Colt MacDonald

The Three Mesquiteers — Tucson Smith, Stony Brooke, and Lullaby Joslin — return with their special brand of triple trouble! Two gunfighters arrive in Los Potros the same day, both seeking Tucson. One is anxious to shake the hand of the man who befriended him years before. The other is a desperado looking for an opportunity to put a bullet through Tucson's heart, in revenge for a beating he once suffered. But when Tucson is shot, the evidence points to the culprit being his friend . . .

HIGH IRON

E.E. Halleran

Old Hannibal Putnam was a man who just didn't know when he was licked. Not only had he set out to build a railroad on borrowed money, it had to be high up in the hills. And now there's a spy in the camp. Someone who certainly doesn't want a railroad built. Someone who would kill — and has — to stop it. That's when Hannibal decides to send for his former shooting partner, Lefty Malone. Only Lefty hasn't carried a gun in years . . .

SIX-GUN BOSS

Clay Randall

The three big cattle outfits of New Orlando are being bled dry by rustlers. Pat Reagan, range detective for the Texas Panhandle Stockmen's Association, is assigned to work undercover as a ranch hand for George Albert of the Box-A, and bring the thieves to justice. But the only law around there is that of the six-gun and the noose — and when the glamorous daughter of George makes a play for Pat, he's heading into deep trouble . . .